DELICATE
EDIBLE
BIRDS

Other works by

LAUREN GROFF

✦✦✦

The Monsters of Templeton

Lauren Groff

voice

HYPERION   NEW YORK

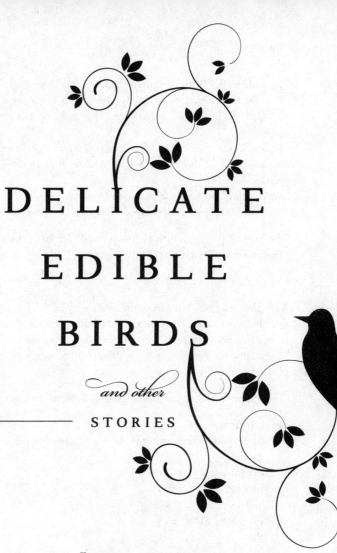

DELICATE

EDIBLE

BIRDS

and other

STORIES

"Delicate Edible Birds" originally appeared in *Glimmer Train*.
"L. DeBard and Aliette" originally appeared in *The Atlantic* and also appeared in *Best American Short Stories* and *Best New American Voices*.
"Lucky Chow Fun" originally appeared in *Ploughshares* and also appeared in the *Pushcart Prize XXXII: Best of the Small Presses*.
"Sir Fleeting" originally appeared in *One Story*.
"Watershed" originally appeared in *The Chattahoochee Review*.

The lines of poetry quoted in "Watershed" are from the poem "Epithalamion" by Gerard Manley Hopkins.

Library of Congress Cataloging-in-Publication Data

Groff, Lauren.
   Delicate edible birds and other stories / Lauren Groff.
     p. cm.
   Short stories.
   ISBN: 978-1-4013-4086-5
   I. Title.
   PS3607.R6344D45 2009
   813'.6—dc22

                      2008044002

Hyperion books are available for special promotions, premiums, or corporate training. For details contact Michael Rentas, Proprietary Markets, Hyperion, 77 West 66th Street, 12th floor, New York, New York 10023, or call 212-456-0133.

Book design by Shubhani Sarkar

FIRST EDITION

10 9 8 7 6 5 4 3 2 1

 FOR CLAY

CONTENTS

DELICATE
EDIBLE

BIRDS

Lucky Chow Fun

EVERY VILLAGE HAS ITS RHYTHM, AND EVERY year Templeton's was the same. Summer meant tourists to the baseball museum, the crawl of traffic down Main Street, even a drunken soprano flinging an aria into the night on her stagger back to the Opera. With fall, the tourists thinned out and the families of Phillies Phanatics ceded the town to retired couples with binoculars, there to watch the hills run riot with color.

Come winter, Templeton hunkered into itself. We natives were so grateful for this quiet—when we could hear the sleigh bells at the Farmers' Museum all the way to the Susquehanna—that we almost didn't mind the shops closing up. In winter we believed in our own virtue, lauded ourselves for being the kind of people to renounce the comforts of city life for a tight community and spectacular beauty. We packed on our winter fat and waited for spring, for the lake to melt, for the cherry blossoms, for the town to burst into its all-American charm, and the rapid crescendo of tourists.

This was our rhythm, at least, until the Lucky Chow Fun girls. That year, the snow didn't melt until mid-May, and the Templeton High School Boys' Swim Team won the State Championships. That year, we natives stopped looking one another in the eye.

I WAS SEVENTEEN that spring and filled with longing, which I tried to sate with the books of myth and folklore that I was devouring by the dozens. I couldn't read enough of the stories, tiny doors that opened only to reveal a place I hadn't known I'd known; stories so old they felt ingrained in my genes. I loved Medea, Isolde, Allerleirauh. I imagined myself as a beautiful Cassandra, wandering vast and lonely halls, spilling prophesies that everyone laughed at, only to watch them come tragically true in the end. This feeling of mutedness, of injustice, was particularly strong in me, though I had no particular prophesies to tell, no clear-sighted warnings. On the nights I stuffed myself with myths, I dreamed of college, of being pumped full of all the old knowledge until I knew everything there was to know, all the past cultures picked clean like delicious roasted chickens.

All March, I skidded home from school as fast as I could in my ratty Honda Civic to look for my college acceptance letters in the mailbox; all of my friends had gotten in early, but because I was being recruited for swimming, I had to wait for the regular acceptances. All March, there was nothing. By the time my little sister, Petra—Pot—trudged the mile home over the snowdrifts, I would be sitting at the kitchen table, having eaten an entire box of cereal plus a bowl of ice cream, feeling sick.

"Oh, God, Lollie," she'd say, dumping her backpack. "Nothing?"

"Nope," I'd say. "Nothing."

And she'd sigh and sit across from me. Her days were also hard, as she was too weird for the other fourth graders, too plump, too spastic. She never once had a sleepover or even a best friend. But instead of complaining, Pot would try to cheer me up by mimicking the new birdsongs she'd learned that day. *"Drop-it, drop-it, cover-it-up, cover-it-up, pull-it-up, pull-it-up,"* she'd sing, then say, "Brown Thrasher," her dumpling face suddenly luminous. That year, Pot was on a strange ornithological kick, as if her entire pudgy being were stuffed with feathers. She fell asleep to tapes of tweets and whistles and had a growing collection of taxidermied birds scattered around her bedroom. I had no idea where she had gotten them, but was too moony with my own troubles to ask. I avoided her room as much as possible, because she had one particular gyrfalcon perched on her dresser that seemed malicious, if not downright evil, ready to scratch at your jugular if you were to saunter innocently by.

Those melancholy afternoons, Pot would chirp away until my mother came home from her own bad day at the high school in Van Hornesville, where she taught biology.

No—my mother never came in, she blew in like the dust devil of a woman she was, stomping the snow off her boots, sending great clouds of snow from her shoulders. "Oh, God, Lollie, nothing?" she would say, releasing her springy gray hair from her cap.

"Nothing," Pot would trill, then leap up to rejoin her stiff little aviary upstairs.

My mother would look at the wreckage of my snack, frown, and hug me. "Elizabeth," she'd say, and I could hear the vibration of her words in her chest, feel the press of each individual bone of her rib cage. "Don't you worry. It will all work out in the end. You're no Podunk idiot like the kids I teach—"

"Spare me," I'd interrupt, and give her a kiss on the chin. Then I'd stand, late for swim practice, and leave my nervous little mother to peep out the window at me as I pulled away. That spring she was dating The Garbageman, and when I came home I may have seen her before going to bed, or I may not have seen her until morning, singing during her preparations for school.

THERE ARE HUNDREDS OF VERSIONS of the Cinderella story throughout the world: Serbian Pepelyouga, Norwegian Kari Trestakk, Chinese Yeh-hsien, German Aschenputtel, French Cendrillon. What most of the stories have in common is both a good, absent mother and an evil, present one. Fairy tales are not like real life in all its beautiful ambiguity.

There are no semigood semiabsent mothers. Or, for that matter, semipresent very good ones.

THAT WINTER, IT WAS ONLY IN THE POOL, feeling the thrust and slide of my body through the water, that I felt good. Only then could I escape the niggling terror of what would happen to my mother and sister when I left them, their sad dinners, my sister talking only of birds, my mother talking only of the crap day she had at school, neither heard by the other, neither listening.

I was the captain and the only girl on the Varsity boys' swim team that year, though not much of a leader. During the long bus rides, I only giggled nervously at the boys' boasts about boning chicks I knew they never touched. I wasn't chosen as a captain because I was a leader, but rather because of my teammates' small-town gallantry and my minor celebrity as an oddity in the papers. I was the fastest butterflier around and could beat everyone, boy or girl, in the region, save for one lightning-swift boy from Glens Falls. The papers all the way to Albany couldn't stop chortling over this fact. They ran photos of me every week, careful to take only my fairly pretty face and leave my—let's face it—overweight body on the cutting room floor. I was very heavy. "Rubenesque," my mother called it, but the boys were clearly no aesthetes because they never looked directly at me, not even when I was on the block, waiting for the start. I was no pushover, though. If a boy made fun of the way I bulged in my bathing suit, calling me Moby Dickless, for instance, that boy would find himself stunned on the pool bottom, having been swum over by my own impersonation of a great white whale.

One Friday night in March, after an exceptionally hard relay practice, Tim Summerton leaned over the gutter when I came trundling in from the last race. He was no looker, all wonky-eyed and stippled with pimples, but he had a heart so kind he never went without a date to any school dance. He spat a stream of warm water into my face; I ducked and spat back at him, laughing. Then he grinned.

"Hey," he said. "The divers and I are going to the Lucky Chow Fun. Want to come?"

I looked at the little clump of divers snapping one another with towels. Those three boys were the exhibitionists of the team, with, truly, a little more to look at in their pick-lesuits than the swimmers had. I would know: I could see underwater remarkably well. "Oooh, Fun, Fun," the divers were saying in a vaguely ethnic impression. "We have fun fun at Fun Fun." They were not the smartest boys, our divers, but I suppose anybody who tries to shave his neck with the end of a diving board must be a little lacking in brainpower.

"Yeah," I said. "Sure."

"Great. Meet you there," he said, tapping my swim-capped head with a pull buoy. I was overwhelmed with the desire to grab his hand, clutch it to me, cover it in kisses, laugh like a madwoman. Instead I smiled then went back under the water, holding my breath until I could hold it no longer, then sent it up in a great silvery jellyfish-bubble of air. When I came up, Tim had gone.

That night, I showered with special care, washed the chlorine off my body, lotioned, powdered. And when I walked out into the cold night, all the gym's lights went out behind me and the last employee locked the door behind my back. I left my hat off to let my hair freeze into the thin little snakes I liked to crunch in my fingers, and thought of moo goo gai pan.

It was a Friday night, but there was a basketball game at the high school, so the town was very still as I drove though it. Only the Ambassador's mansion gave a sign of life, every window burning gold. The Ambassador was our local hero, a former ambassador to France and Guyana, and once-upon-a-time my father's great friend, and I always felt a wash of fondness for him when I passed his fine fieldstone mansion on the river. He was an erect, gray man of eighty years old with thin, bluish fingers and canny eyes. He had, they said, a huge collection of rare goods from all over the world: a room entirely devoted to masks, one for crystal bowls, one for vases, even one for his miniature schnauzer, with paintings done by great artists of the snarly little beast. Nobody knew for sure, though, because when we were invited, we saw only the ground floor. In any case, my family hadn't been invited since we lost my father.

Now, on Main Street, only a few shopwindows had left

their lights on, casting an oily shine on the baseball bats in the souvenir shops, making the artificial flowers in the General Store glow. The Red Dragoon Saloon was open and there were three Harleys in the sludge on Pioneer Street, but still I was able to park right in front of Lucky Chow Fun, behind Tim Summerton's Volvo.

The restaurant was newish, maybe two years old, and the town's first tentative step toward ethnic food, unless one counted Gino's Pizzeria and the Mennonite bakery on Main Street. It was a cheap linoleum joint, with an ugly, hand-drawn sign flapping in the wind off the lake, lit from above by a red light. It served a lot of sticky Americanized Chinese food, like General Tso's chicken and fried rice, and I loved it all, the fat and salt, the scandalous feeling of eating fast food in a hamlet that banned all fast-food places, the miniature mythmaking of the fortune cookies.

That night, when I stepped out of the car and around to the sidewalk, I almost knocked into a small, shivering figure in an overlarge tee-shirt, sweeping the new powder of snow from the walk. "Sorry," I mumbled, and stepped away, not really looking at the girl I had nearly trampled, gathering only a vague impression of crooked teeth and a jagged haircut. She was just one of the girls who worked at the Lucky Chow Fun, one of the wives or daughters of the owners. Nobody in Templeton cared to figure out who the girls were, just as nobody figured out who the two men who ran the place were, calling them only Chen One and Chen Two, or Chen Glasses and Chen Fat. Only later did we realize that no part of their names remotely resembled Chen, nor did the girls resemble the men in any way, either.

I feel the necessity of explaining our hard-heartedness, but I cannot. Templeton has always had a callousness about outsiders, having seen so many come through town, wreak destruction on our lake, trash the ancient baseball stadium, Cartwright Field, litter our streets, and move off. This wariness extended even to those who lived with us; anyone who wasn't related to everyone else was suspect. Newcomers were people who had lived in town for only fifteen years. The one black family who lived in Templeton during my childhood promptly pulled up roots and moved away after a year, and, to my knowledge, there were only three Jewish children in school. The only Asians were preternaturally cheery and popular, adopted kids of the wealthiest of the doctors' families in town. This was a town that clung ferociously to the shameful high school mascot of the Redskins, though if we were any skins, we should have been the Whiteskins. I was born and raised in this attitude. That night, without a second thought, I stepped around the girl and into the fatty brightness of the restaurant, past old Chen Glasses, snoozing over his Chinese newspaper at the door.

The restaurant was nearly empty, the long kitchen in the back sending out a fine oily sizzle, girls like ghosts in white uniforms chopping things, frying things, talking quietly to one another. The back-lit photos above the register struck me so powerfully with their water chestnuts and lovingly fried bits of meat that I didn't at first see the divers, who were pretending to be walruses, chopsticks in their mouths like tusks. When they saw me, they took the chopsticks out so fast that it was clear who they were imitating. I was not unused to this. In fourth grade, the Garrett twins had named their science project, a miniature zeppelin, *The Lollie*. That night, I did what I always did, stifled the pang, pretended to smile.

"Very funny, boys," I said. "Have you ordered?"

"Yeah," said Brad Huxley. He was in my grade and blessed with a set of eyelashes that made every girl in school envious. He gave me a dimpled smile and said, "We each ordered our own. These two freaks don't like sharing," nodding at the others. It was his sorrow in life that he was not endowed with hand-eye coordination; otherwise he would have been on the basketball court that evening with the cool kids. He overcompensated in the diving pool, and in a few weeks, at States, would come so close to the board on his reverse back pike that he flayed a strip of skin from his neck to mid-back and got a perfect score for that dive.

I was standing at the front, deciding what to order from solemn and scornful old Chen Fat, with his filthy apron, when Tim Summerton came from the back where the bathrooms were. His face was drawn and pale, and he looked half-excited, half-horrified. He didn't seem to see me, as he walked past me without a glance. He sat down at the table with the others and began to hiss at them something I couldn't quite make out.

Huxley sat back with a little smirk on his face. "Duh," he

said, just loud enough for me to hear. "Everybody knows." The other two divers looked pale, though, and smiles broke out over their faces.

I was about to ask what they were talking about, but Chen Fat said, "Hem hem," and I turned toward him. His pen was poised over a pad and his eyelids were drawn down over his eyes. I couldn't quite tell if he was looking at me or not.

"General Tso's, please," I said. "And a Coke."

He grunted and rang up the bill on the old register, and I forked over my hard-won babysitting money, two dollars an hour for the Bauer hellions. When I sat down, the boys were already digging into their food, and the girl who had served them was backing away, looking down, holding the round tray before her like a shield. This one was pretty, delicate, with pointed little ears and chapped lips, but the boys didn't seem to notice her at all. Tim Summerton was just pushing around his mu shu pork, looking sick.

"You okay?" I said to Tim. He looked up at me, then looked away.

"He's just a pussy," said Huxley, a grain of rice on his lips. "He's all nervous about Regionals tomorrow. Doesn't want to do the five-hundred free."

"Really?" I said. "But, Tim, you're the best we've got."

"Eh," said Tim, shrugging. "Well, I'm not too nervous about it." Then he blinked and, clearly making an effort to change the subject, said, as my plate of crispy delicious chicken was placed before me, "So, who are you taking to the Winter Dance?" None of the boys really wanted to talk about this, it was clear, but spat out names: Gretchen, Melissa, maybe Gina, maybe Steph. Tim looked at me. "Who you going with, Lollie?"

I shrugged. "I don't know," I said. "Maybe just my friends." Depressing thought: my friends were the girls I ate lunch with, all buddies from kindergarten who knew one another so well we weren't sure if we even liked one another anymore.

Huxley gave me his charming smile and said, "Because you're, like, a dyke, right? You like chicks? It's okay, you can tell us." He laughed, and the other divers laughed with him.

"No," I said, putting my chopsticks down, feeling my face grow hot. "What the hell? No, I'm not a whatever, I mean, I like guys, Jesus." My excitement, the invitation to eat with them, soured a little in my gut. I looked hard at the curls of chicken on my plate.

"Relax, Lollie," said Tim, grinning at me, his wonky eye traveling over the window, where the world was lit pink by the light over the sign. "He's just teasing you. Brad's a dick."

And, charmingly, Huxley winked at me and showed me his mouthful of half-chewed food. "I know you're no dyke," he said. "But you could tell us if you were."

"Yeah," one of the other divers said. "That's totally hot." And when we all looked at him a little funny, he blushed and said, "Well. Maybe not you, Lollie. But lesbians in general." He gathered high fives all around, hooting, until something in me burst and I gave him a little high five on his cheek, and he sat down again, abashed.

IN THE CHINESE MYTH, the goddess Nugua created the first humans from yellow earth, carefully crafting them with her own hands. Though they pleased her, these handcrafted humans took too much time, and so to speed the process along, she dipped a rope into darker mud and swung it around her head. In this way, she populated the earth with the darker mudspatters, who became the lowly commoners, while the handcrafted were the wealthy and higher-caste nobles.

Nugua, they say, has a woman's upper body but a dragon's tail. She invented the whistle, the art of irrigation, the institution of marriage. How terrible that this dragon-goddess is also the one who grants children to mothers; that this impatient snob of a goddess is the intermediary between men and women.

IT WAS LATE WHEN I CAME HOME because we sat around after we ate, as if waiting for something to happen. At last, Tim stood and said, "I'll escort you out, Lollie?" and I had the brief and thrilling fear that he was going to ask me to the Winter Dance. But Tim only opened my car door for me, then pulled off, his old Volvo spitting up smoke. I drove home over the black ice and into the driveway of our cottage on Eagle Street.

My mother's car was gone, and only one light was on in the kitchen when I came in. Pot was sitting in the half-shadow, looking at me with a tragic face.

"Potty?" I said. "What's wrong, honey?" Her little face broke down until, at last, her eyes filled, huge and liquid, with tears.

"I wanted your food to be warm," she said, "so I put up the heat. But then you didn't come home, and it burned a little, and so I put it down. And then I got scared because you still weren't home, and so I put the heat up again, and now it's all ruined." She poked the foil off the plate, and her lip began to tremble.

"Oh, I'm so, so sorry. We went out for Chinese," I said, looking at the charred remains of the chicken and couscous my mother had saved for me. I hugged my little sister until she began to laugh at herself. Then I said, "Petra Pot, where's Mom?"

She frowned and said, sourly, "The Garbageman's." We called our mother's new boyfriend The Garbageman, though he was actually a Ph.D. in garbage science and owned a lucrative monopoly on trash removal in the five counties surrounding ours. He certainly didn't look like a garbageman, either, being fastidious to the point of compulsion, with his hair combed over a small bald spot on his head, his wrists doused in spicy cologne, and the beautiful shirts he had tailored for him in Manhattan. Though Pot hated him, I was ambivalently happy for my mother's sudden passion: since we lost my father, she hadn't seen anyone, and this, I privately assumed, had made her as nervous and trembly as she had been in recent years.

When I say we lost my father, I don't mean he died: I mean that we lost him when we were on a sabbatical in England, in the bowels of Harrods department store. This was back when Pot was five and suffering acutely from both dyslexia and ADHD. Her inability to connect language in her head, combined with her short attention span, frequently made her so frustrated she didn't actually speak, but, rather, screamed. "Petra the Pepperpot," we called her, affectionately, which was shortened to "Pepperpot," then "P-pot," then "Pot" or "Potty." The day we lost my father was an exceptionally trying one, as, all morning, Pot had screamed and screamed and screamed. My dad, having coveted the Barbour oil jackets he'd seen around him all summer long, had taken us to Harrods to try to find one for himself. But for at least fifteen minutes, he was subjected to the snooty superciliousness of the clerk when he tried to describe the jacket.

"Bah-bah," my father kept saying, as that's what he heard when he asked the Brits what kind of jacket they were wearing. "It's brown and oily. A Bah-Bah jacket."

"I'm sorry, sir," the clerk returned indolently. "I've never heard of a Bah-Bah."

Thus, my father was furious already when my little sister fell into an especially loud apoplectic fit, pounding her heels into the ground. At last, my father turned on us. His face was purple, his eyes bulged under his glasses, and this mild-mannered radiologist seemed about ready to throttle someone to death. "Wait here," he hissed, and stalked off.

We waited. We waited for hours. My mother rubbed her thin arms, frightened and angry, and I was sent to the vast deli in the basement for sandwiches. Cheddar and chutney, watercress and ham. We waited, and we had no way to contact him, and so, when the store was about to close, we caught a cab back to our rented flat. We found his things gone. He was in a hotel, he said later when he telephoned. He had arranged our tickets home. My mother shut the sliding doors in the tiny kitchen, and Pot and I tried to watch a bad costume drama on the telly, and when our mother came out, we knew without asking that it was all over. Nowadays, my father lives in an Oxford town house with a woman named Rita, who is about to have their first child. "Lurvely Rita, Meeta-Maid" is what my mother so scornfully calls her, though Rita is a neurologist, and dry, in the British manner, to the point of unloveliness.

But the evening of the Lucky Chow Fun, my father wasn't the villain. My mother was, because who leaves a troubled ten-year-old alone in a big old house in the middle of winter? There were still a few tourists in town, and anyone could have walked through our ever-unlocked front door. I was filled with a terrible fury, tempted to call her at The Garbageman's place with a sudden faux emergency, let her streak home naked through the snow. And then, after some reflection, I realized *I* was the villain: my mother had thought I'd be home by the time she went out, Pot had said.

Stricken with guilt, I allowed Pot to take me upstairs to her own creepy ornithological museum. In the dark, the birds' glass eyes glittered in light from the streetlamps, giving me the odd impression of being scrutinized. I shivered. But Pot turned on the light and led me from bird to bird, solemnly pronouncing each one's name, and giving a respectful little bow as she moved on. At long last, she stopped before a new addition to her collection, a dun-colored bird with mischievous eyes.

Pot stroked its head, and said, "This is an Eastern Towhee. It goes: *hot dog, pickle, ickle, ickle.*"

"Neat," I said, feeling the gaze of the gyrfalcon on the tenderest parts of my neck.

"*Hurry, worry, blurry, flurry,*" Pot said. "Scarlet Tanager."

"Cool," I said. "I like it. Scarlet Tanager. Hey, you want to watch a movie?"

"*Quick-give-me-a-rain-check,*" giggled Pot. "White-eyed Vireo."

"Pots, listen up. Do you want to watch *Dirty Dancing*? I'll make popcorn."

"*If I sees you, I will seize you, and I'll squeeze you till you squirt,*" my baby sister said, grinning so hugely she almost split her chubby little cheeks.

I blinked, held my breath. "Uh," I said. "Where'd you get that one, Pot?"

"That's the call of a Warbling Vireo," she said with great satisfaction. "Let's watch *The Princess Bride*."

My mother was up before we were in the morning, flipping omelets and singing a Led Zeppelin song. "Kashmir," I think. She beamed at me in the doorway, and when I went to her and bent to kiss her on the head, she still stank of The Garbageman's cologne.

"Ugh," I said. "You may want to shower before Pot gets up."

She looked at me, frowning. "I did," she said, pulling a strand of her springy peppered hair across her nose. "Twice."

I took a seat at the table. "That's the power of The Garbageman's scent, I guess," I said. "Indelible. He sprays you like a wildcat, and you belong to him."

"Elizabeth," my mother said, sprinkling cut chives atop the egg. "Can you just try to be happy for me?"

"I am," I said, but looked down at my hands. I wasn't sure what I was happy for, as I had never been on a date, let alone done anything remotely sexual, and it wasn't entirely because I was fat. The hard truth was that nobody really dated at Templeton High. Couples were together, or broken up, without really having dated. There was nowhere to go; the nearest theater, in Oneonta, was thirty minutes away. And though I suspected there was some sexual activity happening, I was mystified as to how it was instigated.

My mother took my hand in a rapid little movement, kissed it, and went to the stairs to shout up for Pot. My sister was always a furious sleeper, everything about her clenched in slumber—face, limbs, fists—and she never awoke until some-one shook her. But that morning, she came downstairs whis-tling, her hair in a sloppy ponytail, dressed all in white, a pair of binoculars slung around her neck. We both stared at her.

"I am going bird-watching on the nature trail," she an-nounced, taking a plate. "I'm wearing white to blend in with the snow. Yummy omelets, Mom."

"Oh. Okay, Honey-Pot. Sounds good," said my mother, sitting down with her own coffee and plate. She had decided when my father left to be a hands-off parent, and went from hovering nervously over everything I did to allowing my little sister the most astounding latitude.

"Wait. You're going alone, Pot?" I said. I glared at my mother, this terrible person who would let a ten-year-old wander in the woods alone. What would she do when I was in college, just let my little sister roam the streets at night? Let her have drunken parties in the backyard, let her squat in the abandoned Sugar Shack on Estli Avenue, let her be a crack whore?

"Yup," Pot said. "All alone."

"Mom," I said, "she can't go alone. Anyone can be out there."

"Honey, Lollie, it's Templeton. For God's sakes, nothing happens here. And the nature trail is maybe five acres. At that."

"Five acres that could be filled with rapists, Mom."

"I think Pot will be fine," said my mother. She and Pot

exchanged wry glances. And then she looked at the clock on the microwave, saying, "Don't you have to be at the gym in fifteen minutes?"

I stifled my protest, warned Pot to take the Mace my mom carried as protection against dogs on her country runs, and struggled into my anorak. Then I stuffed a piece of toast down my gullet and roared off in my deathtrap Honda. When I passed the Ambassador's mansion, I saw him coming up the walk, back from the Purple Pickle Coffee Shop, steaming cup in hand, miniature schnauzer on a lead in the other, and they both—man and beast—were dressed all in white, with matching white pompommed berets. *Curious,* I thought, but that was all: I was already focusing, concentrating on the undulations of my body through the water, envisioning the hundred butterfly, watching myself touching all the boys out by an entire body length.

IN THE GRIMMS' STORY "Hansel and Gretel," it isn't the witch in the gingerbread house who is the wickedest character, as the poor wandering siblings easily defeated her with their small cunning. Rather, the parents of the children were the ones who, in a time of famine, not once, but twice, concocted the plan to take their children into the dark forest and leave them there to starve. The first time, the children dropped stones and found their way back. The second time, the forest gobbled up their trail. The witch did what witches do. The parents were the unnatural ones. This speaks to a deep and ingrained fear: that parents could, in their self-interest, lose sight of their duties to their children. They could sell them to the dark and dank wilderness, send them to the forest, let them starve there. And each time, those two little children, hungry for home, came struggling so bravely back.

BUT NOTHING HAPPENED TO POT THAT DAY, and we won Regionals, as nobody could dent our team that year. It was late when we returned, and I was reading *Bulfinch's Mythologies* for the nth time, under the red exit light in the back of the bus. I was marveling over the tiny passage on Danae: *Daughter of King Acrisius of Argos who did not want her to marry and kept her imprisoned because he had been told that his daughter's son would kill him. Jupiter came to her in the disguise of a shower of gold, and she became the mother of Perseus. She and her child were set adrift in a chest and saved by a fisherman on the island of Seriphos.* There was something so haunting in the story, drama packed so tightly into the words that images burst in my head: a white-limbed girl in a dark room, a chink in the roof, the shower of gold pouring over her dazzled body; then the black chest, the baby squirming on her stomach, the terrifying rasp of the scales of sea-monsters against the wood. A story of light and dark. Purely beautiful, it seemed to me, then.

I was daydreaming so happily as we trundled over Main Street that I didn't at first notice what was happening until one of the freshman boys gave a shout. The bus driver slowed down to rubberneck as we went around the flagpole on Pioneer Street, and I saw it all: all eight of the town's squad cars up the hill to our left, all flashing red and blue in syncopated bolts, glaring on the ice and snow, and the ambulance with the stretcher being swallowed up inside it, the running police, the drawn guns, the Chens, both Fat and Glasses, up against the Lucky Chow Fun's vinyl siding, arms and legs spread. A huddled ring of the Lucky Chow Fun girls on the steps. I could pick out the girl with the jagged haircut, her arm around a plump girl with hair to her waist.

"Ohhhhh. Shit," breathed Brad Huxley in the seat before mine. And then the bus passed the scene, and we rolled down Main Street toward the one stoplight in town. From there, the hamlet looked innocent and pristine, a flurry of windblown snow turning the streetlights into snow globes, icing the trees. Over the hills, the March moon was pinned, stoic and yellow, reflected in pieces on the half-glassy lake.

We were already halfway up Chestnut Street, silently looking out the windows, when someone said, "One too many cases of food poisoning?"

And though it wasn't funny, though we all had the flashing red and blue images lodged firmly in us somewhere just under our hearts, we—all of us—laughed.

I SLEPT LATE ON SUNDAY, into the afternoon. I never sleep late, and I know what this means: the worst cowards are the ones who refuse to look at what they fear. When I went downstairs, my mother and sister were still in their pajamas. Though Pot was almost my tiny mother's size, and twice her width, she was cradled on my mother's lap, sucking her thumb, her other hand up in her infant gesture to stroke my mother's ear. They were watching television, the sound off. I stood in the door, looking at the screen until I realized that the snowy roads I was seeing on the television were roads I knew as intimately as my own limbs, that the averted faces of the men on the screen were men who knew me well, who followed my swimming in the paper, who thought nothing of giving me a kiss when they saw me. Hurrying down the snowy streets now, shame on their faces, shame in the set of their shoulders.

Then came the faces of the Chens—stoic, inexpressive—and the scared faces of the Chinese girls, ducking into Mr. Livingston's limousine. He was my ninth-grade history teacher, and his limo was the only car in town large enough to hold all the girls and their lawyers at once. That car drove legends of baseball all summer from museum to hotel to airport. It drove brides and homecoming queens for the rest of the year. Now it was driving the Lucky Chow Fun girls wherever they were going. Somewhere, I hoped, far away.

I went to the television and turned it off. I stood for a minute, letting the swell die down in my gut, then sat beside my mother and said, "What happened?"

And my mother, who always made a point of being frank about sexual matters, describing biological functions in great detail so that her daughters would never be squeamish or falsely prudish, my mother turned scarlet. "Sit down," she said, and I did. She opened her mouth to speak, then closed it. She bit her lips.

Pot said, pulling her thumb from her mouth, "The Lucky Chow Fun's a whorehouse."

"Pot," said my mother, then sighed. She looked at me, her thin mouth twisting, patting my thigh. "She's right," she said.

"What?" I said. "Wait, what?"

"Last night," my mother said, slowly, as if trying to order the fragmented truths, "one of the girls at the Lucky died. She was locked in her room with her sister—seems they were being punished—and there was some kind of accidental gas leak. One of them died, and the other one almost did, too. And one of the other girls who knew a little English called the police and tried to leave a tip before the Chens found out. But there are not too many poor speakers of English in this town. The police figured it out. They arrested the Chens."

"Oh, God," I said. I thought of the little huddle of the Lucky Chow Fun girls the night before, flushed red and blue in the flashing lights, how quiet they were, how I never saw their eyes. I never looked. "Mom," I said. "Who were those girls?"

My mother brushed Pot's hair out of her eyes and kissed her on the forehead. She seemed to hesitate, then she said, "They were bought in China and brought over here, it seems. They were poor. They worked in sweatshops. The Chens gave money to their parents, promised a better life. Apparently."

"Slaves," I said.

"On TV, they said that, yes," said Pot, stumbling over her words. "And some of them, they said on TV that some of them, they're younger than you, Lollie."

We sat there, in silence, thinking about this. My mother at one point stood and made us some cocoa, but for once, my tongue tasted like ash and I wanted to take absolutely nothing in. I was sick, could never again be hungry, I thought. At last, thinking of Chen Fat glaring at me over his notepad, the sticky smell of the food, Brad Huxley, the delicate girl with the chapped lips, I said, shuddering, "Do they know who visited? Do they have names?"

"Well," said my mother, who paused for a very long time, "that's almost the worst. The Chens wrote down the names of the men who visited the Lucky Chow Fun." It was hard to hear her, even in the preternatural stillness of the town on this day, even in our snow-muffled house. "They had a ledger. They made sure to write in English. The reporters said that they were going to blackmail the men who visited. Apparently, it's not just tourists. Apparently, a lot of men from the town went, too." She looked at us. "You should know. Some of the men you know, some you love, some of them may have gone."

And there was something so uncertain in my mother's face, something so fearful it struck a note in me. I looked at the clock over the mantel: it was already four o'clock, and my mother hadn't left the house yet. Unusual: she was the only person I ever knew who could never sit still. Especially now, when she was dating The Garbageman, for whom she often cooked most meals and who, by this time on Sunday, had usually called our house to chat for hours, as if they were silly teenagers in love.

"Oh," I said. I looked at her face under her mop of curls, the weary circles around her eyes. "The Garbageman call today?"

My mother flushed again and stood to carry the mugs back to the kitchen. "Not yet," she tossed over her shoulder, as if it meant nothing to her at all.

I looked at Pot, who was frowning solemnly on her perch on the living room couch. She looked beyond me at a bird that landed on the tree outside, and cried, "A Song Sparrow! *Hip, hip, hip hurrah boys, spring is here!* That's what they say," she said, beaming. "The Song Sparrows. They say, *Hip, hip, hip hurrah boys, spring is here!*" She was tapping her feet in her excitement, blinking so rapidly and nervously that she reminded me of my mother.

"Pot," I said. "Have you taken your medication today?"

"Whoops," she said, grinning.

"Pot," I said. "How long has it been since you took your medication?"

She shrugged. "A week? Maybe a week. I stopped. I don't believe anymore in medicating children," she said.

I shuddered because I heard in her words the distinct voice of an adult, someone who never saw Pot as she had been in her awful years. A teacher, perhaps, or some judgmental village crone. I went to the kitchen, slamming the door behind me. "Mom," I said. "Pot's not taking her medication. And by the way, don't you think she's too young to understand all this Lucky Chow Fun crap? She's only ten. She's just a baby. I don't think she can handle it."

My mother stopped washing the mug she was holding and let the hot water run. The steam circled up around her, catching in her frizzy gray hair, spangling it when she turned around. "Lollie," she said. "I'll make sure she takes the Ritalin from now on. But nobody in town is going to be able to escape what happened. Not even the kids. It's better that we tell her the truth before someone else tells her something much worse."

"What's worse?" I said. "And I don't think people are made to take truths straight-on, Mom. It's too hard. You need something to soften them. A metaphor or a story or something. You know."

"No," she said, "I don't." She turned off the water with a smack of her hand. "Why don't you teach me, since you seem to know everything."

"Well," I said, but at the moment when we most need these things, they don't always come to us. I couldn't remember a word. I opened my mouth and it hung open there, useless. I closed it. I shrugged.

My mother nodded. "That's what I thought," she said, and turned away.

YEARS LATER, I WOULD HAVE HAD the presence of mind to offer the tale "Fitcher's Bird," from the Brothers Grimm, to offer up an allegorical explanation. I would have told my mother how a wizard dressed as a beggar would magically lure little girls into his basket. He'd cart them to his mansion, give them an egg and key, and tell them not to go into the room that the key opened. Then he'd leave, and the little girls would explore the magnificent house, finally falling prey to curiosity and opening the door of the forbidden chamber.

There, they'd find a huge basin filled with the bloody, dismembered remains of other girls. They'd be so surprised, they'd drop the egg in the vat, and wouldn't be able to wipe the stain away. When the wizard would come home to find the stained egg, he would dismember the girls and toss their remains into the vat.

Eventually, he did this to the two eldest girls from one family, and came back for the third daughter. This girl, though, was uncommonly clever. She hid the egg in a safe place and brazenly went into the room, only to find her dismembered sisters in the bloody vat. But instead of panicking, she pulled their severed limbs out and pieced them back together again, and when the parts were reassembled, the girls miraculously came back to life.

The clever girl hid her sisters in a room to await the wizard, and when he returned and saw she hadn't bloodied the egg, he decided to marry her. She agreed, but said first that she would send him home with a basketful of gold for her parents. She hid her two sisters in the basket, which he carted home, now a servant of his clever bride. In his absence, the little girl dressed a human skull in flowers and jewels and put it in the attic window. Then she rolled herself in honey and feathers to transform herself into a strange feathered creature, and ran out into the bright day.

On her way home, she encountered the wizard, who thought she was a wonderful bird and said, "Oh, Fitcher's feathered bird, where from, where from?"

To which she responded, "From feathered Fitze Fitcher's house I've come."

"And the young bride there, how does she fare?" he asked, imagining his marriage night, and the soft young body of his wife.

And she, smiling softly under her down and honey, said, "She's swept the house all the way through, and from the attic window, she's staring down at you."

When the wizard arrived home to find the skull in the window, he waved at it, thinking it was his bride. When he went inside, the brothers and father of the little stolen girls locked the door, set a fire, and burned the terrible murderer up.

IN THE GRIMMS' STORY, of course, the community at last cleansed itself by fire, and in the aftermath came out righteous and whole. This did not happen to Templeton.

We were under siege. The media trucks were parked all along Main Street. Our town, though small, was famous for the baseball museum and for its beauty, an all-American village. Right-wing pundits on television and in the mega-corporation-owned newspapers held up our town as a symbol for the internal moral rot of America, a symbol of the trickle-down immorality stemming from our Democrat president, who went around screwing everything that moved. People from Cherry Valley and Herkimer roared into town, pretending that they were natives, and the whole country saw us as drawling mulleted hicks in whole-body Carhartt, and hated us more. The handsome newscasters shivered in their fur-lined parkas, sat at our diner, and tried to eavesdrop, but were really only eavesdropping on other newscasters.

Our shell-shocked mayor appeared on television. He was the town know-it-all, a bearded hobbit of a man who gave bombastic walking tours to the tourists and wore shorts all year because of a skin condition. He had to pause to wipe his mouth with a handkerchief, choking up throughout his speech. At the end, he said, "Templeton will survive, as we have survived many other disasters in our illustrious history. Be brave, Templeton, and we will see each other through." But there was no applause at the end, as there were no Templetonians in the audience, composed as it was of disaster-gawkers and newscasters.

Our Ambassador appeared on CNN and *20/20* to defend our town. "We are not perfect," he said in his quivery old man's voice. "But we are a good town, full of good people." His cloudy eyes filled with fervor. It was very affecting.

We stayed inside. We went to the grocery store, if we needed to, to school, and a few of us went to the gym. Our team practiced in virtual silence, the only sound the water sucking in the gutters, the splash of our muscled limbs. In school, the teachers came to classes with red-rimmed eyes, traces of internal anguish happening in the homes of people we never imagined had private lives. The drama kids pretended to weep at lunch on a recurrent basis. There was a hush over the town, as if each of us were muted, swaddled in invisible quilts, so separate from one another as to not be able to touch, if we wanted to. Girls began walking in groups everywhere, as if for protection. The Templeton men did not dare to look at the Templeton women, furious as we were, righteous. And in this separation, in our own sorrow, we forgot about the girls, the Lucky Chow Fun girls, and when, after some time, we thought of them, they were the enemies. They were the ones who had brought this shame to our town.

TWO TERRIBLE WEEKS PASSED. My mother stopped talking about The Garbageman, *tout court*. He stopped calling. She stopped visiting him with plates of food. She grew drawn and pale, and spent a lot of time in her flannel nightgown, watching *Casablanca*. She picked a new fight with the principal and came home spitting. The Winter Dance was canceled: I spent that evening dating a pizza and an apple crumble, watching Fred and Ginger glide across the floor, pure grace. Pot acquired two new taxidermied birds, one finch, one scarlet macaw, its head cocked intelligently, even in death.

One day, I came home, skirting Main Street and its hordes of news cameras. I went to the mailbox and found six envelopes from colleges all over the country, all addressed to me.

I went inside. I sat at the table with a cup of tea, the six letters splayed before me. One by one, I opened them. And what would have been a personal tragedy before the Lucky Chow Fun was now a slight relief. Of the six colleges, all of which had recruited me for swimming, though I had indifferent grades and mediocre SATs, I had only gotten into one.

Rather: I had gotten into one. One, glorious, one.

I tossed out the bad five, and waited for Pot. My tea cooled and I made more, and it cooled again. I peered out the curtains for my little sister, but she didn't come. I made cookies, chocolate chip, her favorite. I had half an hour before swim practice and she still wasn't home when my mother came in, with her energetic stompings and mutterings. "My God, Lollie," she said, "you'll never guess what that ass-muncher of a princip—"

"Mom?" I interrupted. "Do you know where Potty is?"

"Isn't she here?" she said, massaging her neck, peeping in from the mudroom. "She was supposed to come straight home from school to go to the grocery store with me."

"Nope," I said. "And it's getting dark."

She came into the kitchen then, scowling. "Do you have any idea where she could be?" she said. We looked at each other, and her hand floated up to her hair.

I stood, nervous. "Oh, God," I said.

"Calm down," she said, though she was flustered herself. "Think, Lollie. Does she have any friends?"

"Pot?" I said. I looked at her. "You're kidding, right?"

"Oh, God," she said.

"Let's think, let's think," I said. I paced to the window, then back. "Mom. Let's think. Where does Potsy get her birds? The stuffed ones. Do you know?"

My mother looked at me, then slowly lifted her hands to her cheeks. "You know," she said, "I never actually wondered. I guess I assumed your dad was sending them. Or she was buying them with her allowance. Or something. I never wondered."

"You haven't given us allowance in six months," I said. "So where are they from?"

"Is she stealing them?" said my mother. "Maybe from the Biological Field Station?"

"Pot?" I thought of this, wondering if Pot could have the gall to waltz into some place, open up the display cabinets, hide the birds under her shirt, and waltz on home. "I don't think so. It's not like her," I said, at last.

"Well," said my mother, her voice breaking. "Who'd have a collection like that?"

And my mother and I looked at one another. There was a long, shivery beat, a car driving by outside, its headlights washing over my mother's face, then beyond. And then we both ran out coatless into the snow, we ran into the blue twilight as hard as we could up the block, forgetting about our cars in our hurry, we ran past the grand old hospital, over the

Susquehanna, we ran fleet and breathless to the Ambassador's house, and then we burst inside.

The house was extraordinarily hot, the chandelier in the hallway tinkling, and the ugly miniature schnauzer barking and nipping at us. Our shoes slid on the marble floor as we sped into the living room. Bookcases, Persian rugs, leather armchairs—no Pot. We flew through the door, into the library—no Pot. We ran though the hall and stopped short in the dining room.

There, my little sister was dressed in a feather boa and rhinestone starlet glasses, in her undershirt, crouching on an expensive cherrywood chair and looking at a book of birds that was at least as big as she was. She looked up at us, unsurprised, when we came in.

"Hey," she said. "Mom, Lollie, come here, look at this. This is a first edition Audubon. The Ambassador said I could have it when I'm eighteen."

"What the hell are you doing here?" my mother said, snapping from her surprise and charging over to her. She ripped the glasses from Pot's face and pushed her arms into her little cardigan. Pot looked up at her, her face open and wondering.

That's when the Ambassador appeared in the doorway and said, "Oh, dear. I told Miss Petra here she should have been home hours ago. But you know her and birds," and he gave a tinkly little laugh.

"You," I said, charging at him. "What in the fuck are you doing with my sister? Why is she in her undershirt?"

"Pot," my mother was saying at the same time. "Has he touched you? Has he hurt you? Has he done anything to you?"

The Ambassador blinked, his milky eyes canny. "Oh, my," he said mildly. "Oh, I'm afraid there's been a misunderstanding. Pot told me you knew she visited with me."

"We did *not*," I said. "Are you hurting her?"

Pot gave a little bark of surprise. "Oh, God," she said. "No. Jeez, you guys. I mean, like. I don't think he even. You know. Girls," she trailed off.

We looked at her.

She sighed. "No girls. He doesn't like them," she said.

My mother and I looked at the Ambassador, who flushed, ducked his head. "Well," he said. "Well, Petra. Oh, my. But yes, you are right. And no, I have never touched Petra. She comes here after school, and I give her one object of her choice every week. I have no heirs, you know," he said. "I have so many beautiful things. Petra is an original. She is a pleasure to talk to. She will one day be something great, I warrant."

"He lets me wear a boa," said Pot. "He lets me be a movie star. He knew Grace Kelly. And it's always hot in here so I have to take off my sweater. It's always one hundred degrees exactly. I *die* if I don't take off my sweater."

"Yes. I'm afraid I am anemic," the Ambassador said delicately. "I cannot bear cold." He looked at our shoes, dripping slush on his fine floors. He said, "Could I make some tea for you before you three ladies return home?"

My mother and I stared at the Ambassador for a very long moment. And then, in shame, we gathered ourselves up. We apologized, we clutched our little Pot tightly to us. And he, ever the statesman, pretended we hadn't offended him. "These times," he sighed, escorting us to the door, where the wind had blown a great heap of powder onto the priceless rug. "In these dark days, there is so much distrust in this town. I understand absolutely. You never know quite what to think about people you believe you trust." Then he shivered, and Pot reached up and squeezed his hand. In the glance between the two there was such adoration that, on the long walk through the dark, I stole small looks at Pot to try to see what exactly he had seen in her, the budding wonder there. The one she would become, to our great wonder.

IT TOOK A LOT OF TIME. Templeton could not heal quickly. There was still much scandal, many divorces, many people leaving town to start over. The dentist I had been to all my life. The school custodian, the principal, the football coach. My postman, the town librarian, my best friend's brother, the owner of the boatyard, the manager of the Purple Pickle, the CFO of the baseball museum—all divorced or shamed. Brad Huxley sent to military school. The Garbageman moved to Manhattan, though his trucks still rumble by every Thursday morning. And there were many more.

But the newscasters trickled away when a professional football player killed his wife and charged the country with a new angst. The tourists returned as if nothing had happened, and there were motorboats again on the lake, my tearful graduation, the death-by-chocolate binge the night before I drove off to school. The Chens were shipped back to China, and probably set free, and the girls were taken to San Francisco, where most of them decided to make a new life. To heal. I read of their trial in the *Freeman*'s *Journal*, from the safety of my dorm room my freshman year. In the end, time smoothed it all away.

But for those of us who return periodically, there is always a little frisson of darkness that falls over us when we see the candy shop where the Lucky Chow Fun once had been.

ONLY NOW, MANY YEARS LATER, can I imagine what the real tragedy had been. It was not the near-death of my town, though that was where all my sympathy was at the time. I mourned the community that almost buckled under the scandal, for the men in the town, for our women. How we were split. As was my training, I forgot about the poor Lucky Chow Fun girls. Only now, years later, do I dream of them.

ONCE UPON A TIME THERE WERE SEVEN GIRLS. They were girls like any other girls, no cleverer, no more or less wealthy than others in their town. They were pretty as young girls are always pretty, blooming, rose-cheeked, lily-skinned. The factory they worked in was gray, the machines they worked on were gray, the nighttime streets they walked back to their crowded apartments, all gray. But they dreamed in colors, in blues and greens and golds.

One dark night, the girls' parents closed the doors. Conferred. When they came out, the girls were told: we are sending you to America. There should have been joy in this, but the parents' smiles were also taut with fear.

How much? the girls asked, trembling.

Enough, the parents responded, meaning: Enough money, enough of your questions.

And the seven girls were taken to the docks. They crawled into boxes and were sealed inside with water and candy and pills. There, with the bones of their knees pressed to the bones of their ribs, hearing the roar of the tanker, they saw nothing in the darkness but more darkness.

They arrived, weak and trembling. They were unpacked. They were taken to the house where they were trained to be quiet, absent, to press themselves to the mattresses and not say a word. In that house, they slowly became ghosts.

The seven ghosts were put then into a van, driven to a cold town on a lake, where nobody knew who they were, nobody cared if they were living or dead, where they cooked silently, cleaned silently, lay on the mattresses, and did not say a word. Men went into their rooms, men left their rooms, other men came in.

One ghost stopped eating and she died. In the middle of the night, the ghosts were forced to row her to the middle of the black lake. They tied her limbs to grease buckets filled with stones and they dropped her in. She sank under the water and seemed to blink up at them as she went. They rowed back. Wordless, as always.

Then there were six ghosts. The two that were sisters were punished, locked in a room. The air was bad, and one died, the other almost did. And one of the remaining ghosts found the dead girl and her half-dead sister. She touched the blue cheeks of the dead girl, and she felt only cold. Something old rose in her, some small courage. She stole one moment with the phone, spoke words, clumsy, ugly, perhaps, but those words breathed life back into the girls, brought liberty in the form of flashing red and blue lights.

IN THE END, AFTER THE LONG TRIAL, the men who'd imprisoned them were imprisoned themselves. The girls went to San Francisco, where they chose to stay, where, slowly, they went out into the streets. They saw the green of the water, the gold of the sky, and they learned what it meant to be girls again. I imagine them there, together, walking in some garden, their hair gleaming under the sun. I imagine them happy.

And it is a happy ending, perhaps, in the way that myths and fairy tales have happy endings; only if one forgets the bloody, dark middles, the fifty dismembered girls in the vat, the parents who sent their children into the woods with only a crust of bread. I like to think it's a happy ending, though it is the middle that haunts me.

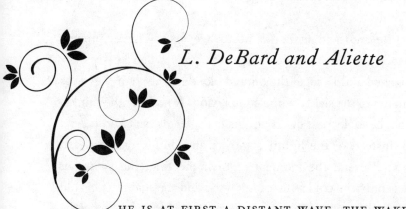

L. DeBard and Aliette

HE IS AT FIRST A DISTANT WAVE, THE WAKE-wedge of a loon as it surfaces. The day is cold and gray as a stone. In the mid-distance the swimmer splits into parts, smoothly angled arms and a matte black head. Twenty feet from the dock he dips below the water and comes up a moment later at the ladder, blowing like a whale.

She sees him step onto the dock: the pronounced ribs heaving, the puckered nipples, the moustache limp with seawater. She feels herself flush, and, trembling, smiles.

It is March 1918, and hundreds of dead jellyfish litter the beach. The morning newspapers include a story, buried under the accounts of battles at the Western Front, about a mysterious illness striking down hale soldiers in Kansas.

The swimmer lifts his towel to gain time, wondering about the strange, expectant trio that watches him. The man in the clump is fat and bald, his chin deeply lined from mouth to jowl. His shave is close, his clothes expensive. A brunette stands beside him, the wind chucking her silk collar under her chin: the fat man's young wife, the swimmer thinks, mistakenly.

Before them sits a girl in a wheelchair. The swimmer's glance brushes over her and veers away when he sees her wizened child's face, the diluted blonde of her hair, her eyes sunken in the sickly white complexion. A nothing, he thinks. That he looks past her is not his fault. He doesn't know. And so, instead of the lightning strike and fluttering heart that should attend the moment of their meeting, the swimmer feels only the cold whip of the wind and the shame of his old suit, holey and stretched out, worn on the dark days when he needs nostalgia and old glory to bring him to the water.

THE SWIMMER IS A FAMOUS MAN. He is an Olympian: gold medalist in the 1908 London Olympics in the 100-meter freestyle, anchor on the 4×200 relay. Triple gold in the 1912 Stockholm Olympics: 100-meter freestyle, 100-meter backstroke, anchor again on the 4×200. He was on the American Swim Association's champion water polo team from 1898 through 1911. He is, quite simply, The World's Best Swimmer.

His name is L. DeBard, though this was not always his name. He was Lodovico DeBartolo, but was taken from Rome at the age of six and transplanted to New York, where the Ukrainians, the Poles, the Chinese couldn't pronounce

Lodovico. He reworked his last name when he discovered in himself literary agility and a love of Shakespeare.

He is a swimmer, but he is other things, too. A forty-three-year-old with a mighty set of pectorals, one chipped front tooth, and a rakish smile; a rumored Bolshevik; a poet, filler of notebooks, absinthe-drinker, cavorter of the literary type. He knows a number of whores by name, though in the wider world he is thought to be a bit queer, his friendships a mite too close with the city's more effeminate novelists and poets. He has been alone in the company of Tad Perkins, C.T. Dane, Arnold Effingham. Something is suspect about a man-poet, anyway, and many of his critics ask one another, pursing their lips lewdly, why he is not in France, fighting for the Allies. The reason is that his flat feet make him unfit for battle.

And today, he is one last thing: starving. Poets and swimmers are the last to be fed in these final few months of the Great War.

The fat man steps forward. "L. DeBard?" he says.

L. wraps the towel under the straps of his suit. "Yes," he says, at last.

The girl in the wheelchair speaks. "We have a proposition for you," she says. Her voice reminds the swimmer of river rock: gravelly, smooth.

THE GIRL'S NAME IS ALIETTE HUBER. She is sixteen, and she is a schoolgirl, or was before her illness. She won her school's honors for French, Composition, Rhetoric, and Recitation for three years in a row. She can read a poem once and recite it perfectly from memory years later. Before the polio, she was a fine horsewoman, a beautiful archer, the lightest dancer of any of the girls at the children's balls society had delighted in staging in the heady days before the war. Her mother died when she was three, and her father is distantly doting.

She knows L. from his book of poetry, which she read when she was recuperating from her illness. She feels she knows him so intimately that now, freezing on the dock, she is startled and near tears: she has just realized that, to him, she is a stranger.

AND SO, ALIETTE DOES SOMETHING DRASTIC: she unveils her legs. They are small, wrinkled sticks, nearly useless. She wears a Scottish wool blanket over her lap, sinfully thick. L. thinks of his thin sheet and the dirty greatcoat he sleeps under, and envies her the blanket. Her skirt is short and her stockings silk. L. doesn't gasp when he sees her legs, her kneecaps like dinner rolls skewered with willow switches. He just looks up at Aliette's face, and suddenly sees that her lips are set in a perfect heart, purple with cold.

After that, the swim lessons are easily arranged. When they leave—the brunette pushing the wheelchair over the boards of the docks, her trim hips swishing—their departure thrums in L.'s heels. The wind picks up even more and the waves make impatient sounds on the dock. L. dresses. His last nickel rolls from the pocket of his jacket as he slides it over his yellowed shirt. The coin flashes in the water and glints, falling.

ALIETTE LIES IN HER WHITE starched sheets in her bedroom on Park Avenue, and listens to the Red Cross trucks grinding gears in the street below. She puts the thin book of poetry under the sheets when she hears footsteps coming down the hall to her door. But the book slides from her stomach and between her almost useless legs, and she gasps with sudden pleasure.

Her nurse, the brunette from the dock, enters with a glass of buttermilk. Rosalind is only a few years older than Aliette, but looks as hearty and innocent as Little Bo Peep, corn-fed, pink with indolence. Aliette tries not to hate her as she stands there, cross-armed, until Aliette drains the glass. The nurse's lipstick has smeared slightly beyond the boundaries of her lips. From the front hall, Mr. Huber's trilling whistle resounds, then the butler says, "Good afternoon, sir," and the door closes, and Aliette's father returns to Wall Street. The girl hands the glass back to Rosalind, who smiles a bit too hard.

"Do you need a trip to the water closet, Miss?" the nurse asks.

Aliette tells her no, she is reading, and that would be all. When the nurse's footsteps have faded, the girl retrieves the book of poetry from under the covers where it had nestled so pleasingly. *Ambivalence*, the title says. *By L. DeBard*.

While L. and Aliette wait to begin their first lesson the next day, the mysterious illness is creeping from the sleepy Spanish tourist town of San Sebastián. It will make its way into the farthest corners of the realm, until even King Alfonso XIII will lie suffering in his royal bed. French, English, and American troops scattered in France are just now becoming deathly ill, and the disease will skulk with them to England. Even King George V will be afflicted.

In New York, they know nothing of this. L. eats his last can of potted meat. Aliette picks the raisins from her scones and tries to read fortunes in the dregs of her teacup.

THEY WILL USE THE NATATORIUM at the Amsterdam Hotel for the lessons. It is a lovely pool of green tile, gold-leaf tendrils growing down the sides and a bold heliotrope of yellow tile covering the bottom. The walls and ceiling are sky blue. They cannot use it during the guest hours and must swim either in the early morning or at night.

Both, insists L., hating to take so much money from Mr. Huber for so little work. He comes early for the first lesson, marveling at the beautiful warmth and crystal water. He leaps from the sauna to the pool, laughing to himself. His moustache wilts in the heat.

When Aliette comes in, steaming from the showers, her hair in a black cloth cap with a strap under the chin, L. lifts her from her chair and carries her into the water. Rosalind sits in the corner by the potted palm, takes out her knitting, and falls asleep.

IN THE BEGINNING, THEY DON'T SPEAK. He asks her to kick as he holds her in the water. She tries, making one tiny splash, then another. Around the shallow end they go, three, four times. Rosalind's gentle snores echo in the room. At last, Aliette slides one thin arm around L.'s neck. "Stop," she says, panting with pain.

He brings her to the steps and sets her there. He stands before her in the waist-deep water, trying not to look at her.

"What is wrong with Rosalind?" he says. "Why is she sleeping?"

"Nothing is wrong," says Aliette. "Poor thing has been up all night."

"I trust that she was not caring for you? I assumed you were healthy," L. says.

Aliette hesitates and looks down. "She was caring for me, yes—and others," she says. Her face is tight and forbidding. But she then looks at him with one cocked eyebrow and whispers, "L., I must admit that I like your other suit better."

He is wearing a new indigo bathing costume with suspenders, and he looks down at himself, then at her, puzzled. His new suit cost him a week's wages. "Why is that?" he asks.

She glances at the sleeping nurse, then touches him where a muscle bulges over one hip. "I liked the hole here," she says. Then her hand is under the water where it looms, suddenly immense. She touches his thigh. "And here," she says. Her fingertip lingers, then falls away.

When he has steadied himself to look at her face, she is smiling innocently. She does not, however, look like a little girl anymore.

"They were only small holes," he says. "I am surprised you noticed."

"I notice everything," she says. But her face grows a little frightened; her eyes slide toward Rosalind, and she gives a great roar as if he'd told a stunner of a joke. This awakens the nurse, who resumes her knitting, blinking and looking sternly at the pair. "Let's swim," cries Aliette, and claps both of her hands on the water like a child.

DURING THE LATE LESSON THAT NIGHT, as Rosalind again succumbs to the heat and damp of the room, Aliette watches with amusement as L. tries to hide his chipped tooth from her by turning his face. He has waxed his moustache mightily, and the musky fragrance of the wax fills her head and makes it swim. She laughs, her face in the water. He thinks she is only blowing bubbles.

BY THE END OF THE FIRST WEEK, Aliette has gained ten pounds. When she is not swimming, she is forcing herself to eat cheese and bread with butter, even when she is not hungry.

father touches his new linen suit with admiration. In Rome, Amadeo was a tailor; here he is a hearse driver. He mutters, "Beautiful, beautiful," and nods at his son, fingering the lapels, checking the seams. L.'s older sister is blind and cannot remark upon the visible change in him.

But in the trolley home, his stomach filled with saltimbocca, L. thinks of his sister when she touched his face in farewell. "You have met a girl," she whispered. Lucrezia has never seen her own face, and cannot know its expressions—how, at that moment, her smile was an explosion.

IN LATE APRIL, THE NEWSPAPERS are full of news of a strange illness. The journalists try to blunt their alarm by exoticizing it, naming it Spanish influenza, *La Grippe*. In Switzerland, it is called *La Coquette*, as if it were a courtesan. In Ceylon it's the Bombay Fever, and in Britain the Flanders Grippe. The Germans, whom the Allies blame for this disease, call it *Blitzkatarrh*. The disease is as deadly as that name sounds.

Americans do not pay attention. They watch Charlie Chaplin and laugh until they cry. They read the sports pages and make bets on when the war will be over. And if a few healthy soldiers suddenly fall ill and die, the Americans blame it on exposure to tear gas.

L. HAS GONE TOMCATTING with his writer friends only twice by the time spring rolls into summer. The second time,

She loosens her corset, then throws it away. At night, though exhausted from swimming, she climbs out of bed and tries to stand. She succeeds for one minute one night, and five minutes the next. She has a tremendous tolerance for pain. At the end of the week, she can stand for thirty minutes and take two steps before falling. When she does fall, it is into bed, and she sleeps immediately, L.'s poetry beating around in her brain like so many trapped sparrows.

ALL THAT WEEK, L. PACES. On the cloudy Friday, he kicks the notebooks full of weightless little words, and they skitter across his floor. He decides that he must quit, tell that Wall Street Huber that he has another obligation and can no longer teach Aliette to swim. Blast her pathetic little legs to hell, he thinks. L. stands at his window and looks down into the dark street, where urchins pick through boxes of rotting vegetables discarded from the greengrocer's downstairs. A leaf of cabbage blows free in the wind and attaches itself to the brick wall opposite L.'s window, where it flutters like a small green pennant.

"*Porca madonna,*" he says. Then, as if correcting himself, he says, in English, "Pig Madonna." It doesn't sound right, and in the wake of its dissonance he finds that he is completely unable to walk to Park Avenue and quit.

Late that evening he sits by the pool. He touches the place on his thigh where Aliette's finger had touched him a week earlier. He does not look up until he hears a throat clearing,

you, you know. Only have to wait me some sixteen years or so. And he'd give her a dashing grin until she fell over on her love-weak legs.

But soon, another creature began to grow in the mother, sucking all energy right out of her, and so the girl learned to totter then run when the mother was taking her afternoon naps. There was a terrible emptiness inside her then, a sickness that her mother used to soothe by her presence alone. Now, she sang to herself, but the songs didn't sound right; she licked the cranberry-glass goblets in the china cabinet to see if they tasted red, but they didn't. And so, rattling alone in the dim house, the girl learned to take off her dress, to slide button through hole, ribbon-end through the bunny-ears of the bow, because the frills and the starch of her dresses were harsh on her skin and she liked the sweep of air much better. And when the mother was weak in bed, and the father snipped violently at the hedges outside, she learned how to take off her little patent leather shoes and her lacy socks and her big-girl diapers with the pink-nubbed pins. She took off her dress, but left the red hairbow in her rag curls. And then she stood in the bay window that gave out onto the busy, sunny streets, the postman coming up the walk, the boys playing dodgeball with a flabby ball, the mothers pushing their babies in their strollers, the little girl stood there and pressed her belly against the cold glass like a sunbleached sand-dollar. She pressed her hands against the glass until they turned into suction cups holding her there. She stood in the window, nude and happy.

But a boy saw her and began to scream with laughter, holding the red rubber ball against his chest, pointing. The other boys began hooting. The mothers covered their smiles with their red-nailed hands, made little shooing motions, and the postman, talking to the father, turned and guffawed. In her pleasure, all the people in the glass laughing, the little girl laughed, too, sending out bell-like peals of joy. She was excited, fizzed to the bone, and clutched her crotch because she had to pee, which only made the boys laugh harder.

Then her father looked up from the hedges, grew pink, and stormed inside, still holding the clippers, so that, for a moment before he grabbed her roughly by her fat forearm, she thought he was going to snip her in the way he snipped the hedges, and she was afraid. She opened her little mouth in a round O and narrowed her eyes and sirened with alarm.

When the father spanked her, she screamed so loudly he thought he was doing her great harm. After he put the diaper and the dress back on and shoved the shoes roughly on her betrayed little feet, he held her so tightly she panted, kissing her until the mother came down from the nap, bleary-faced and asking groggily what had happened.

WHEN THE GIRL WAS BIG ENOUGH to open doors and steal into rooms where she shouldn't be, she peered through the bars of the crib at her small brother, who looked like the baby rabbits that Fritz, the collie, found and ate in the yard. He smelled of celery, of urine, of baby sweat. He looked at her with his pink and quivering face, opened his mouth in a rictus of joy.

You, she accused, are ugly. He reached out his tiny hand and clutched at her nose, sliding his earthworm fingers into her nostrils, grinning his bare-gummed grin. She put a thumb into his mouth and he clamped down on it, and his tongue was hot and squirmy. Some small warmth hatched in her, and for a moment, she forgot the sick feeling that she had felt since her mother was fat with him, since he came home. She sighed. It's okay, she said, taking his fingers out of her nose. You can be ugly. You're a boy. He let out a cackle, as if agreeing, then the sick feeling returned to her.

Girl things were beautiful. Beauty was in girl things. Pretty, she breathed as her mother lifted the charlotte pan from the quivering dessert. Beautiful, she said to her face in the puddle when she took the red berries from the chokecherry and smeared the juice across her lips. Lovely were the dance lessons, the little pink leotards and tutus that made her look like a carnation. There was a lot of jumping and leaping and twirling, and the girls told secrets and pulled their leotards from the necks to show their nipples and sat in the middle of the lesson to cry for no reason. The girl scorned such behavior; *she* did not sit and cry, and for that reason, for the performance, she was the one chosen to be the purple butterfly when everyone else was pink. Her mother spent all night on the clacketing sewing machine creating her wings, vast and fluttery, with wire supports. When she wore them she *was* a butterfly, and at night she would crawl from her sleeping body and go spinning out the window over the rooftops of her neighborhood, flapping about with her spangled wings, looking down upon the daddies like her own, weaving home on the sidewalks and singing slurredly, the mothers like her own in the kitchen, in curlers, in housedresses, flipping through magazines, cigarettes in their downturned mouths. Above their unsuspecting heads, the girl spun unseen in the dark sky, so beautiful, so very beautiful.

She loved the wings so much she wore them on her first day of school. But the wings were crushed when she went out to play on the monkey bars and one boy twisted them savagely. Stupid, he said, You're not no stupid butterfly, you're just a girl. She said, I am so, you *monster*, I am so a butterfly, and she threw her shoe at him and ran away, one-shoed. When her mother came to get her, fat again with yet another baby, she clung to her mother's knees and choked until she vomited. The prettiest thing in the world, her wings, now dead, now gone, now crushed. Pure sorrow.

For consolation, her mother let the girl wear her Hershey Queen tiara and the girl fell asleep with it glittering on her head that night. Her baby brother patted her foot with his dumpling hand, the warmth of his flesh against her foot extraordinary, sweet.

SHE WOULD NO LONGER PLAY on the playground for fear of dirtying her dresses and her father spanking her for it. He had begun to spank her for anything: for talking at dinner, for quarreling with her brother, for hiding the booze when he staggered home at night, calling out to his wife to get her ass down here and help him upstairs, goddammit. Her mother would stand at the top of the stairs, her arms folded over the new baby girl, who looked like a monkey with a bad overbite. She would sigh and finger her sausage curls and send her eldest daughter down, and the girl would sit on her father's lap as he drank the whiskey that, under threat of the belt, she had miraculously found in the pie safe for him. Her back would vibrate under the great warm thumps of his heart, and he would kiss the back of her rag-bound head, kiss without stopping, kiss long after she fell asleep on his lap.

The one day that she wore an old brown dress to school in order to go out for recess, the boys pushed her against the chain-link fence, tied her there with her own jump rope, and lifted her skirt, chanting, I see London, I see France, I see Dummy's undiepants, and the girls shrieked with laughter, and she stood there, furious, kicking at the boys as they gyrated around her. When they set her free, she decked the biggest of them with a swift fist until he cried into the dirt, then she ran off into the classroom. She refused to take recess for the rest of the year, stopped talking in class or singing in choir, shook her head when the teacher asked her to read from the *Little Bear* book, although she read very well.

Because she wouldn't speak, the teacher brought her parents in for a conference in the shiny green classroom. Her father's face was knotted when they went out, but they all went for ice cream, and the girl was sucking a mouthful of strawberry delight when her mother leaned forward, with her smell of lily of the valley and cigarettes. Oh, honey, she said, patting the baby calm, tugging at the brother's tether so that he wouldn't wander. Oh, my little princess, you're going to stay back a year. The teacher says you're behind. Your teacher says you're a little slow, honey. It's okay, some people just take a little longer than others. You understand? You have to stay back.

And the terrible shame in the girl, the way the blood rushed before her eyes, turning her sight dark. The strawberry ice cream souring in her mouth. She did not want it, gave it to her little brother, who smeared it over his sailor suit, and let a passing dog gobble it up.

Then the father said to the mother, as if the girl weren't there, Don't worry, honey, she'll always have her looks, at least. Squeezing the mother's knee, winking at her.

When the mother frowned her carmine lips, the girl said, No, I am not slow. But even though there was a scream inside her, a feeling as if her stomach had had holes punched into it and she was pouring out, she said it so softly that nobody else heard.

ONE DAY WHEN SHE WAS TEN, the father came home early and sat at the table, head in his hands, drinking straight from the whiskey bottle, which he never did, not even when he staggered home late at night. The mother banished the children to watch the cowboy program on the television set while the parents' voices rose in the kitchen. I don't care . . . the girl heard, What are we going to do . . . the girl heard, Jesus Christ, why didn't you get your tubes tied . . . she heard. There was shouting and the girl turned up the television, but it wasn't loud enough to drown it all out. When the front door crashed, the mother came into the den. Go to bed, she ordered the brother, grabbing the girl's hand so that she would stay. Take the baby with.

We got to brush our teeth? said the brother, and the mother sighed. No. Just put your sister in bed, and the little ones went away, and the mother turned to her daughter, and, wordless, put her kerchiefed head in her lap, burying her face on her skinny legs. As the girl stroked her mother's fine hair, she tried to keep down the thing that was rising in her stomach, and the mother kept saying, Oh God, can you believe? Lost his job. Now! Of all times. Stupid drunk, she said. Oh my God. The mother's cigarette trembled in her lips until it ashed itself all over her daughter's legs, but the girl did not move them under the tiny burn.

This was how the littlest baby of the four was born a little clammy and a little dull: every few weeks her father wobbled home late at night and the girl awoke and listened to his curses below, and at school her cheeks were flushed with all that she held in. Her little brother wet his bed, her little sister ate from her diapers, her mother swelled up, pale and bloated, and the neighbor ladies asked curtly for their casserole dishes back. The girl was not surprised when the mother sat everyone down and unveiled the sleeping face of the new child.

She had heard it on the playground. She knew it as a truth: Mongoloids come, she understood, from a lack of love in the family.

ON SATURDAYS THAT BAD WINTER when she was twelve, the girl pushed the three littlest in the swings at the park when her mother was in the church basement, waiting for a boxful of dented cans and dandruffy cake mixes. At home, there were endless projects, her mother bent over the sewing machine crafting trousers out of curtains, remaking some little Anabaptist's dress into something the girl wouldn't hate, perhaps even a skirt the other girls would finger with envy, wondering what boutique it was from.

She was picturing exactly this one day as she watched her brother and sister whip one another with willow branches in one of those sordid little parks beside the more generous churches. The spade-shaped duck pond was filled with cigarette butts and little plastic jellyfish she was too young to know were condoms. The girl was pulling her cold fingers through her curls to keep them from knotting, shivering in the sharp March wind. That was the year she didn't have a winter coat, pretending that three old cardigans and a scarf and some mittens spelled warmth.

She turned her head and he appeared, the young man with thinning hair and irisless eyes and round red cheeks like a doll's. Those cheeks were why she didn't scream when he stood close, closer, why she sat on her bench, frozen, looking up. She didn't move when he opened his trousers and out popped his little worm and he brushed it, hot and silky, against her neck. And then he gave a breathy giggle as her brother shouted at a duck at the far end of the park, and the man pushed the worm back in the pants hole and hurried away over the desolate grass. She watched him go, holding her breath, clutching the bench so hard she felt as if she broke her hands. At home, in the pink bathroom, she scrubbed at her neck with the guest soaps in the shapes of curled nautili, scrubbed until she scrubbed that spot bloody and, eventually, scabrous. That night, sleepless, reimagining the hot brush on her neck, that gulf the girl carried around inside of herself widened with a terrible dull roar. When her daddy came home, silent and sober, the dangerous fire in his eyes snuffed when she shied away from his kiss. He looked at his eldest daughter, her pinched averted face, her bad shoes. I suppose I deserve that, he said, softly.

A DAY CAME WHEN THE GIRL RAN HOME, eyes kindling with excitement. There was a teacher in school who would teach the girls to be twirlers, with fire batons and everything! The mother frowned, put down her cigarette, and stood, arms akimbo, pushing the new baby in his rocker with her foot. Sparked by the girl's excitement, the brother raced out of the room with a Mohican ululation, the little sister did a shimmy to the music on the radio. The mother had to look away when she took a deep drag and, letting it out through her nose like a dragon, told her daughter, No, my pretty one, you know we don't have the money for baton lessons.

The girl struggled with the bitterness that stirred in her. Trained as she was by now, she didn't open her mouth. She bowed her head. Set the table.

It was the face the girl made, sharp as a needle, that the father saw when he looked up through the steam of his sauerkraut and pork supper. And the next day, old Joe Helmuth came into the kitchen with one hand behind his back, his favorite bitch clicking along behind him. He leaned over to whisper in his stepdaughter's ear. Her puffy, once-pretty face lifted, broke into wonderment. She clutched his hand and put her cheek on it, wordless.

Then old Joe Helmuth looked at his stepgranddaughter as she pinned the hem on a dress across the table and asked her what she thought he had behind his back. She guessed a silver dollar, but the hand came out waving a baton in saucy imitation of a twirl. Give your old granddaddy a little kiss, he said, and she did, a big one, and didn't mind his scratchy moustache or the way his lips lingered a half-second too long on her own.

Now the father worked at the kennel all day, mucking the dog shit from the concrete floor, no matter that he had two years of college, no matter that he had once been a government employee. And with the father at work so long, the mother was able to finish her chores before supper, and the girl had time to practice. Lordy, did she practice. She took that hollow ringing in her and twirled it away, twirled in the basement in the foulest weather, when her hands stuck to the metal in the cold and she could not practice on the lawn. In her bed at night, her fingers flicked imaginary batons in the air. She sent batons spinning up like whirligigs into the night sky, batons flipping around her body like ions to her atom, batons spinning about her like glittering wings. She twirled through her legs and over her body as if her batons were her very own limbs. The mother paused to watch her daughter practice out the kitchen window and plum forgot to bread the chicken. The father took her in the early mornings to the far-off competitions, drinking coffee from a thermos as she snoozed against the car door, and praying a little to his forgotten God before she marched onto the field.

A natural, said the baton teacher, clasping her hands to her breast, rolling her eyes cloudward. A natural, smirked the boys on the football team as she marched at the head of the marching band in her knee-high boots, in her spangly little leotard, in her hat like an upended loaf of bread. She was the head majorette in her sophomore year of high school, hers the sole white costume amid the others' discontented blues. The other twirlers dropped, one by one, nastily, all humdrum twirlers compared to her, until, at last, she stood alone. Before the thousands of awestruck fans, she tossed her solo batons until they spun above the bleachers on the football field. The fans lost the thin bands in the dusky sky and gasped when they fell into the girl's hands, streaking stars.

THE GIRL SPENT HER EVENINGS plucking her eyebrows, hair by hair, until they were as thin and arced as scythes. She swabbed the roots of her hair with cotton soaked in peroxide until she was blond as the day she was born, reduced with cottage cheese until her arms were twigs, smeared petroleum jelly over her lips and hands to keep them supple. She hemmed her skirts to mid-thigh, then hemmed still more. She wore her sweaters tight until her brother, embarrassed by his horn-dog friends, asked if she didn't think her sweater kittens were going to freeze, exposed as they were. She looked at him coolly and changed into an even tighter sweater, so tight one could trace the label on her brassiere.

And she said Yes to the boys who called for her, despite her daddy, who snarled and barked at them, and Yes to the football players who jogged after her before practice to ask her to the movies, and Yes to parking in the makeout lane, and Yes to their hands under her skirts, and Yes when they pushed their jeans down their thin hips because by then she forgot what it meant to say No. She caught her father in her room one evening holding her underwear up to the window, panty by panty, examining. She caught him staring at her above the goulash and she had to look away, in confusion, a dank feeling in her stomach. When Stepgranddaddy Joe Helmuth came for Easter supper, he settled his bitches in the corner with a bone, and Fritz the old collie wobbled over and sniffed them with panting eagerness. After Joe Helmuth said the prayer and the rest of them dove into their food, he looked long and hard at the girl, her makeup, her hair, the neat halves of each portion left on her plate in service of her diet. Then he said to her mother with a mouthful of lamb, Better watch my little wifey like a goddamn hawk, else she's going to turn into her mother, my dear. He pointed at the girl with the tines of his fork, and the father dropped his napkin and pushed up from the table and went to pace the lawn, kicking at the dropped chokecherries.

The girl then looked at her mother with the purple sleepless bruises around her eyes, at her smallest brother, who drooled in bubbles and seemed only to have attention for the way the cigarette smoke shattered against the overhead lamp. And there was something icy in her gut then, something hard, and she stopped saying Yes. She stopped saying much. She smiled, coquettish, and posed for the photographs for the school paper, for the Harrisburg *Patriot-News*, and she twirled, but no longer went out with the boys.

Instead, she spent her nights and weekends at beauty pageants. Why not? she'd decided one Saturday night, restless and imagining the boys with their boy smells. Why not? She already had the sparkly leotards. By Monday she had stitched together an evening gown. By summer, she had won enough for a coughing blue Hornet and went chugging around the state, preparing for Miss America. She dreamed of the big payout, the scholarship to the college of her choice, vague classes with lab coats and fat books and professors with leather patches on their coats, four years, a real college, not two at a stupid technical school. But when she brought home the sashes and the crowns, the bouquets of red roses, she didn't tell a soul where she'd gotten them, not even her mother, who had smoked herself foul-smelling and unpretty. In a box under her bed the girl buried Miss Hummelstown, Pennsylvania Milk Princess, Miss Lancaster County, Central Pennsylvania Cheese Duchess, and even Hershey Queen. All that long hot summer, the smell of chocolate rose from the factory, a memory made sensual, all that she'd won.

Her mother watched her come into the house, this fine, thin girl. She pulled her sudsy hands from the sink and she walked toward her, holding them out to the girl as if to clutch her, to hold her, even briefly, before she had to let her go. But the daughter backed away from the soapy arms with a look of disgust, and fled the kitchen to the room she shared with her incurious, moody sister, to recount her tiaras and to straighten her sashes in order.

AND SO IT WAS UNTIL THE DAY in her junior fall when the girl was outside with her fire batons on a day her father was burning leaves. She was spinning them skyward, where they blazed bright against the glum fall sky. Her monkey-faced sister was raking leaves, sulking in an old red sweater of their brother's, and everywhere the glorious smell of singed leaves, smoke as thick as wool.

The girl sent the fire baton into the air with her left hand as she did an Around the World with her right. When the baton fell, it fell a little askew, and she missed catching it with her palm; it fell on the ratty fringe of the old jeans she was wearing, they flamed up, and she stared at the bright blaze, blank, for a couple of seconds before she began to scream, Help me, help me, help!, clapping at the flame. The father dropped his wheelbarrow and ran, but for the younger daughter, for the red sweater—he tackled the younger daughter, and smacked out the flames of her red sweater before he realized they weren't flames at all. By the time he reached his eldest daughter and put out the fire, holding her as the sister ran for the telephone, there were black scorch marks on the flesh of the girl's shins and calves, and she had gone limp and unconscious.

When the girl awakened, she was in the burn unit, tubes in her arms, her legs bandaged and elevated and feeling as if they were packed with clay. Her idiot brother was kneeling on a chair beside her, nobody else in the room. He rubbed her cheek with his finger and cooed.

Oh, little guy, she would have groaned if she could only get her mouth to work. Oh, little guy, what happened? She only remembered the flames when she saw, on the stand, monuments of flowers, from the principal, from the football team, from the boys who knew every inch of her skin rather well, from her calculus and biology teachers, from her stepgranddaddy, from her baton teacher's good-looking husband. All, she realized, from men. She picked up a novel her mother had dropped there, and she read to escape the thought.

By the time the flowers wilted and dropped their petals one by one, the girl had devoured a tower of books. She was a religious convert for books, parched and feverish. While she spun her batons she had forgotten that terrible ache; the books made her forget for longer. She gave up the idea of Miss America with nary a pang; nobody wants a singed beauty queen. And when she began walking again with her skinny, tender legs, and zipped up the long boots she would forevermore have to wear with her skirts, and she realized her grades were not good enough to slide into school on them alone, she began twirling again. Only halfheartedly. Only to stay in the light. She was good at it. It would take her where she would need to go: to college, that distant horizon.

In the summer, she was selected to be the head majorette for Big 33, the state high school football championships, and as such, she choreographed the routines of forty-five of the state's best twirlers. On the big day, she did a perfect routine with three fire batons. On television, in front of everyone, Joe Paterno watched her and gave a little smile and said, Hell, if I had any say over the Penn State band, that young lady would be my number one draft pick.

Flushed with her success, knowing this was the pinnacle of her half-abandoned life as a majorette, she drove home in her coughing Hornet, her father by her side, her mother crammed in the back. And perhaps it was what Paterno had said, but her father looked at his firstborn, and his eyes filled, and he couldn't say a word, only turning away from her, to look out into Pennsylvania flying by. The girl felt the heat of his gaze, and then the relief as he looked away.

Though that autumn her history and English teachers had a great blowup in the faculty lounge about who, exactly, should take credit for the girl's turnaround, neither was responsible: after the fire, after Paterno, the girl read at night until the books made her fall asleep. That was how she earned herself a full scholarship to Lafayette College, near Allentown. For their first coed class, the admissions committee wanted a diverse group of girls. She fluttered her eyelashes. She aced her interview.

THE SERENITY, THE BEAUTY, the aged brick of the campus stirred in her something close to exploding, something sweet and good. She smiled, she got along well with her roommates, both city girls, both rich. She borrowed their White Shoulders, their miniskirts, their brandy; their bracelets chuckled on her wrists. And though the football games were quieter than her high school ones—the team was awful, the fans more interested in smoking pot and watching the clouds above explode into psychedelic shapes—every weekend, she put on her flabby handed-down uniform and twirled mightily and gained a few fans.

Hey, Darlin', war protesters outside the union would shout at her as she crossed the quad, Hey, Majorette. Come twirl over here to protest the war.

And when she'd give them a shy smile at halftime as she marched out for the routine, one boy with gleaming reddish hair and a sweet face under his glasses would trot before the bleachers and woo the sky, singing, One, two, three, four, we don't want your fucking war! And the crowd would raise their fists and say, Five, six, seven, eight, twirl them sticks to set them straight!

And the girl, under the spinning batons in the air, would laugh. She'd give a little antiwar shuffle to the beat of the chant. And then she would think of her glowering father if he were to see her, and become scandalized at her own daring, and flush and run off.

She didn't know that the redheaded boy was in her biology class until the day she saw him as she was coming down the steps of the lecture hall to hand in a test. Her skirt was the miniest she had, her boots white platforms, and he dropped a pencil to peer up the stretch of her legs. He grinned at her, and, despite herself, she grinned down at him, and this is how they met. He was in premed, he said, because his draft number was ridiculously low, and if he didn't get into graduate school he'd be in some Asian jungle somewhere, torching babies.

What do you think? he said, naked, gleaming with sweat on his frat-house bed, looking at her anxiously. If I don't get into med school, would you go to Canada with me? For weeks her greatest anxiety had been how to hide her seared calves under his sheets, but now she forgot her own body entirely. And she looked at him, began to blink, and as she blinked, there was a tremendous shifting as if something began to strain closed inside her. He frowned. What's the matter? he said. And she said, Nobody ever asked me what I thought before. And he said, That's silly, you must have been asked what you thought at some point, and she said, No, and he said, Well, you have to have opinions, everyone has opinions, and she said, I don't. I don't know. I don't know how to make opinions. And he pried her hands from her face and kissed her on the nose, and instead of saying, as she thought he was going to say, Well, I'll have all the opinions you need, little missy, he said, Well, you can have all the opinions you want around me. Go ahead and practice.

And she looked at him, at the laughing redheaded boy who squinted at her presbyopically, she saw the lick of salt from the dried sweat on his forehead and said, I think you are the kindest man I know. And he said, Well, that's a good one. You're about the only woman in the world to ever have that opinion, and they laughed together, and he stopped laughing and he looked at her very seriously, brushing the bleached hair from her face. He opened his mouth. And when all the other men she'd known would have said, Baby, you're so beautiful, he didn't. Instead, he said, Beautiful, you *are* smart. Believe it.

Then she burrowed into him, tried to fit her whole head into the hollows of his torso. Oh, she wanted to weep, but not from sorrow, from confusion. She felt as if all her life she'd been carrying this black sack filled with cobras, and the redheaded boy had swept it from her hands and given her a different one, filled with something soft, and said, Listen, this, too, is yours, and you can have it, and didn't you know there are millions of different things to carry in the world, darling? And she thought of her father, of Joe Helmuth and all the other hard, dark men in her childhood, and had to blink to see the redheaded boy with his big nose and his sleepy, molelike eyes as the same genre of human as them. Later, she let the sheets fall off her legs, let the boy exclaim and hold her calves in his hands, and she explained the burns, told the story for the first time of her own small revolution. As she watched him sleep that night, she thought a very definite Yes.

THIS IS HOW A LIFE FALLS INTO PLACE. A graduation, a wedding with her pale, redheaded groom sneaking into her room before the ceremony for a prewedding snuggle, the reception with Joe Helmuth in a fine blue tuxedo, spinning her around the dance floor, his white moustache twitching with pride as she smiled up at him in her lace dress. A hot day outside, the chocolate factory perfuming the wedding, like a blessing bestowed by her hometown. Her parents looked small and nervous at their table, her father becoming so drunk he wept openly, smacking his forehead with his palm, smacking, smacking, until her mother stubbed out her cigarette, and took his hands in her own jaundiced ones, and held them to her lips and kissed them until he leaned his forehead against hers. They sat there, calm, eyebrow to eyebrow. Her monkey-faced sister, who turned out to be quite pretty in an overbitten Betty Boop way, swept her retarded brother around the floor, both laughing like fools, and the bride's younger brother pressed her to him for one brief moment after the dance, unable to speak, his eyes full of tears. He smelled the same as ever: celery, sweat.

Then she was the breadwinner, putting her husband through medical school, drawing blood samples from small Amish boys who never so much as whimpered at the needle. Her father, resenting this—It's not natural, he said, it's not right; a man should provide for his wife—began to only grunt in her husband's presence, always seeming to have a tool in his hand. Joe Helmuth tried hard to provoke her husband to bickering and when her redheaded husband only laughed, refused to bicker, he at last relented, giving them a basset puppy that grew up fat and gentle. With the residency came the years of joyous scrimping, years of making baskets for gifts and canning her own vegetables, and hovering over her first child, a beloved son, whose birth was the best day of her life, at least until the birth of her daughter, an even brighter day that seemed to engulf her, drown her in its fearsome miracles.

When she unwrapped her daughter for the first time, she touched the tender folds of the baby's body, the warm little tires of her neck and lips and eyelids and kneepits. And she, the new mother of a daughter, felt a fierceness come over her that seized at her heart, that made her feel as if her bones were turned to steel, as if she could turn herself into a weapon to keep this daughter of hers from having to be hurt by the world outside the ring of her arms. If her daughter cried at night, she stood and slipped into her room and kissed her to sleep. She nursed her and felt herself grow softer, her hard edges sanded off, as the satiated mouth grew slack.

And she watched this daughter grow, grasp at words as if they were bright things, shove everything the world offered into her mouth, as if to taste it all. She watched those little legs in their corduroy pants pump like pistons down the lawn after her older brother, she watched her build forts of sticks and stones and tree stumps, make soft beds for herself of thick moss. The delicate things her daughter crafted with her hands she held in her own and wondered over, as she wondered over the fierceness of the girl's bright force as she shouted and pulled at a stranger's mean dog that had attacked their family's golden retriever, at how, so young, the power of her fury drove the mean dog off. The years of dancing to suburban hip-hop in the kitchen as they did dishes, of bent flowers ripped from the ground in a pitcher for Mother's Day, of the hurling of words more painful than any thwack of her own daddy's belt, her daughter screaming words at her, spiny with superiority: You're so fucking superficial; It's the nineties; Make Dad make his own sandwich, for God's sake. And then the swallowed sorries and bittersweet repentance: Mom, you know I love you. Her daughter grew tall and muscled, fierce and laughing, so terrible that the girl scared her mother, her brother, her small and suspicious grandparents. Joe Helmuth laughed and laughed at her. My girlfriend, he said with admiration, Such a spicy jalapeño. Her mother watched her, awed, this mountain of a girl; she saw how the hunger in her was different from her own, greedy, not empty.

Should a life be lived with such intensity? the mother asked her husband as he read a magazine before bed. Should life be lived with the intensity our daughter lives it? He put the magazine down, smiled, the skin behind his glasses crinkling. He was bald now, plump. What do you think? he said. She did not answer him at first, spent a few minutes looking through the dark panes and into the city where they lived, far from Hershey, far from her childhood. She thought of her mother's cigarette smoke as it spun a blue web on the ceiling. Yes, I think it should, she said, and then put out the light and folded herself under the covers, rested herself against him. Her old body against his old body, unbeautiful in aging. But together, they were still beautiful, somehow.

In the end, it was volleyball that was her daughter's steady passion, the sport for leaping Amazons. The mother sat in the honeyed high school gymnasiums, the college gyms, and watched the stony look come over her daughter's face with every stuff, dig, kill. In the stands, the mother touched her ravaged calves. She was still so lovely in her increasing years, her hair dark now and straight, her lips glossed, eyebrows grown out to a normal thickness. When the ball shot toward her girl, the mother leaned forward and waited.

She saw her daughter's thigh muscles bunch as she readied herself for the jump; she saw one beautiful summer night at her parents' years ago. Her children had been tiny then, running around with glass jars to collect the fireflies, her retarded brother was singing a song under his breath. Tang of daiquiri in her mouth; lick of cigarette smoke curling into the night; scent of the middle-aged chokecherry pricking her eyes. She ran inside and dug in the basement for her fire batons and came out onto the lawn, setting her mother's lighter to the ancient ends, flinging them one, two, three, four, into the air so they spun into the starred sky, one after another, outglowing the stars. She saw herself reflected in the faces of her family, twirling, the children spellbound; she saw how they looked at her with surprise.

In the warm glow of the gym she closed her eyes to imprint her daughter upon her eyelids, stilled her in midmotion. As the game went on, she held her daughter leaping. A wonder, this girl, who knew already how to catch herself.

Blythe

THE YEARS BEFORE BLYTHE WERE A KIND OF beautiful limbo, sticky with juice boxes, scented with leaf mold at Wissahickon Park where I walked the babies, bookended by the hordes of Catholic schoolchildren in their uniforms who flitted down the hill in the mornings, drawn by the ponderous bells, and dispersed in the afternoons like handfuls of moths. Sue and Mackenzie would press their faces to the window and watch the children pass with toddlers' fixed awe, and I would watch my girls and think with a fierceness I still sometimes feel, *Not yet*. When I'd remember the law firm where I was supposed to return to work, panic like a cold finger would press my heart, and I'd think the same thing: *Not yet, not yet, not yet*.

My husband tells me I romanticize those years, that in reality I was lonely and wept a lot and complained about betraying my principles by being a lowly housewife. He claims I called the girls little vampires, sucking the life out of me with their constant need. His version would explain the electric jingle of my nerves the day before that first poetry class, why all afternoon I caught the girls watching me carefully, as if they were afraid I'd suddenly explode. The class that evening seemed at once the most difficult thing I'd ever attempted and the most immensely silly. It was, of course, Sam's idea. I had been absently filling scraps of paper with the words that bubbled up in my brain as I cleaned the house, and Sam had found them, and enrolled me in the class for my birthday.

"Harriet Buxbaum," he scolded after I'd refused his gift. "You have talent. And you seem so tired. Your very soul seems tired." True, I was deeply tired, but I believe I would have skipped the class entirely had Sam not come home that night with a weary pale face and a briefcase of papers he still had to wade through before sleeping. I kissed him, smelled the law firm on his skin, and was chased out of the house more by a desire to never return to that life of codicils and affidavits than by anything else.

On the drive from Manayunk to the University of Pennsylvania that night, the streets seemed made of wet tar, and inside the building the corridors smelled of mushrooms and raincoats. I was in such a flutter of panic I could barely clutch my pencil or look at the other students in the circle about me. All I wanted was the warm effacement of home.

When the room had filled, the teacher, a slight man with a quivery Vandyke, began rustling his papers and hemming to begin. Before he could, though, the door opened again. A subtle shifting in the chemistry of the room; like everyone else I found myself looking toward the doorway. There, smiling, stood a fashion model. Surely a mistake. I waited for someone to tell her that the life-drawing class was down the hall, but the woman stepped inside. She was tall, her dark hair shot with copper and studded with tiny white flowers.

This was Blythe Cantor, extremely thin back then and making one of her brilliant entrances. She looked nothing like anyone I had ever known; my familiars were floury types, wholesome and good. My friends, my family, potato knishes all.

"Poetry?" Blythe said in a husky voice.

"Yes," said the instructor, pulling at his bowtie. "Please, sit."

Blythe glided across the room to fold her long self into a chair beside me. I felt resentful at the scent wafting from her, cigarette smoke and perfume like some overblown peony about to shiver apart. When I looked at the frumpy people about me, I knew this woman had no right to be in the room. *We* were serious poets. *She* could be only a dilettante. A WASPy poetaster. She seemed raw in the way silk can be raw, and still shimmery, elegant.

That's when I felt my ambitions begin to solidify, if only to defend them against fakers like this woman.

So I fumed until the teacher began to speak, and Blythe leaned over to me, green eyes brilliant with tears. She whispered, "Lord. Lord. I am so very frightened. You'll be my friend, won't you?" It was only when I smelled bourbon on her breath and watched one of her flowers unpin itself and fall down her collar that my heart fell for her with a decided plunk, the sound of a stone dropping into water. I squeezed her hand. Blythe wouldn't let go, not throughout the entire hour, though I had to take unruly notes with my left hand, or even afterward in the beer-stinking undergraduate bar where we'd fled after class was over.

I had planned on going home directly after class—I knew Sam was waiting for me—but that night seemed to ring with a new kind of freedom, and so I followed her. The bar was so dark that at first all I could see of Blythe was a series of sparkles: eyes, necklace, glossy lips. We perched on our stools, and, over the first round of stingers—her choice—we found out that our children were the same age. She lived in Merion, a place that evoked Tudor-style manors and tennis courts and Katharine Hepburn; we were renting at the ridge of a steep hill between Manayunk and Roxborough, where old men would sit on their porches in their wife-beaters and drink homebrewed beer from mason jars. From her clothes it was clear that Blythe had few money worries, while Sam and I lived a series of small economies, our law school debts enormous, my salary gone when Mackenzie was born.

That night we talked and talked. Even then, Blythe had the ability to look at you as if you were the most stunning person in the world, and I, who had spent years as a ghost, basked in this new sun. We discovered that I had been in law school with a cousin of hers; she remembered visiting my parents' candy store when she was a little girl; I had an uncle who once worked in her father's investment company. With every particle of ourselves that we brought up we found a connection, a subtle link. I know now that if one digs enough one can find such confluences with practically anybody, but that night, under the spell of her magnetism, those connections seemed miraculous.

"Do you know what this means?" said Blythe. "Harriet, we're destined to be best friends." She clasped my hand and kissed it. Then she frowned. "I should tell you something before we fall madly in love, of course, which we will. It's just that I'm probably crazy."

"Me too," I said, tipsy and laughing. "The girls drive me nuts all day long."

"No," said Blythe. "I mean I've been in the hospital. I've tried to kill myself three times. In July, I left my littlest son in the car and tried again. Bridge. I came home from the hospital a week ago. I'm only in this class because my shrink said poetry is good for me." She rolled her glass in her hands and gave me a strained smile. "Now that you know, you don't have to be friends with me. I'll understand."

But my whole good self had cracked open that night like a walnut; I felt fresh. Blythe was so little like me—plain, quiet—that she seemed like hope embodied. Besides, other than a maniacal professor in college who began hooting like an owl during an anthropology class and had to be escorted from the room, I'd never known anyone who was actually clinically insane. I thought of Sam, my gentle parents, my sensible activist friends. "Oh, Blythe," I said. "I don't think there's been *enough* madness in my life."

Blythe raised one eyebrow. "Careful what you wish for," she said. Then she grinned and kissed me on the temple and raised her glass so that the liquid swung in the light. She said, "To us." She downed her drink, wiped her mouth with a delicate pinky finger, and signaled for more with a coy little wink at the bartender.

A FEW WEEKS LATER ON THE LAST moderate afternoon of the year, my girls and I were paddling around the Cantors' pool like ducks. It was a chilly day and fog lifted breathlike from the heated water, but Blythe lay on her chaise longue in a bikini that showed off her smooth waist and lovely small breasts. It seemed vaguely obscene to see how eagerly her nipples pushed against the fabric. I tried not to look.

That day, Blythe's sons hovered around their mother, small satellites. Tom carefully conveyed ice cubes from the kitchen in silver tongs, to deliver them one by one to his mother's glass of vodka like an officiant. Bear, the baby, was playing with his blow-up floaty at Blythe's feet, from time to time patting them as if reassuring himself that she truly was there. Both boys wore a calm film over their faces like plastic wrap. Sometimes when the film slipped I saw fear beneath, and I had to look toward my own babies: Mackenzie, three, strawberried by the sun, pudgy little Susan, a joy.

I spun Mackenzie in the water and when I looked up, Blythe

was blowing twin strands of smoke from her nostrils and frowning at us. "I could never have girls," she said. "I don't know how my mother did it. Three girls. Hell on Earth."

"That's awful," I said. "My girls are sweet. They're going to be my best friends someday." Mackenzie squeezed my neck furiously and breathed her wet breath into my ear.

Blythe smiled, said, "I'm sure. But girls are just so needy. *I* had to sleep in my mother's bed until I was almost sixteen. Plus, all the world wants to get into their panties, and you have to protect them, even from their own fathers and uncles and grandfathers. Boys can practically raise themselves. At least with them the Oedipus complex thing is simple. Screw Mommy, kill Daddy. Easy enough." She laughed.

The four children all paused and looked at Blythe, but she lowered her glasses and winked at them and stretched like a great sleek cat. They returned to their play. Only I could have taken this seriously, and I wasn't about to ask her to stop talking like this: nobody I knew was ever so reckless, and it filled me with a kind of ecstatic terror. When I looked toward the kitchen, I saw Pritch, Blythe's husband, moving behind the window, wearing an apron and making dinner. He was a stocky man with the face of a Boston terrier, condensed features and bulging eyes, and I always expected his tongue to loll pinkly out of his mouth on a hot day. I feared him a little, for no reason I could figure out, and knew if he heard his wife saying such things before the children he would grow angry in his quiet, flushing way. I said, "Blythe. Maybe now's not the time."

"Oh, Harriet," said Blythe. "We've both lived through all that feminist crap, probably even joined some of those clubs." I blanched: I'd been the president of the Feminist Alliance in college. She said, "You were a lawyer, I did advertising. And here we are, housewives. No matter what we choose to do from now on, that's what we are. We won't be taken as seriously as the boys. We'll be inferior, even if we could write rings around them. Which we can."

"You're wrong," I said. "I believe the cream rises to the top." I really did, back then.

Blythe carefully put out her cigarette. "Not in America, darling," she said at last. "Here, the scream rises to the top. Home of the squeaky wheel, land of the knave," and she laughed, pleased with her rhyme.

I went underwater to think. When I came up, I pushed my springy hair from my eyes. "Fine," I said at last. "Then scream."

Blythe gave a funny smile. "I intend to," she said. She stood and walked to the diving board. Bouncing a little, she raised her arms and grinned, and then, despite all of my expectations to the contrary, she gave a rather clumsy dive, shaping herself like a candy cane and dropping deep with a splash.

I NEVER FELT COMPETITIVE WITH BLYTHE. I was skinny and small and plain, far poorer, far less charming. I'd never been to Europe; I'd never eaten escargot. My mother was from a small village in Latvia, my father only finished three months of college. Blythe's family could recite all their ancestors since the *Mayflower*. I was not in the least the magnet for strangers' eyes that Blythe was, with her stunning looks, her tight clothes.

Yet, for a long time, Blythe was a horrendous poet, writing song lyrics and thinking they were lovely. I had to tutor her, and I held tight to the small comfort of this superiority. In our class, I was the teacher's pet, the one who could give moderate critique, the one whose poems he held up to the rest of the class as examples of anaphora, ellipsis, tone. And I would allow myself one tiny lick of judgment, like a child with a secret lollipop, when Blythe would sit across from me in the bar and breathe out the stories about her lovers; the undergraduate's sweaty garret, the poetry teacher's lust for clamps and rubber tubing, the way her shrink's head resident (Blythe's shrink refused to have sex with her) delighted in the cold examination table on his buttocks. I would never do any of these things myself, but did have a voyeur's delight in hearing about Blythe's doing them. In those days she seemed the distillation of life, and I felt some of my own returning, breath by breath, in her presence.

We grew close, then closer. *L'amour fou,* Sam called it, with a wry look on his soft face; *folie à deux*. One night in bed after a dinner party where the tiniest derogation had sent Blythe into a frenzy of sorrow (*Blythe's a princess,* someone had said, and her whole face had crumpled), my husband assessed my friend with affectionate exasperation. "Like a

Chihuahua," he said. "Precious, trembling, breakable. She's skinless, that girl."

But I clicked my tongue and pulled my pillow from under his head. "You have it all wrong," I said. "She's something wild and sensitive and overbred. Like some Arabian stallion or something."

"She can't be a stallion, she's a girl. You mean a mare," said Sam, laughing.

But I was thinking of the way Blythe seized life with two greedy hands and gobbled, the bell-like laugh, the conviction in her voice when she spoke of her former sadnesses. I said quietly, "That's where you're wrong," and wouldn't respond even when Sam put a hand on my waist in apology.

Our class ended, the long winter passed, and in the spring Blythe and I both signed up for advanced poetry. Something subtle had been shifting in my friend for a few months: she had begun to come over during my children's naps when I tried to clean the house, and sat at the table, twittering gaily about small things until Mackenzie and Susan woke and called to me from their rooms. One cold day she brought over a frosty fistful of crocuses, and while she talked her eyes followed me whenever I moved. I wondered about Blythe's boys, if she'd left them alone, but knew that she had the money for a nanny. Not even Blythe, I hoped, would leave them alone, I thought, and hated myself for doubting her.

Then, the phone call in the middle of the night when, in the bolt-upright moment just before the phone rang, I knew it was Blythe, and that there was something wrong.

"Hello," I said, but she was already talking, her voice vibrant in the dark.

"Harriet, Harriet, I've done it," she said. "You have to see." And before I could respond, I heard her drop the phone, her footsteps running from the room.

"Sam," I whispered, putting the phone back in the cradle. "I think there's something wrong with Blythe."

"She's crazy, dammit," he muttered.

I had almost fallen back asleep when I heard the squeal of tires around a corner, and I ran downstairs in my pajamas. Through the screen I saw Blythe's car ram the curb and narrowly miss the crabapple in our minuscule yard. The car ground to a stop and, its headlights still on, Blythe burst from the driver's seat and hurried up the walk. Her hair was wild and her nightdress eerie in the stream of brightness and shadow. I cringed, expecting the lights to come on in the neighbors' houses, but this was a place used to teenagers' heavy metal past midnight, where neighbors inserted themselves into marital spats through the open windows of houses. Blythe's behavior didn't warrant a dog barking. She leaped the steps and thrust a paper in my hand. "Read it," she said and gave a little crow. Then she grasped the poem back out of my hand and said, "No. I have to read it. It's the performance that counts."

Blythe stepped down onto the lawn and tilted the paper into the headlights' beam. She let the paper drop so it floated down, and raised her arms so her sleeves were filled with light. And then she declaimed her poem at high voice. The neighbor's beagle bayed along with her: she swept her arms up and out of the light, then back in, out, in. She was conducting the midges, the wind along the rooftops, the Schuylkill glimmering at the foot of the hill, I thought. Later I would read the poem itself and think, *Eh*, but in her mouth that night the words were full of needles and music.

I watched Blythe, so gorgeous and fluttering in her iridescent nightgown, a winged thing, and said, "God." I had never been religious, and even if I had been, my God would have been much more ancient and angry than Blythe's prim Episcopalian one, but still, I sensed the hand of something vast in this swift transformation.

When Blythe clasped me about the neck at the end, I thought I heard her say something strange over the wind and the idling engine: *Oh, Mother.* Later I dismissed what I heard and climbed back into bed to fall asleep, happy for my friend.

BLYTHE AND I TOOK SHOPPING trips with the children, long walks, and soon we began to spend mornings in our separate houses on speakerphone to read a poem aloud (me), and to talk about additions to pieces (her). She'd been to the galleries downtown where she'd seen performance art for the first time, and she wanted badly to create her own. Blythe's new subjects were fanged, bloodthirsty: insanity, suicide, adultery, incest, masturbation, wanting to kill her own children. She wrote things so internal they still had the slick and beat of an organ when they came from her.

"Listen, Harriet," she'd say. "I know what I want to do so well. I want to mix my words with movement, you see? *Visuals*. Public, not static. In the moment. I want to crack open the words so people can step in. I want to *give* them to you, not just present them on a paper. I want whole rooms full of naked women smeared with blood, you know?" Her voice was hushed, and we held the moment until a child shrieked somewhere. The silence broke, and Blythe laughed at herself, at her solemnity, at my speechlessness.

Blythe was making up what she was doing as she went along. She began to work with food, smearing the dark red jelly her mother made on her face as she chanted; making an igloo of the housewife's best friend, frozen peas, and saying a long prayer-poem; shoving a grape into her mouth with each new line of a dialogue about her sons so that she almost choked herself at the end. She showed me her food log, hardbound sketchbooks in which she had noted every morsel that passed her lips from age fifteen to twenty-one, which stopped abruptly when she tried to kill herself for the first time (aspirin, in her parents' pool house, she said, with a low laugh). She watched me as I read parts of it, growing nauseated at the annotations beside the biggest binges: *Nasty, nasty, hog* beside *three cheesesteaks and a case of Coke*; *Filthy bitch* beside *entire red velvet cake*.

"I want to use these," she said. "I'll record these entries and play them over a loudspeaker and eat an entire *picnic* of food in front of people until someone throws up."

"Jesus," I said, which sometimes seemed like the only thing I could say.

I admired how Blythe used her body, the shock of her, but there was too much Milton and Frost in me for my own stabs at such dramatics to be anything but undignified. While Blythe created new pieces at a fevered pitch throughout the summer and fall, I wrote of gardening and politics, of sense and memory, of things safely domestic. I saved the secret thrill of transgression for Blythe's work, proud to help her birth her strange little creatures, because it *was* midwifery. I was the one to contact the galleries, to drive Blythe to the theaters, to call the press, to organize. I was the woman behind the camera for the videos of her performances, Blythe's very first audience. All the while I scribbled poem after poem in the ragged notebooks I salvaged at the end of my daughters' school year, and only dared to show Blythe the best.

SOON THOUGH, BLYTHE BEGAN to sleep very little and ate nothing, sipping only what she called her "magic potion," a Bloody Mary with extra vodka. I could see the ridges of her back through a cardigan. And in November, fourteen months after we'd met, there came another midnight call. Blythe was sobbing this time: "I've finished the best, I've finished *Darkling*. I've made a sculpture of alphabet pasta, I am going to eat it. I'm going to eat my words. I need you to organize it."

I had just nursed the babies through the chicken pox and was exhausted. I closed my eyes to the bluelit bedroom and leaned against my pillow. "That's wonderful, B. I'll do my best," I said as Sam cursed into the mattress.

Blythe gave a half-wailed, "Oh," and put the phone down. I waited again at the front door, shivering with chill, but this time there was no squeal of tires or Blythe spinning merrily across the lawn. This time, there was a heavy silence all night and into the next few days, then a call from Pritch a week later, on Blythe's birthday. The girls were out gathering armfuls of leaves from the lawn. I pressed my hand to the glass, as if to protect them, when he asked me to watch the boys for a week. Blythe had had another break, he'd said, and under his words, I understood that something terrible had happened. My core felt frozen, and I began to shiver.

"It was so strange, Harriet," he said. "She was wearing this disgusting lace dress that she'd had since she was nine. It's this horrible thing she couldn't even zip up. As if that was part of a formula. Vodka, pills, dress. So strange. Such a goddamn cliché."

I said soothing things, but mostly to keep myself from panicking, from throwing the phone across the room. He seemed calm, but when we'd already said good-bye, he said, "I forgot." Now his voice seemed just on the edge of breaking. "Some big gallery downtown wants Blythe to come and do her newest piece. *Darkling*, I think she's calling it." Then, hesitant, "I've never seen it. I've never seen anything she does. I won't understand it, I'm not artistic, but I think I need to. Do I, Harriet? Should I look at the videos you made? Or should I read the work? Would that help?"

A long, cold moment passed before I could react. In one performance, Blythe had made a net of Pritch's ties, and, catching herself in it, entangling herself, gave a monologue in which she used the lines "and wives are made / for fucking." In another, she'd smeared red jelly across her face as she delivered a poem about one of her abortions. I had to turn away from my girls, whose hands were full of leaves burning red and orange, in the thinning afternoon. "Oh, Pritchard," I said. "No, I really don't think you should."

All afternoon, watching the four children playing a board game, I couldn't shake Pritch's quaver out of my ears. I had been a bad friend. I had been too busy with my own life; I hadn't taken care of Blythe. I could have stopped her free fall, if only I had been paying more attention. I knelt and buried my head in Bear's mop of hair, ferociously breathing in his musky boy smell. Never, never would I make that mistake again, I promised. I would stop the despair the next time it came around and the next and the next, however long it took.

THAT WINTER AND SPRING I LEARNED the dark strain of recovery. Blythe at the hospital; home, but not allowed to be alone with the children; crying, gray and languid; then suddenly, as if infused with someone else's blood, in a gallery, creating *Darkling* for a solemn audience. It was a long and painful piece: Blythe singing the same poem to herself as she ate the woman-shaped sculpture of alphabet noodles, until her voice cracked and her lips bled and she sank to a squat. She had insisted on performing it until Pritch and I had both caved in. When we did, she dimpled, kissed us both on the cheek, and we were charmed, despite ourselves.

Her slow recovery was sped by a front-page write-up of *Darkling* in the Arts section of the *Inquirer*. The reporter, a recent women's college graduate, said her whole world shifted when she saw it. "Through Cantor's work," she rhapsodized, "we see the plight of the housewife in contemporary America, pulled between the competing obligations to her family and a career of her own, the sad legacy of women's liberation in this new decade of ours. It is a terrific sight, and one this reporter won't forget for a very long time."

After that, Blythe still spoke in a little-girl voice at times, still clutched me too hard around the waist. But for long stretches, weeks at a time, she donned a personality she'd concocted for the reporters who came to interview her: brash, chain-smoking, hinnying like a horse, raw with sex. I liked this new Blythe. I was afraid of her. She appeared so hard, though all the while, if I was in the room, Blythe held my hand and stroked it.

I adored her, even during those dark hours when she'd turn herself off, slip vegetative into her sadness. I saw her vision, and it shook me. What talent I had was quiet and web-like, a connecting of seemingly scattered elements, while Blythe imprinted herself upon the world with a grandiosity that awed me. She had a vast generosity, a daring charm. She brought armfuls of Gerbera daisies into my house because, she said, they were beautiful and I was beautiful in the same way, ruddy and angular and strong; she mixed me drinks until we were drunk by the pool in the early afternoon; she slipped off her heels with the gold buckles and handed them to me because I loved them. She laughed when her boys turned to me with a wound, and allowed me the pleasure of comforting them. Those boys, with their translucent little faces, their wariness, the way they sidled up to me shyly whenever I was around, broke my heart.

One day, in late summer, in the ladies' room at the zoo on an excursion with Blythe and the boys, Susan looked up at me with a grave frown as I tried to wrestle her pants up her legs. "Mom," she said, "which kid do you love most: me or Mackenzie or Blythe?" And though I felt terribly guilty later, at that moment I only stared at my littlest and broke into a surprised roar, and didn't end up answering my daughter at all.

THOSE FIRST FOUR YEARS I had only seen Blythe's mother once, though Blythe and I were more like sisters than friends. I doubt Blythe had ever truly told her about our friendship. The old crone was fearsome. I discovered this only by accident; one day I'd hurried through a department store with my hands full of bargain goods—Mackenzie needed shoes, money was tight—and I saw Blythe at the café with an older woman. They were dressed in suits identical save for their different shades of blue. The older woman was Blythe with a thinner face, gray hair, a wicked bauble on her finger, and she was avoiding her daughter's hungry stare by addressing her remarks to the embossed tin of the ceiling.

I approached, eager to introduce myself, but stopped when I heard the mother's voice. It was clipped and cold. "Shameful, really," she was saying. "I must speak out: your sisters fear you, you know, and Pritch is useless. Why would you wallow like a pig in your *episodes*? Why? I tried to come to one of your performances, you know, and couldn't stay for more than a minute. So dark and ugly. Why must you insist on making yourself so ugly, rubbing things all over you, saying those horrible things? Blythe, darling, we all wish you wouldn't, you know. They're no one's business. Your boys will never get away from them. You will end up making them just like you, and I, well . . . It's simply unfair," she said.

Her webbed eyes fell from their focus and she saw me standing behind Blythe, staring at her. I was holding Mackenzie's hand so tightly the poor child was squirming. Blythe's mother pursed her lips and narrowed her dark eyes, which were so like my Blythe's, but hard where her daughter's were liquid. I suddenly felt so dirty and ugly and vulgar with my cut-price shoes that I turned and fled, despite Mackenzie's whining, despite my own curiosity. And from then on I couldn't help grimacing whenever Blythe spoke of her mother, because she always did so in a voice redolent with love.

BY THE TIME MY GIRLS were in school I had stopped writing poetry. Blythe was already making great waves with her pieces, and in the maelstrom of her success I began to lose my love for my own poems. I make no excuses for myself: had I been a real poet, her fame wouldn't have affected me at all. I would have kept on writing my quiet things, sending them out, collecting the rejections and rejoicing in the few acceptances. But under Blythe's reflected light my poems seemed so paltry and meek. I kept my love for poetry in general and for the more serious fiction I was reading in gulps, and it was this love that made me return to school for a Ph.D. in English. I would still be thinking deeply of writing and art, would still be doing what my poetry had been doing, trying to connect distant pieces of the world and draw them closer.

I could never tell Blythe why I had stopped writing: she needed the fiction that I was there solely for her. "Without you, Harriet," she'd cry in her exuberance after a performance, "I'd be nothing, nothing." We both knew it was true; only I knew it was bittersweet, and that before making my decision, I spent long nights at the kitchen table, my eyes sandpapered with sadness.

The day I was accepted at UPenn, Sam said, "You, Harriet, are going to be the most overeducated mommy in the world," and I couldn't tell you then why that statement seemed to suck the air right out of me.

Her new celebrity made Blythe grow first indiscreet, then downright flippant, about her lovers. She even invited her most recent beau to a February party she threw to celebrate her new artist's grant. He was a florid Montana painter, tall and moustached, so full of himself that he didn't seem to notice the inappropriateness of his presence or the poisonous way Blythe grinned at Pritch all night. As at all of the Cantors' parties, there was too much whiskey, too little food, too loud house music. Their parties had such an air of permissiveness that inevitably some actor would paw his pretty-boy date in the corner or some matronly woman would disapear conspicuously into the bathroom with a man decades younger than she was.

I should have put a stop to Blythe's display, I knew. But I was drunk, loving the silver bangles that chittered on my wrists when I danced, celebrating my own minor victory: I'd just had my first book review accepted for publication. So I thought, *Yummy*, looking at the cowboy-painter, instead of *I'd better go stop this nonsense*, which was more like me.

Just before dawn the second-to-last couple staggered out with the Montana painter to give him a ride home. Sam and I were left to pick up the empty glasses and clean the ashtrays and turn off the music. In the new silence, Pritch's and Blythe's whispers boiled up into shouts in the kitchen. Sam seized my arm, pulling me to the door, but I shook free to listen.

"Had to bring him here, in front of our goddamn friends. In our goddamn house with our goddamn children sleeping upstairs," Pritch said.

"What do you want me to do? I can't touch you, Pritchard. You make me sick," said Blythe. There was a horrible sound of hand against flesh, a fall, a shattering of glass. Sam and I ran to the kitchen. Blythe was sitting in a pile of broken tumblers, bleeding from her hands and clutching her left cheek.

Before we could rouse ourselves, Pritch bent down and scooped her up as if she were light as a doll. Blythe buried her face in her husband's chest and threw her arms around his neck, murmuring, "I'm so sorry, I'm so sorry." Pritch gave me a stern look, then turned away, carrying Blythe upstairs. Sam cleaned up the blood, the glass, as I stood there, burning. We let ourselves out into the dove-gray dawn in silence, clutching each other's hands with all the force we could muster.

Yet, when we were safe in bed that morning, I resisted sleep. All night there had been a strange lightness in me, and as I listened to Sam's breath, I imagined vivid impossibilities. A dark bathroom, the heartbeat of a party downstairs, tile cold against my hands and knees. One silky moustache tickling my ear.

I NEVER GREW USED TO BLYTHE'S CRUMBLINGS, or how they could come along so suddenly. One happened before my eyes when we were thirty-eight, and Blythe had been manic for quite some time. She'd put a great deal of weight on her bones and though the lithium had given her odd twitchings, weird darts of her tongue, it made her skin glow and her sore chapped lips swell and ripen, a postcoital look.

Throaty, glittering, these were the years she was performing naked, glorying in her thick body, in her shame. She sat in a bathtub made of ice as she said, *And the sweet wet slide of my son into water / a dive / how he beats like a pulse before bursting / into air.* Severe, incantatory, she made an electric chair of willow rods as she repeated, *Give us the brank / give us the switch / we are all witches / we terrible ones.*

Blythe was still the darling of New York, of London, but I saw that she had begun to repeat herself, that her vision had narrowed, that she was growing only more extreme, not more subtle. I tried to tell her, but even small criticisms were treason to Blythe. She would shout so much that I learned to stay quiet and watch. I thought she would do what she wanted to no matter what I said; that I would be a better friend by being purely supportive.

The night of her collapse she was in an elegant gray silk suit, flushed and victorious from a performance that held the critics in thrall: these were her AIDS years, and she had black male models and white female models walking in a tight room, brushing up carnally against one another. Blythe was in the center, touching everyone who passed by like an enormous, ravenous spider. Afterward we had returned home to her Merion house, and she thrust open the French doors so the sunset threaded her bob with veins of bronze. In that moment, she had transformed into a figure of bliss. She turned to speak to me, to hold my face in her hands and kiss me on the forehead in her excess of joy, when the phone rang and she went to it, all a green-eyed dazzle.

Her face fell and she said "No" in a very low murmur. She grew pale, seemed to shrink, and her eyes darkened until they were black. The moment after Blythe hung up the phone and just before she looked at me and spoke of her mother's sudden death, I couldn't find my friend in her transformation into a dull and bloodless woman.

That was her most decided collapse yet. She grew querulous, fought more. She grew plumper, then outright fat, though her new flesh was creamy and somehow beautiful, making her even grander. Pritch stayed away from the house for as long as possible, as did the boys. Tom and Bear turned my rec room into a foot-smelling sanctuary for themselves, and they slept there, on a bunk bed I'd bought them, more nights than not. Once, despairing at her weight while Pritch was on a business trip, Blythe trashed all the food in her house, and the boys had no meals for a whole day until Tom called me, crying. She even turned on me when she seemed strong enough to do something bad and I stole her pills. She would throw glasses and lamps, whatever was at hand, until I fled.

It felt inevitable that I would come upon Blythe lying on the hideous dress on the sofa, senseless, so I was calm when I called the ambulance. Blythe had shouted at me when she awoke to the hospital's buzz and bleachy sheen, "How dare you, Harriet? How dare you? You're not my friend," and she refused to talk to me for the three weeks she was in the hospital. Then one day she called to chat as if nothing had happened.

Those years I awoke at night many times in a panic of sweat, having dreamed of falling. Such constant urgency began to feel routine, Peter and the Wolf on repeat. I began to ignore the histrionics, and a few times refused to come to the phone when I sensed Blythe was on the other line and only mildly insane.

Then came the fall morning when the boys were at school and Blythe slipped from the house and drove to the Jersey shore, where her mother's family had had a summer house for generations. She went to a cup of light at the top of the antique curving stairwell. In that smell of salt and fish, under the rattle of the bubbled windows, she slit her wrists, letting her blood dribble in rays down the stairs. But the man the family hired to check on the house grew suspicious on seeing Blythe's car in the drive and entered, and she was saved, yet again.

THE CHILDREN WERE IN MIDDLE SCHOOL when Blythe began spreading rumors about herself. She was quite large by then, and reporters had stopped taking pictures of her. Plus, her newest performance was not going well. Africa had grown popular as a cause: the extent of the genocide in Rwanda was emerging, and Blythe had orchestrated a piece in which she'd "borrowed" Tutsi orphans, some as old as three, and put them naked in a close, white room, to be suckled by extremely pale women. The babies sobbed and soiled themselves and the women, though they had been told to hold still, grew anxious, wanting to clean the babies, to comfort them. I could only stand to see it for a minute before I walked out. The critics had the same reaction I did.

Blythe had always been a canny marketer; her new rumor campaign had a sort of sidewise brilliance. Some of what she spread was true, some was flagrantly untrue, but everything had an element of reality to it. These are only a few of the many rumors I heard:

That Blythe had found Christ by seducing a Catholic priest. True.

That Blythe had spent an entire semester as artist in residence at Bryn Mawr sitting with her back turned to her students and saying nary a word. Untrue.

That Blythe had found herself a lesbian lover. True; the lover was an unattractive fifty-year-old psychiatrist from Plymouth Meeting with whom she had a yearlong affair. At its denouement, the lover showed up at my house weeping, wanting me to explain Blythe to her. I could only give her some warm milk and send her home.

That Blythe had found herself wandering naked in South Philadelphia. Semi-true: she had been wandering naked, but it was on the Swarthmore campus.

That Blythe had had sexual urges for Tom, her son. This scared me the most. I longed to ask him, to make sure he was all right, but it is hard to meddle with a family, and I couldn't hurt Blythe like that. I watched him and hoped. I still had faith in Blythe.

I had tried to protect Blythe from these rumors for a long

time; I had no idea she was the one spreading them. But one day when she sat on my veranda, nursing a glass of ginger ale, she began telling me a strange dark fable in which, a year earlier, she had been abducted by a man at the grocery store, held for twenty-four hours in a small apartment, and repeatedly violated. She had given the man her engagement ring, and when he was out pawning it, she escaped, half-naked, and caught a ride home in a taxicab. She had actually rather enjoyed the escape, she said. I should tell my girls and any other woman I knew, she said, because that man could still be out there in this horrible world of ours.

She told me this, looking beyond me and nodding. I watched her, ill. There was no twenty-four-hour stretch in the past year when I hadn't spoken to Blythe. There was no twelve-hour stretch. I was there when she lost her engagement ring down the pool filter, and cried for four hours, for fear of Pritch. Her story was horribly false.

But I knew what harm I could do by showing disbelief, and said, "That sounds awful," then asked her how her Rwandan piece was doing.

She gave me her old dazzling smile and leaned forward. "Darling," she said, "I'm doing it for the Museum of Modern Art in New York. I'm officially famous."

She was, and she had been even before that moment, and she would remain so for these five years since. All this time Sam and I have become more comfortable, moved from Manayunk to a house in Rittenhouse Square, spent our weekends fixing it up. I gained some small celebrity with my critical pieces, perhaps mainly because I had tried to eschew the savagery that was so common in my field, and instead tried to locate the piece I was considering within the larger web of art, to consider it under those lights. I was afraid of what I would discover if I considered Blythe's. I never did.

Blythe once read a piece of mine, a five-thousand-word essay in *The New York Review of Books*, then waved it at herself, as if it were a giant fan. She said, "This is great and all, but, Harriet, doesn't it make you sad to do this kind of stuff? You were such a good poet, remember? Writing about writing just seems so, I don't know. Meaningless. Or masturbatory, or what have you."

I had to control my voice. "I think," I said, "that criticism can be just as meaningful as the art it considers. It creates a dialogue."

"Art creates dialogue," said Blythe. "Critics are just vultures." She watched my face with her sharp green eyes, then laughed. "Not you," she said. "You're too sweet for carrion." She poured me another glass of iced tea and chattered away until my irritation dissolved and I found my resistances collapsing, found myself sinking into her again.

IN THE AUTUMN THIS PAST YEAR I went to Blythe's house, prodded by a bad feeling, and found a spout of Pritch's clothes issuing from the bedroom window, a hailstorm of shoes. Pritch was in the yard, red-faced, gathering his things from where they fell into the piles of leaves. "Harriet," he spat when he saw me. "If she doesn't do it herself, I swear to God I'm going to kill her."

I looked at Pritch. He stood, his arms heaped with suits, and sighed. "She's insisting that we get a divorce. Out of nowhere. Not to mention hypocritical for a born-again Catholic. I'm apparently the one that makes her crazy."

"Oh, Pritch," I said. "Oh, no." His eyes were red-rimmed. I said, "You're the one who keeps her sane."

"You are," he said. "We both know it." Pritch dropped his face into the bundle of clothing and held it there for a long time. "Harriet," he said, looking up at last, "I give up. I'm so tired. It's up to you now, kid." He walked to his car and shoved the things into the backseat, then sat on the bumper and buried his head in his hands again.

When I went inside, Tom was sitting on the stairwell. "Oh, Aunt Harriet," he said. "I'm so glad you're here." Tom was seventeen, a beautiful boy though almost too graceful, with worry marks etched in his forehead. He still spoke with a lisp. Of all my children, and I include Blythe's, he was the one who gave me heartache; his happiness seemed the least sure, his life to come the hardest. I gave him a kiss on the way upstairs, and he squeezed my hand as I passed. He smelled of pine and, surprisingly, jasmine.

When I opened Blythe's door, she was in the middle of the floor, nude. She was pulling her hair with both hands. My friend had gained a great deal of weight again, and I looked at her body with a little thrill: my own aging one was so lumpy compared to hers. Her fat was smooth, her body beautifully large. I lay down beside her. She rolled over and buried her hot, wet face on my chest, and I rubbed her head until she calmed.

"I hate him," she mumbled. I could feel her mouth move warm on my breast and, to my shame, felt my nipple harden. "I figured it all out. I wasn't really crazy until I married him. And then I had his kids, and poof! I'm insane. I'm getting a divorce. I'm getting it tomorrow. Just wait and see."

I just stroked her glossy hair, wondering when she'd begun to get those few white hairs, when the crows'-feet had pushed themselves more deeply beside her eyes. I didn't know how to say that I was tired, too. I had just that morning refused a wonderful offer to teach in England, and had refused many more lectureships in the past, because I couldn't be away from Blythe, for fear that her world would crash down and I wouldn't be there to salvage what remained. I didn't know how to say that I wished she could safely go to the beauty salon without me, to the grocery store, to the movies. That I wished she were a stranger, and I could walk away. That I wished to go to sleep for just one night without the fear of awakening into a shattered world.

I couldn't say this, of course. So I said nothing.

For a long time we lay there as the sky darkened and small rain fell through the open window. Downstairs, we could hear Bear's television nattering and Tom moving about the kitchen, making dinner. "Oh, Harriet," she sighed into my chest. "My Harriet." She drew her head up. Her eyes had gone slate gray and narrow. She leaned forward and gave me a long, lingering kiss. Her lips were very soft and tasted like whiskey.

I can't say that I didn't like it. I can't say that somewhere in me, for twelve years, I had not longed for exactly that. To be, for a moment, the center. To, finally, *take*.

She nuzzled my cheek. When she gave a seductive little laugh, a laugh that spoke of practice, of seduction, I felt a break in me.

I pushed Blythe aside and stood, shaking. I went to the door. And I didn't look around when I said, "Blythe, honey. Get dressed and come downstairs. Take a deep breath, and do whatever it is you want me to tell you to do."

I left. My call awoke the kindly gentleman in England, who had been so disappointed when I'd refused the lectureship that morning. He was gracious and pleased that I had changed my mind. Weeks later, when the plane lifted from the runway for the transoceanic flight, I felt as if I were a great plant being ripped from the ground, roots snapping below me with great shudderings.

AT THE END OF THE TERM I flew home for Blythe's party in honor of her grandest award yet. When the plane circled down into polluted, glorious Philadelphia, I felt I willed it down myself. But I didn't have time to do much more than hug my girls, take one long look at my Rittenhouse Square garden, with its wisteria climbing the latticework, and then Sam and I hurried to the party. In the tight space of the car, my husband seemed a stranger to me, and we held the shyness of a first date between us, sweet and awkward.

"It's been so hard without you," he said when we turned into the driveway of the monstrous modern house in Paoli where the party was to take place. In his words I felt his giddy relief at my return. Then he added, "Not just me. All of us. Mack and Sue went nuts somehow. Blythe, too. Harriet," he said, watching me in a sidelong way, "I'm afraid that Blythe is going again."

I nodded. All summer I sensed a growing problem, and had called Blythe twice a week. And just before I returned to America, I received a package from my friend, two inches thick with her new piece she'd been creating at a white heat since spring. *Bombing the Wreck*, she called it. As far as I could tell, it was only a collection of loose, troublesome lines: *and so I choose the bloodsnake / the writhing shades in the eggs it makes / curls like smoke and licks my life / for I have wearied so of water.* The accompanying drawings for the performance made no sense to me: Blythe in a swimsuit, majestic, chained underwater in a great glass aquarium. This was not a performance. I didn't quite know what it was.

The party was enormous, more than two hundred important people, and Blythe was late, of course. One hour rolled into two and I stood alone at the edge of the living room, growing furious. I could be with my girls, I thought: they had surprised me with how leggy they'd become in the few short months I'd been gone, and I wanted to touch them again, to know how they had changed. In the living room of the modern house, the cement walls had been scattered with random-seeming windows, and the party, growing edgier by the minute, was reflected back at itself. I searched the windows for a reflection of Sam's dear bald pate, my one comfort, but couldn't find him. I felt a little bereft at the lack.

At last, some of the guests began to slink home and the hostess finally gave up on Blythe. She gathered people at the buffet, though the meat was now rubbery, the shrimp pale, the potatoes cold.

Only then did the sliding doors thunder open, drowning out the light techno on the air. A jolt, a buzz, recognition: Blythe had arrived. I was too angry to look up, but heard her husky voice saying, "Oh, darlings, I am fearfully late, so sorry. A car crash! It was awful."

The irritation in the room disappeared like smoke. I peered at Blythe in the concise reflection in the window. She wore a golden-brown velvet minidress, a thick gold cuff on her bicep, one arm in a sling. Her head was thrown back, hips forward, the good arm akimbo on her hip. All adazzle, as usual. She was magnificent, as shocking as she was that first night I saw her, if mainly because of the warp of the glass. I also knew that when I turned, I would see Blythe as she actually was, the lines on her thin skin, the lickings of her lips, the great broad bulk, the panic in the eyes whirling up as soon as she saw me, that need.

I thought: *I will turn around now. I'll pull her back again.* I gave myself to the count of three, but kept counting to thirty, and didn't turn. *Come on, Harriet,* I scolded myself. But I was so very weary. I just couldn't do it. Not again.

Instead, I looked into the glass, into the darkness of the October night. I thought of how, out there in a Pennsylvania pond, near some sleeping farmhouse, there was probably one old catfish caught and released so often her gills were scarred and stiff, barely filtering the water anymore. When I took a step closer to the wall of windows, I saw my own face grow large and pale. Beyond, the moon and the dark lawn seemed to shrink the closer I came to them. I took another step, watched them shrink again. Blythe spoke, and though I couldn't hear the words, I heard the hunger in them.

I would release her. She'd swim into whatever dark and terrible place she needed to go. I could do no more. I took one more step toward my face, toward the landscape, a chill draft from the loose casing stroking my cheek. One more step. Then I watched it all, miraculously, bloom.

The Wife of the Dictator

THE WIFE OF THE DICTATOR IS SALLOW AND strange. She's a plump woman, uncomfortable here in the hot sun with our cocktails and croquet. She has not yet learned to perspire with grace; in one hour her gray silk dress is dotted, then black with moisture. She speaks little, moves in a series of small fidgets, wears a corset. When she stands to excuse herself and gives us her hand it is so soft it seems almost to not exist at all.

What has been reported is true: the dictator has brought back a wife from his last visit to America. It is also true that she is not one of us.

We survey the hole in the air where she had been sitting, let it fill for a moment with the scratchy tenor on the gramophone. The children shriek at the edge of the lake with their nannies; we mix more gin into our drinks. When the dictator's black car slides from the compound, dips from sight into the city, and later beetles up the hill toward the pink palace glistening in the sun, we, at last, feel free to wonder.

The dictator is an enormous man with a cruel mouth: we like to watch him on his chestnut charger when his troops are doing maneuvers on the parade grounds. Wherever could he have gotten this plump sparrow of a wife? And why, when he could have plucked one from the ten thousand good families of his own country, trembling girls with downcast eyes and charming virginal figures? If he must marry an American to discharge what secret debts he holds, could he not have chosen one of our daughters or one of our friends, some fine, laughing girl who would know how to entertain us at the palace, a girl who would at least look good beside the dictator on horseback?

The tiny monkeys chew red fruits and cast the sticky seeds down into our hair.

Her family must be very rich, we say, and imagine train lines, coal mines, houses in Newport. Woozy under the sun and drink, someone says she looks like a medium, and we imagine her in a dark room, ectoplasm spinning from her mouth, voices of the dead rising from within her to enchant the dictator into an occultish love. Or maybe, we say, she sat opposite him on a train, and her plainness moved the dictator to pity, his hard heart dissolving into a thousand small butterflies that flitted away with his sense.

We drink, we speculate, until our heads ring wild. We are ossified, we laugh; we are zozzled. At home, in a pique, we put our good dresses away; they hadn't been worth wearing, now, had they. The evening cools and from the city smells of strange cooking waft up to us. When our husbands come home from the Company, from the Embassy, we sit beside them as they eat their supper. Like our children who hold up for our scrutiny the strange stones they find by the lakeside, green-veined, bulb-shaped chunks of this country, we hold the dictator's wife up for our husbands' amusement. We exaggerate her oddness, say she reminds us of our mothers' generation, conservative and dark, of Queen Victoria. We turn her this way and that, and, in the process, we make her an object of wonder.

THE DICTATOR IS ONLY two years a dictator, a man from an obscure mountain city. There had been unrest in his country for a decade, bloodshed and bandits; from the turmoil the dictator was spat into power, as smooth and hard as a gem. This city is still ensconced in the nineteenth century, with its alabaster gas lamps and carriages still more plentiful than automobiles; his grandeur suits it well. There is something in him that makes other men smaller. At the few dinners to which we were invited when he was a bachelor, we watched his tanned, scarred face, his hawk nose, the vast breadth of his shoulders, and when he put his eyes on us we might as well have been nude.

By hints and dribbles we hear of the dictator's wife in her former life in Saint Louis. To escape the humid fug we float in the women's pool, waiting for the cocktail hour, and talk of what we've learned. She is four years older than the dictator, we know now, the widow of another man, the mother of a dead son. She was born into nothing, a provincial dull family, married a boat captain on the Mississippi. On their boy's ninth birthday his father took him on a trip. A flash flood, and the ship foundered and sank, drowning her husband, her boy.

In grief, the dictator's wife took up painting. She painted scenes of epiphany, revelation, saturated with color, details to make grown men weep. She is Catholic, like the natives, we hear: and we can't help but see her in the confessional, the grille casting shadows like lace on her skin, her thin mouth hungry for grace.

When next we see her, dutiful at the dictator's side at a dance, we watch her delicate hands with a new interest, see the poignancy of the gold cross at her throat, study the way her dark hair frames her face. We feel a warmth not unlike pity in our chests. This surprises us.

Mater dolorosa, she has become newly interesting. A dark flower of sorrow transplanted to the strange soil of this bright place; a woman famous for painting angels.

THE RAINY SEASON ARRIVES and we can no longer swim in the pool, or walk by the lake, or play croquet, or complain about the heat. We can no longer stand on the hill and watch the young officers through our binoculars. There are the endless tea parties, the dramatic recitations of Shakespeare, the new Chaplin we love no less for being a whole year late.

The remaking parties when we take apart our old dresses and refashion them according to the magazines our friends and sisters send us, letting down the waists and necklines, heaving up the hems. We smoke cigarettes out the windows, eat pastries until we gasp for air in our clothing, squash spiders under our thumbs, too weary to make much of a fuss. Affairs spark up during the rainy season and fizzle along in the dampness. Our husbands eat their lunches at the club and we are relieved that we don't have to entertain them, too. When we are reduced to watching the pots of geraniums on the verandas fill with water and overspill, we scold our servants for their lapses in housekeeping. They stand, eyelashes on their cheeks, until we release them. We're sure they talk about us in their language in the kitchen. It aggravates us until we want to slap them. Sometimes we do.

We watch the pink palace on the hill, a subdued coral now that it is wet. We wonder if the dictator's wife ever slaps her servants. We doubt it, and we resent her for it.

The rains let up at last and we allow our children to play in the mudpuddles. The dry air in our chests feels like a long sob. Some of our servants' sisters work in the palace, and it is from them that we hear that the dictator's wife is now thickening around the middle.

When we meet one another on a clear, cool day, we laugh behind our hands. So *that's* what the dictator and his wife do when it rains, we giggle. Though the image of the dark plump woman and the grunting vast man together is surreal, it does make a certain sort of sense.

We have asked our sisters and friends to send us articles about the dictator's wife and her art. Famous people consume us because we are bored. In the articles she is described the way we see her, but in kinder tones, words like *pale* for our *sallow*, *unearthly* for our *strange*. She describes her art as products of visions, ghastly revelations that would not let her sleep until she set them down as exactly as possible on her canvases.

When, at one of our bridge parties, out of boredom or tipsiness, we blurt out a question about her painting, she flushes. She looks down at her jostling knees, and in her quiet voice, she says, *But I no longer paint, you know. I haven't needed to since I married the dictator.*

We are so flabbergasted that hers is a talent that can turn on and off like a fountain, according to need, that it is only later, when we are alone and drifting off to sleep, that we realize how odd it is that she, too, calls her husband *the dictator*.

OUR HUSBANDS AT NIGHT tell us a story. The dictator took a few of his generals, some of the higher ranking of the Company and Embassy, over to his hunting camp where the sugarcane meets the jungle. A party of thirty, plus servants, they were there to hunt boar.

They awoke before dawn, when the jungle was filled with hooting monkeys and great cats slinking in the shadows. When the thrashers at midmorning rustled up an enormous boar, grunting with horrific power and fury, the men circled their horses and waited for the dictator's command.

In lieu of bringing the gun to his eye and simply killing the beast, though, he slid down and put his gun on the ground. He approached the boar, which fell silent, watchful, as he neared. When the dictator was a mere foot away, the boar bowed his head, the prelude to spearing it up and gutting the dictator with his tusks. But before he could, the dictator planted his knife in the base of the boar's neck and the great beast collapsed in a geyser of blood.

When our husbands tell us this story, we wonder what it is like to be married to a man who could kill such a beast with his hands. We look at our husbands' balding temples, their concave chests, their pale shoulders, and try not to laugh.

That isn't the end of the story, our husbands protest. They prop themselves on their arms, leaning over us in their eagerness. As he drove the knife in and the boar collapsed, there was a smile on the dictator's face. It was a sweet, shy look, our husbands say: it was the kind of smile better worn by a man in love.

WE HEAR REPORTS: there is unrest again at the country's edges. If possible, the dictator grows even more stern. Our husbands tell us not to listen to the radio, that we should not worry one whit, and because we know not to ask what they do at the Company or the Embassy, we take them at their word. There are few cars in this small country, and those that pick our husbands up in the morning, whether from the Company or the Embassy, appear to be the same.

When the wife of the dictator is six months expecting,

the dictator rides off with a few battalions to quell the militants. Over the city falls a new gentleness, a new quiet, and in the trees land flocks of strange green birds that end their rills with metallic clicks. When the birds startle at a sound, it looks as if the trees are tossing handfuls of their own leaves into the skies. We can hear the bands in the square at the bottom of the hill; we find ourselves dancing to them as we ready ourselves for bed. We Shimmy, we Charleston, we Bunny Hug; we imagine ourselves at great gay parties where these things come to us with ease.

The night the wife of the dictator goes into labor, heat lightning branches blue across the sky and our hair yearns staticky toward our brushes. We can't sleep. We sit on our verandas, smoking our clandestine cigarettes and across the compound see other embers floating, fireflies of disquiet.

The electricity breaks around two with a thunderclap and torrential rain. We are chasing frogs from our porches in the morning when we hear the news. The dictator charged into the city on his wheezing horse in the midst of the storm and hurried into the palace. The mud clotted thick and black on the carpets behind him. When he reached his wife, his face was so dirty and wet she screamed as if he were a baboon come in from the jungle. The dictator knelt, he shuddered. He held her little pale feet in his hands, as if they were delicate as teacups, and he kissed them.

With the last push and convulsion, the dictator's wife near dead with fatigue and fear, the tiny baby emerged at last, all skinny and blue. The dictator sat back on his heels, country-style. And when the doctor at last got the baby to breathe and mewl, the dictator stood and left the room, because she was only a girl.

WE SEE THE DICTATOR'S wife everywhere, it seems, and nowhere: while the dictator is fighting the rebels she pushes her babe down by the lake in her perambulator, trailed by the useless, pretty nannies the dictator hired. She refuses a wet nurse, which is not done here, and the native ladies have turned indignant. We hear they have refused to invite her to their teas; we wonder at her solitary life now. It can't, we think, be a hardship for her.

The news from the border is not good. The opposition forces, they say, are resilient and clever at blending into the countryside. The papers hold photos of the dictator, enormous and severe, in his command tent in the jungle. When we see them, we are filled with a hot thrill and wish, briefly, that we could read the language and understand the captions. Some of our husbands are sent to the plantations, the mines, the Embassy, with more frequency, and when they return they stare at their knees with a blank look. But a few days soaking in the gentlemen's pool, a few nights at the club, and they are normal again. We have our charity bazaars for the victims of the dengue fever, which is gripping certain tight-packed segments of the city. We have our ice cream socials. We keep busy.

Our servants' sisters who work in the palace relay rumors

that the dictator's wife sometimes awakes shrieking in the nights. They say she wanders the white marble halls in her humble slippers, passing like a ghost through the shadows. When a servant comes upon her, she does not appear to see, and passes as if her eyes are fixed on another world. We wonder what the dictator's wife is thinking of at those times: her dead son, her dead husband, those two souls lost under the thick murmuring water of a distant river. Or if, like us, she dreams of a vaster country, one where she is not caged in the palace as we are caged in our compound. Or if she ever longs to take up brush and palette again, paint that old life away until the grief rises, time and again, gently back into the heavens.

THE DICTATOR IS SHOT in the foot. He returns home to the palace, gray-faced and grim, to recuperate. He has left his generals in charge in the jungle. The little girl is walking now, an unfortunate small replica of her mother, and in public she shrieks into her mother's skirts and hides her face from our children, who would not hurt her.

The dictator's wife is wearing new colors, greens and purples and indigos, and on her head she now wears hats with chin-length veils. When we search out her eyes we believe we see bruises around them, and from that moment on we don't search them out anymore. Later we wonder if they are not bruises, if she is simply exhausted from all of the sleep she has been missing. When they are together in public, the dictator rarely turns his eyes from his wife. We almost never hear her subdued voice now.

A BRIEF RESPITE: a cruise ship needing repairs docks at the marina, and there descends into the town a pair of celebrated lovebirds weeks into their honeymoon. They are known to everyone who knows anything about the theater. Our magazines are months behind; only recently have we gotten hints about this romance. The actress is golden as a songbird with a sharp little face; the actor is a small man with a barrel chest. When we hear they are in the port, we leave the pool in a hurry, still smelling of the oil we spread on our skin, and try not to run to the bazaar, where they are buying armfuls of textiles and tin sculptures.

When we arrive, however, so does a car for a luncheon arranged with the dictator's wife. We can hardly see the actors before they are whisked away. Morose, we buy drinks at a bar that we believe has only ever known men, and sit at the tables abandoned by the chess players when they saw us coming. We move the pawns about, dreaming of what we would do with this country if we were the dictator's wife, flicking the bishops and kings with our fingers.

In an hour, the car hums down the hill again. When the actors climb, laughing, from the car, after them climbs the dictator's wife like their single dark shadow. She is smiling, we see: she follows them to the gangplank and they give her elaborate kisses on the cheek when they part.

The boat's lines are thrown, the boat edges away from the dock. And when it is heading firmly toward sea again, we watch the small form of the dictator's wife as she stares after it. When she turns, we lose the sharpness of our envy. Always pale, she is deathly white, and though she was plump when she came to the country, her clothes hang on her loosely now.

We wonder if what the servant girls say is true: that she sleeps very little any longer, that she spends her nights staring out the window, horror on her face. That the last time the dictator was home she ducked away when he tried to embrace her.

THE RAINY SEASON COMES and goes; our beautiful young lovers are gone in the war and we must content ourselves with books turned stale with humidity, phonographs playing the same fatigued songs. At our tea parties there fall long swaths of silence, which in earlier times we'd break by laughing, saying *an angel is passing over our roof,* though we do not bother now. Our servant girls bring reports of starvation in dark parts of the city, but when we go down in an investigatory cluster to see what we can do, the smell is so terrible we do not go again. We see writing on the buildings that appears to be angry, and there are people who stare at us with frowns on their faces. Our children seem pallid and whiny, mere specters of children. Our husbands are gone for longer stints and will not tell us where they have been when they return.

We pay the servant girls for their rumors, and the rumors

trickle in more thickly. The guerrillas, they say, are peeling the dictator's forces back, pushing them toward the city, decimating the ranks of those beautiful young men. Because we can do nothing about it we pretend not to know.

And we hear, now, worse rumors about the dictator, what cruelties his armies are unloosing. Suspected insurgents punched in the stomachs while their heads are held in buckets of water; almost drowned this way, they cough up any confessions that are suggested to them. A special battery hooked to the nipples, a special torture. Phalanxes of hooded insurgents marched somewhere, never seen again. Villages in the way burned, survivors gutted. We hear that there is an ex-butcher on the dictator's special team called the Flayer, and we must stop ourselves from imagining what he does.

One day, before our husbands rise to the breakfast table, we flip open the newspapers and see the photograph on the front page. The dictator is frowning in his tall boots, and there is a pole suspended between two lieutenants beside him. Strung like beads on the pole, threaded through the tongue, are the decapitated heads of men. Each died grimacing.

We are modern women; some of us bob our hair and wear trousers at home; we are not the fainting types our mothers were. Still, after this, even we walk around the house feeling weak, feeling as if our legs are made of air.

OUR HUSBANDS COME home early from work one evening and tell us, grimly, that the barbarians are at the gates. The dictator has been useless, they say. When we press, they say that there are other forces at work; we should not worry our heads about it.

We wait. The pool is a blue stone inlaid in the ground, untouched. The monkeys get into the kitchens, leave floury imprints on the pianos, and we let them. The city itself seems to draw its tentacles in. Things are so quiet we can hear the distant sounds, the low dull explosions and the cracks of the guns. Some of our servants go home at night and do not return in the morning. We have difficulty finding coffee, then bread.

The dictator's wife comes to sit with us on the overgrown lawn, the bougainvillea threatening to swallow the tennis court. She has been to the cathedral, she tells us, but the doors were closed. She found a side entrance to the priests' house and found the priests at the kitchen table, eating toast, still in their pajamas. They would not look her in the eye. They would not give confession, she says. They silently refused.

She says this, her body still, this woman who jitters when calm. Never beautiful, she has become ugly with fatigue, her skin lined. Her daughter hides behind her chair, and we notice the girl's mouth is the dictator's own. One by one, she plucks out gray hairs from her mother's head, and though her mother winces with each pluck, she allows it. We have little to offer the dictator's wife now, except our silence and more tea.

I have dreams, the dictator's wife starts to say. When she raises her face, her pupils have swallowed her irises. We are reminded again of a medium in mid-séance, of the plain, quiet widow she had once been in a Saint Louis parlor, limning a canvas with her paint and visions. *I know everything he has done,* she says.

In the middle of the night, a knock on the door, and we who have packed everything get into the cars and glide down the hill. The younger children are sleeping against our shoulders, and there is the smell of smoke in the air. Our husbands are grim and do not speak. We do not say good-bye to our remaining servants, or to the booze we cannot take home to our dry country. We do not say good-bye to the compound, our lovely houses, the pool in which we have spent so many of our years. The darkness swallows it all. The marina is protected by a line of our own officers with guns on their shoulders. If the natives know we are leaving, we do not see them in the night, and it would not matter, we cannot take them. In the distance there are terrible sounds.

When we are on the boat, we breathe again. Not one of us asks our husbands to fetch the dictator's wife, who is alone in the pink palace on the hill, her daughter sleeping beside her. We have made our own choices in this life; the dictator was hers. There is something that unfurls in us when we think this, and we dare not examine what it is.

Still, as the boat unhitches from the dock and quietly moves into the harbor, we see the palace dwindle into a dark lump on the hill and imagine her there, in the gilded chamber, the dark carved bed swinging with velvet drapes. We imagine her at the window, watching the fires roil from the edges of the city. The sky is touched with a terrible glow and our ship is a dark spot fading against the greater darkness.

Then, in the moment between the thump of one heartbeat and its sweet sliding after, we at last see what is before her eyes. We see great flights of angels in flapping robes descending upon the city, their faces terrible with bloodlust and fury; we see the furious melee, the young boys falling, the old people huddled in their apartments, the dictator wild on a screaming horse and the boar-hunting knife in his hand. In this moment we know his strength is only her own last strength, which he pulls from her, for that is what this marriage was; the dictator coming into the gallery in Washington, feeling small under the power of those paintings, turning to the little dark woman standing patiently beside him in her widow's weeds, knowing in that moment the terrific power in her, everything he could use of hers. We watch through her now as she sees the ragged bandits crash in one great wave, then two great waves against the palace, find entry. She closes her eyes and leans her forehead against the window. Like that she is emptied, at last.

We will not tell one another what we knew just then; we are not sure we will ever admit it to ourselves. As we see the city dwindle into a small speck of light, we lean against our husbands, who are not strong and do not fight, but at least have gotten us away. They, wanting to comfort, put their arms around us. And they are comforted for all their own errors, in their turn.

Watershed

A DIVER WE KNEW ONCE TOLD US A STORY. We were at a wedding, and all night he had watched us with a curious look on his face. At last, he loomed up from the corner of the tent, already talking, drunk, breathing his winey breath into our faces. You clutched my knee under the table to keep from laughing. The diver didn't notice, just kept on talking.

When he was young, he said, he dove to a wreck beside a deep, dark chasm. It was cold down there and in his lights the wreck seemed strange, scabbed with rust, the fish pale and shiny as they darted before him. His dive buddy was a man he had been paired with, barely an acquaintance. That far down, a diver should be wary of nitrogen narcosis, with its hallucinations, its emotional swoops, its blackouts. At one point, our friend turned to make sure everything was fine with his dive buddy, and saw him falling quietly, spread-eagled, into the abyss.

Our friend had two choices. He could watch the man disappear into the dark, knowing he had fainted and would never awaken before he died. Or, he could set off after him, risking a blackout himself, certain death for both of them. That deep, he gave himself a five percent chance of catching his buddy while he was cogent enough to bring them both to safety. He paused here in his story, looking at the dancers on the floor swaying to "Our Love Is Here to Stay." We thought he was trying to build suspense. We cried, Well, what did you do?

The diver blinked and returned to us. Oh. Well, I just dove, he said.

The water was heavy, and just before his hands touched the other fellow's arms, our friend began to laugh. It came from nowhere, the laughter, and though he was daring death, he couldn't help it. He laughed so hard he almost spat out his regulator so he could laugh even harder. But he didn't. He grabbed his buddy, inflating his buoyancy vest a little. It was only when they rose out of the chasm and into the lighter, greener waters above the wreck that he stopped laughing. He watched the other man awaken behind his mask, open his eyes, confused. As they floated at twenty feet below the surface, decompressing the nitrogen from their blood, they clutched each other. They watched the waves wrinkle and break like silk against the boat's prow, the elegant blue of the sky beyond.

I held that guy, said the diver over the empty wine bottles, I held him so hard. On land he'd never have been a close friend. But waiting to emerge into the air, he said, I have never in my life felt a purer love for a human being. I have never loved anybody as much as I did that stupid man at that very moment.

Without another word, our friend stood and moved off. We watched each other in the candlelight and suave music, and because laughter was the only weapon we had, we laughed until the chill of his story faded, and was gone.

YOU'LL REMEMBER THIS SPRING, how, after the snow melted, the lake rose and didn't stop rising. March was soggy with rain, April drenched. In the hills, the beaver dams broke and spread diseased water into the rain-slapped lake until it was the color of a bruise. The river couldn't drain it fast enough, and roared thick and brown over the bridges, carrying the bloated bodies of unwary cows and deer down the current toward Harrisburg.

By June, our basement walls wept between the stones. Water seeped to ankle level, then to mid-calf. In the corner, the cardboard boxes weakened then broke apart, and when they did they spilled still-wrapped wedding gifts into the murk.

IT IS STRANGE to find myself living again in our chintzy hometown after fifteen years away. It was a tiny thing, really, that brought me back to stay: a high school friend of ours was getting married last autumn, and I was almost late for the wedding. I slid into the pew with four seconds to spare and was still so flustered throughout the benediction that I began to tear the program into tiny pieces. I may have ended up shredding a hymnal or the offertory sleeves, or even my own hem, had a man's hand not reached over into my lap and gently took hold of both of mine, and held them still until the end of the service.

I stared at those strange hands until it was all over. I could do nothing else, and they were large, callused, with swirls of dark hair below the first and second knuckles, neat nails and pretty moons in the nail beds. Very strong, very warm. But I didn't dare peek at their owner until the bride, beaming, swooshed back down the aisle in a cloud of lily scent and Pachelbel and lace. Then I glanced at you and had to quickly look away. You were almost too handsome, though I know now that's not how you strike most people. What, to others, was a too-big jaw and too-ruddy cheeks, a prominent forehead, the blue shadow of a beard under freshly shaven skin (I could smell the cream you'd used), was, to me, breathtaking.

Hello, Celie, you said, grinning.

Hello, I whispered.

You cocked your head. You don't remember me, do you?

No, I said. No.

Well, you said, and stood when everyone else did, and took my arm. Your date gave a dismayed squeal (I remember her only as a brown silk frill, some kind of gold shoe that was kicked at me after she grew drunk at the reception), but we ignored her. We walked out of the warm church and under a hail of rice that wasn't meant for us; we went over the hard-frosted grass and through the first door we could find, the rectory, empty. You plucked a piece of rice out of my hair, and leaned me up against a stained-glass window depicting John the Baptist, baptizing. A cloud slid back outside and in the brief burst of sun, your cheek was dyed red and yellow and blue. I hid my hands behind my back to keep them from shaking.

Think hard, you said. You *do* know me.

Nope, I said. Nothing. We maybe went to high school together?

You gave a little grin and clicked the bridge of your four top teeth out of your mouth so that I was staring through a great gap at your pink tongue.

I was startled and drew away against the cool glass. And then I laughed, with wonder. My God, I said, it's *you*. You sure have grown up, I said.

Boy, have you, you said. And like that, four front teeth in your hand, you kissed me.

YOU WERE A FRIEND so old I had forgotten about you. The little boy down the street, but a year younger than I, and my brother's buddy. So, invisible. Still, there are family pictures you snuck into, and I was there when my brother judo-kicked you in the mouth by accident and you lost those front teeth. You were there the day of my eighth-grade cotillion, and said nothing when I came down the stairs in my royal blue satin and sparkles, just ran off to do what seventh-grade boys do behind locked doors.

I loved books like people; I liked real people less. You

were wild and left clumps of mud from your soccer cleats everywhere. I sometimes tried to speak all day in perfect rhyme. *I will take some flakes to break my fast,* I'd say in my poetically gauzy nightgown, *For that alone is a fine repast,* and my siblings would groan and my father snort into his coffee, and the little neighbor boy who was always hanging around would give me a bright, shy smile.

You didn't laugh much, but when you did it was a goosey honk you never quite lost.

My parents weren't from this village, had four graduate degrees between them, and expected their children would do the same. My siblings—a doctor, a lawyer, an architect—left and only returned to visit. Before I came back I was a professional storyteller, a glamorous title that means a life of public libraries and wailing children and minimum wage.

Your family has been rooted in our village for six generations and though not poor, were not well-off, either. Your father is the town's florist and a hard, mean man; he'd replace the twelfth rose of a bouquet with baby's breath to cut costs. Your mother, a housewife who clipped coupons. You came home after two years of college to buy a snowmobile store, which turned into an ATV store in the summer.

All that time, you said, you never forgot me. There were many dates, many girlfriends—a ridiculous number—but they were never serious. Because, you said, there I was, riding along with you all that time. A leech, a lamprey, a fluke.

I went off into the world and if I ever thought of you, it was as a small child, hair sticking up everywhere, a snot-bubble in your nose, that peculiar wedge-shaped face. A brown little boy in too-short jeans. I remembered an androgynous shirt you wore then, a cheery blue with a rainbow on the front. At one end of the rainbow, a beaming sun. On the other a white cloud spilling rain down your spindly, wriggling, little-boy rib cage.

EVERY MARCH OF MY CHILDHOOD, my father would uncover the pool to reveal the greasy green water, still frigid with winter. There'd be frogs kicking toward the gutters, masses of insects, dead leaves. One year, when my mother was away for the evening and I was about seven, he gave us a dare.

Whoever can stay in the water longest gets five bucks, he said, laughing, figuring thirty seconds would be enough. We stripped down and climbed in, careful to keep our heads dry. My little brother got out immediately; cold wasn't his thing. My older brother and sister lasted two minutes, then came out muttering *retarded this, retarded that*. In the end, the only ones left were you and me, and though I was a princess I was fierce. I would die before I'd be beaten by a younger boy, a boy whose nipples were turning purple, whose whole skinny body was shuddering.

I hope I would have gotten out had I known what five dollars meant to you then. To me, it was another book from the bookstore that I'd half-understand; to you, it was a birthday present for your little sister.

Twenty minutes in, my father was no longer amused and

had begun to have visions of the emergency room, explaining to the mothers and his doctor colleagues why, exactly, two kids left in his care were hypothermic. He said, Enough, blinking quickly behind his thick glasses. We were both blue and quaking. But I was laughing because you went up the ladder first, and I thought that made me the winner. My father held the fiver in his hands and seemed for a second about to be Solomon, to rip the bill in two.

It's okay, you said, still shaking under the warm towel. Celie can have it.

It's yours, said my father, handing the bill to you. You earned it.

I began to squawk and my father said, Hush, hush, you'll have one too, as soon as your mother gets back and I can get it from her purse. Then he gathered us both up under his arms and carried us in and dumped us unceremoniously in the shower. Don't tell your mothers I let you do that, okay? he said, looking abashed.

Okay, we said, but when my father left, I stared angrily at you as you lost your blue and began turning pink under the warm water. *I* won, I said.

We both won, you said. You'll get your money when your mom is home.

It's my dad's, I said. His money and my pool, and I should get it first.

You shrugged and soaped yourself, singing a little song.

I climbed out and dried off, and, seeing the wet wad of a bill on the sink, took it.

At dinner, you said nothing about the missing money. Even when you started sneezing you said nothing; even when my father dug into my mother's purse to give me a five (the other bill wadded wetly in my underwear, imprinting my skin), you said nothing. When I took the money from my father's hand and ran away from the table and to my room and locked my door, you didn't come knocking, and the next time I saw you, after the fever that had kept you from school for a week subsided, you still said nothing.

Years later, I asked if you remembered this.

Of course, you said. It was one of the great traumas of my childhood.

You should've punched me, I said. I was such a jerk.

You were you, Celie, you said. I couldn't have been mad. Even then, you were beyond my anger.

ONCE UPON A TIME, my life began with *Once upon a time*. I didn't have a passion when I graduated from college, and I floated from profession to profession: bartender, newsletter editor, grant writer, finally a temp. I liked the anonymity of temphood, the office supplies, the interchangeability of one cubicle with the next, but was an atrocious typist and had no math skills at all. When I was kept on for a long time, it was because the workers had gotten to like me, despite my lack of ability.

One morning my temp coordinator called me about a job: a literacy fair in Cambridge sponsored by a fruit company. The afternoon storyteller had gotten sick in the hundred-degree heat and I was to fill in. I'd have to wear a banana suit all week, she said. I laughed and said, No way. She laughed and said, Forty bucks an hour; I laughed and said, Call me Banana.

The first two days were hell, the suit soggy with the morning storyteller's sweat before I even put it on, the children whinging, my stories duds. But on the third day, magic happened: I began spinning a story and the children stopped fidgeting, their parents leaned forward in their seats, and I was able to forget the sweat streaming down the inside of the suit. The story carried me until the cool evening wind rose and the heat scaled back and the children went home, one by one, small pools of sweat where they had sat, entranced, for hours. When I took off the banana suit that evening, soaked and weak with elation, I had found what I was meant to do.

Storytelling is simple: selecting a few strands from many and weaving them into cloth. My life was retranslated, made neater. The tale of the neighbor boy and the pool became an epic of redemption: in retelling you became older, charismatic, quick, a bully; *you* became the robber of *my* shivery winnings, and I was the wounded little stoic.

AT THE WEDDING RECEPTION the day I rediscovered you, years after we had left childhood, I don't think I ever found my table or had a bite to eat. We were at a teahouse in a private garden right on the lake, and the stalks of summer's plants were brown and frostbitten. In the dusky fog, every dead plant seemed imbued with meaning, which I thought I could decipher if I only concentrated hard enough. We walked in the clammy dark garden, listening to the music and voices from the teahouse, sometimes talking, sometimes not. When dancing started, we came into the bright house and danced, too, my cheek only as high as your shoulder. Your date kicked her shoe at me, and was escorted away by the brother of the groom; the bride chortled and threw her pretty arms around us, squeezing us, telling us she *loved us, loved us, loved us*. At the end of the night, after the garter, the bouquet, the slow slipping away of the guests, we were the last ones in the teahouse, urged by the tired father of the bride to turn out the lights when we left. We laughed in the wreck of the feast, and sat down on a bench.

There are only a few moments in every life where the world becomes entirely real: that night, the lake, the fog, your face so startlingly near, crystallized in me.

You took my foot and rubbed it. So, you said. Do they have snowmobiles in Boston? Because I'm going where you are.

Oh, that would be a mistake, I said, too quickly. I'd had a thought of my tiny apartment, the marmalade cat I'd taken to help a friend, a nasty squalling beast I hated. I imagined you, hulking and strange, inserting yourself into my solitary life there.

A cloud settled over your face and your hands fell from my foot. In your scowl, I recognized the little neighbor boy, and it felt the way it did when I began to tell that first real story in the banana suit, a good weight, deep within.

You don't understand, I said. I touched your cheek. I'm staying here, I said.

I WAS THIRTY-TWO then, thirty-three now. I'm a feminist if they'll still have me, though from the way my friends reacted when I told them that I was staying in my little hometown it seems doubtful I'll be welcomed back into the fold.

A friend from Boston, a tenured professor in anthropology, said, Good God, Celie. "Stand By Your Man" is only a song—you're not supposed to take it *literally*.

A friend from my years in Philadelphia said, But what are you going to do in Podunkville? (I don't know.) How many people live there? (Twelve hundred.) Do they even have a movie theater? (No.) Aren't you going to die of boredom? (Possibly.)

A friend from my years in Wisconsin said, suspiciously, I thought you always said you didn't believe in marriage. Catering to the hegemony, yadda yadda. Wait a second; you can't be Celie. Who *are* you?

But my best friend from college was silent for a long time. She, of all of my friends, had seen the parade of sad wrecks through my life, date after bad date after bad boyfriend. She was the one who'd picked up the pieces after the musician, the investment banker, the humanitarian who was humane to everyone but me.

When at last she spoke, she said, Oh, hell.

And, after that: Hallelujah.

I AWOKE IN YOUR APARTMENT over the pizzeria to the sound of eggs cracking on a metal bowl. I called my mother so she wouldn't worry, and whispered where I was. She let out a whoop and, delighted, said, Nice job, honey! That's one good-looking boy.

You came back in then, holding an omelet, coffee, toast. When I bit into the omelet later, my teeth would grind against eggshells and the coffee would be harsh and overbrewed. But at that moment, it looked perfect.

I said, Let's fly to Las Vegas and get hitched.

You deposited the tray on the bed and folded your arms, frowning. No, you said.

Oh, I said. I flushed and looked away, now doubting everything: the night before, the brilliant morning, the man standing before me in the too-small robe.

Oh, no, you said, sitting down. I'm going to build you a house, then we'll get married. I already have the land ready to go.

You said, without any irony, Every bird needs her nest.

I felt dizzy, spun back to a time when this may have been an appropriate thing for a man to say; I wanted to protest, or at least to scoff a little. But something in me felt like a bubble popping, the fear I'd carried around under my sternum, the ugly balloon that expanded a breath with every passing year, the one in the shape of the word *spinster*.

So I said, Oh. Well, then, yes. A nest sounds nice.

It was my fault that I didn't say what I should have: that I wasn't the bird type, or maybe the nest type. To watch out, to think this over carefully, because it wouldn't be easy.

EVEN IN THAT FIRST hot flush I knew you were human, flawed. You had false front teeth, an annoying laugh, a streak of stupidity that made you once lose a pinky toe to frostbite and another time vote for Ross Perot. You became belligerent when soused, held half-baked convictions about politics, made messes (of clothes, of facts, of women), adored cooking but cooked inedibly, and from the beginning loved too-proud, too-angry, too-mean me. And that, in the tally of flaws, was one that even your friends tried to talk you out of.

She's a tough cookie, they warned. She's used to things we don't have here.

You nodded gravely, then gave your crooked smile. I'm pretty tough, too, you said. I think I can tackle tough like Celie's any day.

WE SPENT THAT FIRST WEEK in bed. The whole world was indulgent, and we could hear the smiles in people's voices when we called to abandon our responsibilities; the snowmobile store could be run by the boys there, my family was fine gathered in the house together without me. Stripped of almost everything, eating crackers and single-serve pudding with our fingers in the sheets, all we had left were our stories.

Mine were elaborate, and when I retold them I always changed them. Yours were simple and neat and didn't change at all.

This is one of mine: I was out on a sailboat in Lake Tahoe with an old boyfriend. The wind died down, and as we were waiting for it to start up again, he told me that a famous diver, the one on all the documentaries, was hired to film the bottom of the lake. Nobody had ever done this before; it was too deep. The diver went down and came back up sooner than the people on the boat expected. When he hauled himself over the gunwale, he was pale and shaking and wouldn't speak a word, but when they were at last on shore, he swore them to secrecy, then told them what he'd seen: all the victims of mob hits from the casinos, their feet in buckets of concrete, perfectly preserved by the cold down there. Dozens of them, in a tight space, no more than fifty feet by fifty. Some faces still frightened, frozen in quiet screams. Fat men in business suits, skinny men who looked like jockeys, one woman in a spangled dress, her hair shifting in the current. And this is what scared the diver the most: their hands were floating at breast-level, beseeching.

I told this story to scare you, I think, but instead you laughed. Urban legend, you said, resting your heavy head on my chest.

I believe it, I protested. When the wind rose and the boat

was flying again over Lake Tahoe and the water was splashing everywhere, I screamed every time a drop hit me.

That's your problem, you said. You have way too vivid an imagination. Now, let me tell you a real story.

Oh, goody, I said, a little smug: I was the one, after all, who once made an entire kindergarten class cry fat tears of sorrow for my own little mermaid.

You put your hand on my mouth to make me hush. Now, I saw you once in your Wisconsin phase, you said, when you came back to town for the holidays. It was Christmas Eve, Midnight Mass at the old Presbyterian church, lit up with the candles we were holding. You were with your family in front, and me and my family were in back, my cousin and me passing our traditional flask of bourbon under the hymnal. I look around, bored, and I see you there. Wearing this jacket with fur around the collar, holding the candle under your chin. One more inch and you burst into flame. So thin I could almost see through you. Then everything ends, we do the singing thing, blow out the candles, I was about to go talk to your parents and your brother, say hi to you, when you just walk by and I'm struck to stone. You looked sad, like you needed someone to just come along and make you happy. I took a good look at myself and knew I didn't have what it took. So I let you walk away.

Oh, I said. That's awful. Five years down the drain.

No, but, listen, you said, though I already was listening. Listen, if had I gone to say hello then, we wouldn't be here now. Now we're right, the timing's right, but before we weren't and it wasn't. We were lucky, you said, turning your head and kissing my lowest rib, gently. Timing is everything.

In the window an icicle caught the sun and burst into a thousand shards of light on the walls. I watched it burn there, dripping. I said, Your story was better than mine.

AT THE END of that week, we emerged into the cold world blinking like newborns. In our absence, the village had been swaddled with thick snow. There was the first skim of ice stretched taut across the lake, a canvas waiting for the brush. When we crossed the crashing river, I couldn't help myself, and said, *Where a gluegold-brown marbled river, boisterously beautiful, between roots and rocks is danced and dandled, all in froth and waterblowballs, down.*

You looked at me. That's so damn pretty, you said, and, for such a tough country boy, there were tears in your eyes. That's the prettiest thing I ever heard, you said in such a voice that I couldn't ever tell you the words weren't mine.

WE WENT TO BOTH Thanksgiving dinners, the early one at your mother's, with her frozen corn and box stuffing, the later one at my house, with homegrown Brussels sprouts and orange-nutmeg cranberry sauce. I preferred your mother's. Over dessert, we settled on late May for the wedding.

Immediately, the fights began.

In December, I scratched off the bumper sticker on

your truck that endorsed the worst president in American history.

In January, when we started building the house, though you tried to stick to my eco-structure mandate, I freaked out when I saw the workmen lowering a standard septic tank into the ground.

In February, I decided I wouldn't take your name, even though your mother sobbed over the dishes about it and your father stomped around saying that your name was as good a name as any name in the dadblasted town, and they'd been here longer than some snooty people he could name and where do I get off saying his name wasn't good enough, he would like to know that, he would like to dadblasted know that.

In March, we almost came to blows over something you said that I wasn't supposed to hear, a joke at the bar involving terrorists and nuclear bombs. I, who had just come into the busy place, and had been about to put my hands over your eyes and plant a kiss on the back of your neck, stalked out of the bar, your friends looking away.

In April, in the height of wedding planning, we fought once a day.

Still, there was no other valve for everything building up inside us, and we always made up beautifully. You were kind. You had a certain delicacy that, when either of us was at the point of broaching a real darkness, allowed you to suddenly capitulate. Your face would pale and you'd nod once and say, Okay. You're right. I would stare at you, disbelieving, the horrid thing I was just about to say still crawling on my tongue.

Stupid me. Those months, I thought your capitulation was weakness. I now know it was everyday kindness.

IT WASN'T EASY to come back to a little town when I was used to cities. Our hometown is tiny and obscure, an upstate village with a cheap-looking Main Street, cracked sidewalks, public buildings of brown brick and particleboard, weathered plastic wreaths on the neighbors' doors. Townspeople gave me befuddled looks when I said I was staying: Really? they said. I saw my stock sink in their faces. The produce manager in the grocery store snorted at me when I suggested he start up an organic section, and when I looked at the sorry state of the conventional pears he had, I understood what he meant. I couldn't find enough space in town to walk, and when I went into the hills where the dogs are never locked up and unused to pedestrians, I was attacked by a furiously droopy basset hound. I was impatient with the Saturday night choices: the movies thirty minutes away, or television, or a bar, or a board game. I felt like a teenager again, stifled and bored, without even the possibility of babysitting and snooping around in other people's business. I attempted to have a storytelling hour at the library, but the time ticked by and not one child came, and the librarian muttered with a sideways glance that I shouldn't be surprised: there was a high school basketball game that afternoon, after all.

Yet, as winter dribbled into spring, I found myself paying more attention to the tiniest things: a crocus furling out of the ground, the way the two old women who sat in the diner from opening to closing greeted each other with only a wet sniff every day. Because I had nothing to do, I finally began to understand the rhythm of the village, its subtleties that I had been too impatient to recognize when I was young.

Are you happy here? my mother said once in April, pouring coffee into my cup. I don't mean with him, she said, nodding toward the living room, where you and my father were shouting at some sports team thousands of miles away. But here?

I considered this, the bones of my hands warming against the mug. I said, slowly, I can feel the beginnings of happiness sort of seeping into me.

My mother nodded and looked out the window, though she couldn't see anything through the downpour. She sighed and said, Oh, that damn rain.

IT HAD BEEN RAINING constantly since late February, and of course it rained at our wedding. In the receiving line, nearly everyone whispered into my ear, *Rain on a bride means good luck,* and kissed my cheek and went on to the buffet.

I didn't care. I beamed. I'd had the flu for a week, but had taken nuclear doses of medicine and all night felt like I was floating. I danced and ate and drank, and when we came home to our new-smelling house, with the floors still unfinished and the walls still unpainted, you tossed aside the umbrella (we found it the next day halfway up a blue spruce), swooped me up into your arms, kicked open the door, and carried me over the threshold, to where it smelled of sawdust and plaster; you kicked the door shut behind us and carried me up the stairs and the rain on the roof was thrumming, and opened the door to the bedroom, the one room in the house you'd finished and furnished with castoffs from my parents' house. Candles were aflame, and your florist father hadn't held back, filling the room with ferns and lilac, lovely garlands across the walls, huge vases overflowing with greenery.

This was a surprise to you, too. You started and almost dropped me, then filled our new house with your honking laugh, populating it with an invisible skein of ducks, until I had to laugh, also, at your joy.

AND THEN, THE DENOUEMENT. One week and two days after the wedding, you were in your work clothes, crouching in the living room to put in a baseboard over the freshly painted walls. Outside it was raining, of course, but harder than it had rained for the past few months, so thickly we couldn't see out the windows at all. I had squelched through the mud with eight sacks of groceries and had just finished putting them away in our cabinets.

My flu had redoubled: I saw the world through a feverish haze. I hadn't slept in what felt like weeks and had reams of thank-you notes to write, never actually written. Exhausted, I put my head down on the counter and began to cry.

You heard and came in, alarmed. What? you said. What's wrong?

I don't know, I said. I'm just so sad here.

Here? you said, looking around with dismay. In this house?

In this whole goddamn town, I said. I'm so freaking sick of it. I hate it, I hate everything about it. Freaking small-minded people, fat stupid idiots.

You hate everything about this town, Celie?

Everything, I said, savagely. Everything. The stupid grocery store where they don't even have portobello mushrooms. God forbid a freaking mango. God forbid an open mind. Only things they can think about here are sex and hunting and football. I *hate* it here.

You looked at me coldly, jaw tensed and eyes narrowed. I'm so sorry, Ms. Big-shot Storyteller. I guess it's all my fault, you said, huh? Dragging you away from civilization?

I hated the coldness in your voice, what I took to be a sneer on your face.

Yes, it's all your fault, I said. Hurt, I burned to hurt in turn.

And that was it, a petty quarrel when I was soaked and sick and overwhelmed.

You dropped the hammer on the ground, where it made a dent in the floor that's still there; you went outside, leaving the door open to the wickedly driving rain. I couldn't see the truck or hear it pull away, but I felt it. Later, I'd hear that mine had been the last car they'd let over the bridge on my trip home from the store. After me, the swollen river was too dangerous and they closed it off. I like to think I would have run after you had I remembered the policemen in the orange vests, the sacks of sand they were dragging, that I would have tried to chase down the truck, apologized. But I was sunk in my misery, my flu, my soaking clothes. When I had cried myself out, I stood and shut the door and went into the bedroom and took a long nap, only to awaken to the phone call almost exactly an hour later.

A RIDDLE: WHAT HAPPENS when a lake and a river both overflow their banks, forming a pond where the bridge should be? When an angry man drives too quickly away from his harpy wife, from the house he worked so hard to build for her, when he turns the bend and hits the water and hydroplanes? When the old red truck blasts into the stand of trees and a branch goes through the windshield, through the man's chest; when, at the same time, his head hits first the steering wheel and then the seat back, hard? When, a half hour later, someone comes along and sees the wreck, and pulls the man from the red truck, with the branch still in his chest? When the ambulance arrives the long way, the bridge out, and wails off to the emergency room, and the doctors on staff are so worried about the stake through the lung and the loss of blood that they don't do a CT scan for about eight hours, all the time it takes to extract the branch and bring the hysterical new wife in, and draw enough blood from the shaken family for a transfusion, for his blood type is hard to match, and there isn't enough in the banks for him; and then, when he's stable, they finally figure out that he is in the deepest sort of coma, a three on the Glasgow Coma Scale, no eye-opening, no response to physical stimulus or verbal cues? What happens when the doctor puts up the results of the CT scan and his eyes narrow and he looks at the ghostly vision of the brain on the screen and claps his hand over his mouth? What would be the most fitting, apt, apposite diagnosis in this set of circumstances? The punch line at the end of the joke for a man at whose wedding a little more than one week earlier it had rained and rained and rained?

The answer: Hydrocephalus, of course.

I SAT IN THE EMERGENCY ROOM with the town around me, your family (father weeping, smelling of roses), your shaken buddies pale and trying to hold it in with whispered jokes and chewing tobacco, your mother blissed out on tranquilizers, my family a protective ring around me. My father was giving me the rundown on hydrocephalus in a whisper, and I was dry and dim and stupid, but drinking it in.

There is a fluid in the brain and spinal cord, my father said, called cerebrospinal fluid, which is constantly created throughout the day. Normally, this can be flushed by the body, but when someone has a hemorrhage that bleeds into the subarachnoid part of the brain, the fluids can't drain, and so they build up pressure in the ventricles. The pressure can cause damage. The neurosurgeon, as soon as he gets here, is going do a procedure called an endoscopic third ventriculostomy. They put a hole in the ventricle and a shunt in the hole. The shunt drains the pressure. My father paused, and looked at me.

Will he be all right? I said. Will he be the same?

My father blinked rapidly and took off his glasses. He wiped them with his sleeve, and when he put them back on, he took my hand. I don't know, he said, looking away. It's too soon to know.

THE NEUROSURGEON DID HIS WORK late into that first night, until the sky was just turning the viscous gray of yet another rainy day. He was a tiny man who looked the way I thought a priest should look, ashy and stern and ascetic. He took my hand in his small, cool one, and pressed it.

I've done my best, he said. We'll have to wait and see.

I looked through the little porthole and into the scrub room, where the nurses were wearily taking off their paper gowns and hats and masks. You were in there, I knew, tubes perforating your wounded flesh. My hand in the doctor's shook, and I squeezed until I could feel my fingernails press into his soft skin.

Wake him up, I said. Make him wake up.

He patted my cheek with his other little hand, and said, I wish I could, darling. When he pulled away, I could see my nail marks like little crescent moons in his skin. He flexed the hand I had gripped all the way down the hall. I hoped I had cracked those delicate bones.

THE FIRST TWO DAYS in the hospital I couldn't eat, though people pressed food on me. I put the cups of coffee and doughnuts and apples underneath my chair, and paced some more. I liked the harsh rasp of thirst in my throat, the way that it hurt every time I swallowed. My body soured and whenever I moved the smell would rise up in a wave and wash over me.

When your parents and I were at last allowed to go into the room and see you, I took a step inside and then turned around and around and around in a little circle on the floor. Your mother pushed past me and began a dovelike sobbing, *hoo-ooh-ooh,* sinking into a little chair, and your father walked back out of the room.

I went over to you and took your cold, stiff hand in my own. I kneaded it, staring down at the mass of purple and red and yellow and blue that they said was my husband, at the white bandages and the tubes sucking fluids out of you, putting other fluids in. That first visit I almost said nothing, although the nurse had told us we should talk to you, that it was possible you could hear. We sat there, your mother and I, until the end of the visiting hours.

When we were asked to leave, I leaned close. You didn't smell like yourself; you smelled of gauze and something bitter and wet. I said, Damn you, and left that ugly little present in your ear.

IN THE MIDST OF EVERYTHING, I would go outside the hospital and the world would be swollen, juicy, runneling. The sky overhead a warm wet washcloth pressed to my brow, the trees lascivious with wet. Everywhere, the smell of things awakened; the fevered ground, the upswell of mud. Down the hill was the river, the breeding carp pushing against the dam's concrete frame.

I understood in those moments all those surreal ancient stories: water flowing upward from earth to sky, rains of blood, plagues of frogs. Abominations or miracles seemed likely in those hours. In the Canticle of the Sun, Saint Francis of Assisi praises God for water: *Praised be Thou, O Lord, for sister water,* he says, *who is very useful, humble, precious and chaste.* But I would stand there, my head bowed to the rain, eyes closed, braced between each thunk of each fat drop of rain on my skull, each a blow, hard to predict, a punishment.

AFTER FOUR DAYS, no sleep, little food, no showering, no improvement in your condition, I began to see things that didn't exist. Rats scuttling across the floor, gray curtains flapping at the edges of my vision. Infants with your face, beard and all. Many of your friends had returned to their lives, coming to the hospital periodically with grave faces and comforting things in their hands. I paid no attention to them. I was concentrating, as if listening for music very, very far away, which if I heard it, would make everything all right.

On the evening of the fourth day, my father helped my mother sneak me into the attendings' locker room, where there were showers. I let my mother bathe me, as if I were a little girl, and put lotions on me, and dress me. Her face was pinched and gray; she looked old, I noticed with surprise. I could have done all of this myself, but I was concentrating too hard on the impossibly distant music.

You appeared before me in the murk and cold of my mind, your dark body. Over and over again my hands grasped your arm and I began to pull you upward, airward, skyward, again.

When I was clean it was time to visit. I went in and began to tell stories. I had grown used to this changeling in the bed where my husband should have been, and told him stories he had told me. But I embroidered them, perverted them, willing him to wake up and correct me. The first time he killed a deer, a twelve-point buck. The first time he ever had sex with a girl (Jinny Palmer, on the Fairy Springs docks, in broad daylight). That crazy night in his freshman year in college when those boys did everything they could to get arrested, short of murder or rape, and were never caught.

Did I imagine the tightening of your thumb on my palm? The flicker across the face? The swallow? Did I imagine you would open your eyes and wheeze out, That's not the way it went, not at all? Did I hope you'd be angry when you opened your eyes and say, You have the story all wrong, Celie, you have it all wrong?

I did. I do.

On the fifth night there was a commotion, running, loud beeping noises. My father was summoned from my side in the waiting room, where he and my mother were spelling each other, and he was gone for quite some time. It was very late and your family was at home, trying to sleep.

When my father came back, his face was red. Oh, honey, he said. I'm so sorry.

Just say it, I said, my voice rough with thirst.

He said, A mistake. Too much drainage. The vesicles collapsed. He's gone. I'm so sorry.

Dead? I said, very calmly.

Oh, said my father, stricken. Oh, honey. Not entirely. But in a way, yes.

WHEN YOUR FATHER heard he roared. He stomped down the corridor, shouting, We're suing, we're suing the goddamned pants off this goddamned hospital, until my brother, home from Boston, slipped a tranquilizer in his iced tea and put him out for a few hours.

When your mother heard, she pulled herself up and nodded, and went out for a walk that lasted four hours. When it grew dark we sent teams out to look for her and one of your friends found her sitting on one of the boulders at the lake, shuddering in the dusky drizzle, and staring at the swollen water. She was soaked when she came back, and came over to me, lifting her hands like cold wet lumps of paper to my cheeks. She opened her mouth and everyone hushed to hear what she was about to say. But she just breathed and blinked and closed her little mouth again.

GRIEF IS becoming a stranger to oneself. It is always a surprise to see how old, how womanly, one actually is. The crow's-feet by the eyes, the lines by the mouth, how, translucent, a woman's temples bare their tender blue veins to the world. That gold band hanging loose, so much flesh lost over the past few days. Down the empty corridor, ringing with voices and distant sounds of the hospital, steel and mop and rubber shoe. Into the vague green room, thick with shadows that waver like seaweed in the corners.

See the strange woman look around, make sure all are assembled. On the other faces, there is more than fury and sadness. Also a fatigue, a relief. The darkened room. The quiet machines. The sheet pulled over the body that is only flesh, over the bruised face. The turning away.

I SEE YOU NOW just leaving rooms I am in. The hem of your khakis flashing beyond the door frame. The wind in the room still shifting. The smell of you, musk and clove and even the stink of your fatigue when you've come in from a long day outdoors, hunting or snowmobiling or cross-country skiing; all this, a moment before I turn around.

Is that you? I call, but there's no answer. Just this house still empty of furniture. I turn to my books but can't read. Maybe the telephone rings then and breaks the jangling quiet, or a crow flies past the window with a songbird in its beak; carrion comfort. I hold on to the tiniest of visions for as long as I can, savoring them like the aftertaste of a long-gone cup of tea.

OUR DIVER FRIEND, the one from the wreck and the falling dive buddy, changed his song. He chose an odd moment for it, at the wake, avoiding my eye over the cold cuts (funeral meats, I thought; terrible expression). He grabbed my elbow hard, whispering urgently. I let him. There was a comfort in his wine-tart breath in my ear, and I watched the window as he whispered to me. Outside, it still rained and rained.

He told the story again from the beginning: the scaly wreck, the chasm, the strange fishes. He broke off where he had before, where you and I had once thought he'd paused to build tension. Watching his buddy fall and be slowly swallowed by the dark chasm, teetering between his own life and the chance of saving another's. Now, under the strange slow hush of Bach and conversation, the diver blinked and blinked and shifted the glass in his hand.

Instead of telling me about his decision, though, the quick flipping down into the dark maw, the laughter, catching his buddy, he said, Listen. I have to say it. I didn't go after him.

What? I said. I heard him through the gray felt I'd thickened around myself since the phone call, the hospital.

I watched him go, he said.

What? I said, again.

By the time I saw him, he said, he was too far gone. I had to let him go.

I pulled away, my fists clenched. But your crazy laughter, I said.

He looked at me, the very whites of his eyes wine-stained.

But the love, I said.

That was all true, he said. Only after I couldn't see him anymore. When I was just staring down into that trench, just suspended there alone.

I stared at the diver, his purple face. He was trying to tell me something, but it was too raw. A story can also be cruel. And when I remember this scene, I remember it static, my hand in mid-slap, hovering near his left ear. On his face a curious look, almost voluptuous, his cheek tilted up as if to accept the blow, eyes closed and lips nearly bent in a smile.

IN JULY, THE SUN at last came out, dried the mud, sopped the wet from the air. The bodies of water abated, and the greens were so green they filled all of us with wonder. So many different shades lived in the world that summer. For some moments, in some especially strong lights, I felt the generosity of such green as a salve, drawing the sick grief from me.

But even in those deepest greens, hiking in the hills (the maples, the ferns, the pines, the scuttling toads), I caught a memory. When my heart at last righted itself, it beat, but furiously.

Fuck you, fuck you, fuck you, it said into the lovely day.

Long ago, before I found you a second time, when I must have been in college, I was home, driving on East Lake Road. It was a cold day but the lake hadn't yet melted and large pieces of mist flaked off the lake in pastry layers. I was listening to public radio. On one of the shows, a narrator, his voice soft but emotionless, was telling a story about Niagara Falls. There was a sound effect of roaring water—harsh, impersonal—behind his words, a strange contrast to his hush.

In one very poor town near the Falls, he said, there lived an old couple. She was dying of an old-age disease, and her husband was taking care of her. I pictured an orange afghan, a half-drunk cup of tea, a room with olive paint so peeled it was as if the walls were shrugging out of their skins. I pictured a bent old man in suspenders, hovering over a tiny woman, all bones.

The narrator continued, saying that one morning, after the woman had had a very bad night, the couple's son stopped by on the way to a night shift. He found an empty house, no parents, everything tidy. He grew alarmed and drove to all of their places: the diner, the theater, the library, the hospital. They weren't anywhere. He didn't know where else to drive, and at last, to pull himself together, he drove to the Falls. It was almost dawn now; there was a pink cast at the edge of the sky. When the son climbed from the car and went to the fence at the edge of the Falls, he found two pairs of shoes polished to a brilliant shine. The tiny black shoes of his mother, the cordovans of his father, pointing, eloquently, toward the water.

The old man had taken his wife in his arms, hot, sick; he had stood there in the dark predawn with her in his arms. He looked into her old face. Then he jumped.

I had to pull my car over because of this story, because of those lonely four shoes at the annealing edge of the Falls, right where the water hesitates and seems to catch its breath before shattering downward. And, later, during that long winter when you made me come home, I thought vaguely of this story, again and again. Not because I wanted to die, of course. But because I thought I had found exactly that, someone to take me to old age, someone who could take me beyond, if it were necessary and right to do so.

There is no ending, no neatness in this story. There never really is, where water is concerned. It is wild, febrile, kind, ambiguous; it is dark and carries the mud, and it is clear and the cleanest thing. Too much of it kills us, and not enough kills us, and it is what makes us, mostly. Water is the cleverest substance, wily beyond the stretch of our mortal imaginations. And no matter where it is pent, no matter if it is air or liquid or solid, it will someday, inevitably, find its way out.

Sir Fleeting

THE WINTER IS INESCAPABLE HERE. HALF OF my walls are glass, opening to a Central Park vista of naked trees with branches like grasping fingers, and down in the courtyard, even those floozies, the cherry trees, have turned spinsterish in the cold. In my modern apartment their bare limbs are doubled upon the shining walls, the stainless-steel kitchen, the mirrors. What doesn't reflect trees reflects my face, which is not always a welcome variation. Last week, for instance, after my granddaughter visited, full of plans for her wedding and honeymoon in Argentina, I showed her a picture from my own trip so many years ago and upset her; after she left I stood for a long time palpating my cheeks, watching the woman etched in the steel elevator doors do the same.

I don't know why I said what I did. I suppose I was piqued when she held the old photo by its edges, and said, "Oh God, Nana, you were so beautiful."

I took the picture from her. That eighteen-year-old idiot, squinting in the Argentine sun? A pretty face, yes, a girl with a clever hand at dressing well with no money. But fat. A Wisconsin farm girl raised on apples and whole milk, a body carved out of a slick ton of butter like those statues at the state fair.

"Darling," I said, "I was a ball of lard." My granddaughter, bless her heart—she's nothing close to the pudge I was—actually hissed at me. "No," she said loudly. "You were beautiful," and she stood to go, and I couldn't press the check into her hand before she left.

Afterward, I watched that lady reflected in the elevator door and I didn't like her much. Whatever it was I'd had in that picture had seeped away over the years, a rubber tire with a long, slow leak. In the days that followed, I tried to push that image in the elevator door out of my head and go about my life—the yoga, the hairdresser, the charity luncheons. The photo stayed where it was, facedown on the glass table, for days, until it woke me up in the middle of the night and insisted that I look at it again.

I walked through my dark apartment and flipped the photo over to see it in the moonlight. There she was again, that bride, beside her new husband, leaning on the hotel's Corinthian columns. Buenos Aires, 1956. I could feel the warm sun on my face, my first husband's hand in my own. It was spring in Argentina, and the city was full of flowers, great washes of buds bursting open, red hibiscus on our balcony, roses and bougainvillea in the parks. The day of the photo, a fluke of wind from some distant jungle had carried a gigantic cloud of iridescent blue butterflies into the city, and we had run outside to see them. The city seemed to pulsate under the beat of those many wings. In the black-and-white picture the butterflies are blurry streaks behind us, though one creature has settled on my husband's breast pocket like a boutonniere. He is scowling in the sun and I am grinning, not at the butterflies or even my new groom, but, rather, at the man holding the camera.

Once in a while, I like to say the name aloud: *Ancel de Chair.* That name alone seems to bring warmth to this wintry city. We overlapped for only a short time in Argentina when we first met, but a sort of static cling brought us together again and again throughout our lives. My husband and I had already been in Buenos Aires for two weeks by then, though I don't believe we did much during those weeks save eat enormous, glistening steaks and run back upstairs to bed again where we had discovered, to our virginal disbelief, our own bodies. Before marriage we had fallen into an itchy sort of lust, and, good children, we had waited until we were married to scratch it. On our honeymoon, sex was still strange to me: the awkward fittings of parts to parts, my poor husband sobbing after his every achievement, me wide-eyed and wondering if there wasn't something I might have missed in those few frenzied minutes. I'd found my most voluptuous tenderness in stroking my husband's furry ears, and hoped there was more to learn in what I thought would be our eternity together.

How sophisticated we'd thought ourselves then, we inno-cents. I'd had a scholarship to the University of Wisconsin, a farm girl with six sisters, a talent for sewing, and a sharp brain for math, and had spent my freshman year lonely, refusing dates, taking the train home on weekends to help with the chores. When I met my first husband in a social theory course and heard how well the man could argue, I was like a match sparked alight. I used to long to lick his face in the middle of class.

Poor man; I believe he is still alive somewhere like Scottsdale or Santa Fe, an old immigration lawyer turned fat and wheezy. But when I met him he was a child from a New York family that I, with my scant knowledge of wealth back then, thought inordinately rich. He had a cashmere coat and smoked pipe tobacco constantly, something my father was able to treat himself to only once a week, at most. My hus-band had blazing eyes, an attractive nervous energy, and a passion for justice that transmuted, over time, into a Commu-nist zeal that eventually broke up our little union. When my first husband told me his family drank wine at meals, argued about books, and had a strongly Socialist bent, it took my breath away, daughter as I was of a farm wife with chicken blood on her hands and a stony Libertarian with one penny in his pocket that longed for a mate to jingle with.

When my husband and I came to New York after we were married so that I could meet his family, his mother (tweedy, with the face of an Afghan hound) took one look and broke down sobbing on her husband's shoulder. I suppose it was swell to embrace the masses in theory, but she never thought the masses would be quite so blond and blowsy in practice.

Off we flew to Buenos Aires, my husband in a rage about how his parents had treated me. By the day the butterflies landed in the city, I had become slightly bored by his wiry body, and by our tall white room and its balcony. A sign on the door told me the same joke every day; the English translation of a notice to the guests, in which the greeting, "*Señor Pasajero*"—Dear Guest—had been somehow torturously translated to "Sir Fleeting." The first day my husband and I had laughed until we cried about it, called each other Sir and Dame Fleeting, but soon the joke had gotten old. Soon we avoided it as if it were a faux pas we ourselves had made, some stink in the room with an unknown provenance.

So I was restless on the night we first saw Ancel de Chair, made more restless by our dinner company, another newlywed couple we'd been palling around with since we arrived. It was a lukewarm friendship, sparked by proximity and youth rather than true alignment; the man had the personality of a sheet of waxed paper, and the woman was a small, brown field mouse from some excellent English family who read the gossip magazines and relayed everything to us whether we cared to listen or not. We were chatting about Rio de Janeiro, where we were going after Buenos Aires, when the door opened and in walked a couple so striking that our conversation stopped. The woman was a blade, all bones and angles, black hair cut severely to her chin, French by the quiet words I overheard. He, on the other hand, was the distillation of the heroes in the books I loved, a smiling, dapper Mr. Rochester, Rodolphe Boulanger, Sir Percy Blakeney. He had a handsome face with a fine, thin nose, wide-set green eyes, hair as black and shining as a puma's fur, which I'd later find was slicked back with some sweet-smelling oil. The enormous yellow diamond on his tiepin caught the candlelight and winked merrily at us.

They sat at a table by the window, and our table's conversation began again. My gossipy friend gave a chirrup and leaned toward me.

"I can't believe it, I can't believe it," she whispered, her face animated as I'd never seen it. "Those people," she said, "are Ancel de Chair and Lulu Fauré."

I must have looked blank, because she spooled out what she knew, how Lulu was a painter, French, daughter of someone I didn't catch; Ancel de Chair was, well, a playboy. Had a yacht, sailed it all over the world, child of a French baron and his Austrian wife (he has a title!). Impossibly wealthy. He spoke fifteen languages, she said (when I asked him later, he laughed, said, No, only about seven or so). Always had a pretty woman on his arm and never seemed to want to marry her. Played cards for money. Bet on horses. Did all sorts of naughty things, and his picture was *always* in the magazines.

I looked at the man quietly forking up pasta at the table by the window. His companion sat back from her untouched meal, smoking, pouting. "He sounds like a made-up gentleman from a book," I said.

Our giddy companion tossed her head, affronted, and said, "That sort always does, but that's how you know they're real. Besides, see the diamond on his tie?"

"How could you miss it? Nearly put my eye out," sneered my husband. I'd already come to suspect that the poor man was a secret snob, someone who scorned Europe but checked us into the best hotel in Buenos Aires, who pretended he liked humble food, rice and beans, but couldn't repress a greedy gleam when a plate of foie gras was set before him.

"That diamond is his signature," said our gossipy friend. "They say it belonged to his great-great-grandmother who was the mistress of some French king. And seeing it in person, well, I do believe it," she said fervently.

"I'm sure you do," said my husband, and soon started a quarrel with the woman's husband over an entertainment we were going to have that evening. We finished our meal and said good-bye coldly and for good and my husband and I went up to our room, the evening's entertainment dropped, of course, to my annoyance.

"That vulgar busybody," fumed my husband, "is not a suitable influence on a girl like you." Anyway, he said, he didn't want to go out, he'd been thinking of this fun thing that we could do. . . . But I had had enough of our room and paced wildly until he gave up coaxing me and fell asleep, face wedged in a book. I was still dressed, and went out into the hall, intending to use my respectable married state to sit at the bar, have a glass of wine by myself, perhaps watch the people pass on the street out the window. I called the elevator up, tapping my toe, adjusting my suit so it didn't look quite so homemade, refreshing my lipstick.

There was a chime, the noise of the elevator whirring to a stop. The golden doors slowly slid open and my heart burst into a full gallop, for there, slouched in the corner, was Baron Ancel de Chair himself, with an unlit cigarette in his hand. He stood straight and his eyes twinkled gleefully at me when I stepped inside.

"Well, hello," he said, as the door clanged shut. "Why, aren't you a lovely thing. Wait, don't tell me. You're Norwegian, wife of some diplomat, aren't you?"

"No," I said as the elevator lurched and we began our descent. "I'm from Wisconsin."

"Oh! Wisconsin," he said. "Exquisite. What an accent, so charming, so rustic."

Slowly, slowly, the elevator crept down, past the third floor, the second, while Ancel de Chair smiled at me with a perfect mouthful of white teeth. Sliding toward the first floor, he pushed off the wall and loomed closer and closer until we were a mere hairbreadth apart. I held my breath. He dipped his head down, as if to kiss me—I'm sure I would have let him, he was so very handsome—but he only buried his nose in my neck and took a long sniff.

Then he backed away, his eyes closed, and sighed delightedly. "That's what I thought," he murmured. The door opened. He gave me a bow and walked into the lobby. I stood, stunned, in the elevator until the doors closed again and it chugged upward once more.

The next morning, I was dreaming of that odd, electric moment while I waited for my husband to finish getting ready for breakfast. To pass the time, I peered out the window at the park below and watched an old woman creep by with her shopping. She sat on a bench and put her groceries at her feet. Slowly, she brought her trembling hands to her face; a dark stain was creeping over her blue skirt. She'd lost control of her bladder. She was weeping in shame. I was so young, only eighteen, and I felt so much pity for the old lady I almost wanted to strike her. I looked away, thought again of Ancel de Chair in the elevator, and when I looked again at the old woman, she seemed ten times shabbier, twice as comical, with her big ears and a man's boots on her feet. I called my husband over and pointed her out, because a joke seemed the only thing I could do to make her bearable, and we were still laughing when we stepped into the breakfast room, incandescent with light from the tall windows.

It was early, and the tables were empty save one by the windows, where Ancel de Chair and his girl were sitting. He stood when he saw us, pulled out a chair, and beckoned us over. We found ourselves sitting beside them, chatting over our coffee.

"I told Lulu here all about you," said Ancel de Chair to me, smiling. "A fresh-cheeked American, I told her, pretty as a shepherdess. We've been calling you just that. *La bergère*, you know. Lulu has been eager to meet you."

Lulu's eyes flicked over me and she muttered, "*Bof, la berceuse.*" Though my French was poor, even I knew that meant *nursemaid* from a painting I'd seen in an art history class. I blushed hot, and Ancel de Chair laughed until he saw that I understood. Then he said, "Oh, you must forgive her, this crazy girl's an artist, she has no manners."

She gave a click of her tongue, and was about to launch into some hotheaded comment when a blue butterfly sailed in its wobbly flight through the window. I can still see it before me in that bright white room, how it seemed so breakable.

"Look!" I said as it settled on the dip of a silver spoon, and the others turned to look. Three more butterflies fritillated in after the first.

"It's an infestation," cried my husband, cringing. But Ancel de Chair leaped up and said, "My God, no, no, it's a miracle." He ran to the window and looked out, and said, "Hurry, hurry outside, everyone, we *must* get pictures of this."

It was an order: we hurried. The butterflies seethed over the streets, turned buildings into shuddering things, turned the most stoic of people into sleepwalkers, marveling at the delicate dreams at their feet. Ancel de Chair took hundreds of pictures. Lulu tried to set up her easel before birds fluttered down and picked off every simmering beast. We left her there, and my husband and Ancel de Chair and I walked around the city for hours until, with another gust of wind, the butterflies rose as one and vanished. On the ground wings lay broken, trampled, and in the trees sparrows sat puffed, eyes closed, sated almost to bursting.

When the last butterfly had gone and the streets had

returned to their old, prosaic selves, I felt a deep grief, a loss of something I didn't know I'd had. Ancel de Chair, too, turned to us, his eyes wet. He cleared his throat and mopped his forehead and said, Now, my friends, it is time for a small celebration. Though my husband protested, Ancel de Chair took us by the elbows and led us into a shiny café and made us drink whiskey. We were completely blotto by mid-afternoon. I remember once asking about Lulu, and his giving a European shrug and saying, "Oh, she's a big girl, she can manage." At some point, there was a dinner, a terrific sausage, and whole rivers of wine and waiters with perfect teeth leaning over me. My husband lay down in the middle of the dance floor so we loaded him into a cab, and he waggled his hand at us papal-wise, telling Ancel de Chair to take good care of his wifey, and the cab drove off and the baron and I were left alone. I knew my husband, knew he had always congratulated himself for seeing the allure of a farm girl he thought other men would overlook. In his mind, I was in no danger of sparking an international playboy's lust when compared to whittled, elegant Lulu.

But when we were alone together Ancel de Chair leaned close to me and whispered things in my ear that made me gasp and turn pink and very warm. He kissed each of my fingers, one after another; he sent a trail of kisses up my plump upper arm and nestled his lips in my collarbone. Later, on a street lit by gas lamps, a tiny, wizened old man took hold of me, humming a tango into my bosoms, which was as high as his head reached. I was crying with laughter and unable to dance; he, obstinately, kept trying to make me follow his feet. From a dark doorway where he was smoking, Ancel de Chair's eyes gleamed, watching me.

My husband and I awoke at noon the next day, shattered. We could barely call for food, and moaned in bed until it came. When at last the cart was rolled into the room, in addition to the eggs and the coffee and the toast, there was a tiny, perfect bouquet of tea roses. I peered at the card until I understood what it said, and my husband took it from my hand. He read it out loud: *"My dear bergère, Lulu has insisted on a hasty departure and we are off again. So sorry we couldn't say good-bye in person. I feel certain, though, we will meet again, and I will insist on my tango then. Yours, Ancel."*

My husband flipped the card to see if there was anything written for him, then he read the note again. "Tango? Yours, Ancel?" he said darkly. Jealousy twisted his mouth and he looked ugly to me for the first time. Lord knows, it was not the last.

"Listen," he said, "last night did you do anything—"

"No," I said, impatiently. "Of course not." I said this, although I had a brief flash of a slow and salty kiss at the door, a hand on my breast. I turned to my new husband and laughed at him and said, "Why would I ever do anything with that old continental fop when I have you right here." And, "What, you think I'm so irresistible an international playboy couldn't keep his hands off me?" I knew that he didn't. That bleak morning I understood that it would be the essential rift in our marriage, my husband's belief that he had married down.

I cajoled and teased until he smiled and we soon forgot about the eggs turning to rubber on the plate.

Life went on, less magical every year. Ancel de Chair would certainly have devolved into a story I told at dinner parties had I not, shortly after my first divorce, seen him again. I was still young and so recklessly poor that I was fashionably skinny for the first time in my life. I had a part-time position as a secretary in a medical office, and my husband had refused alimony, damn his cheap heart. His new girlfriend, you see, had three children and he was straining to make ends meet already, what with the Party's poor excuse of a paycheck, he told me, and like a stupid soft-hearted sot, I bought it. That was the last I heard of him. I lived in a converted closet in Chinatown and had a hot plate on which I made my food, and accepted every date I could get in order to eat on someone else's dime. Cockroaches rained to the floor like bullets when I turned on the lights; I woke up one night to find a man, who had crawled in through the window, watching me sleep.

"I'm giving you ten seconds to leave," I said in a very slow voice, and started to count. He was outside by four.

Yet that was, in general, a glorious time. We girls from the office would mix malt liquor with gin and powdered punch, pour it into martini glasses that someone had bought at the Salvation Army, and get crocked, and we'd swear it was better than being at the nightclubs downtown. When we had the money, we'd go to a fancy restaurant and order only coffee and pie, and sit for hours living the high life, until we'd picked up enough men or had been politely asked to leave by the maître d'.

In one of those restaurants, I saw Ancel de Chair. I was draped on the couch, laughing, when I felt a hand over my eyes and heard his voice crooning in my ear, "Well, *bonjour, ma bergère*, I hardly recognized you." I leaped up in delight; he looked as suave as ever, catlike in the dim restaurant. He suggested going somewhere else for a drink; in three heartbeats, I left my flabbergasted girlfriends behind. He was in town, he told me as we walked, for only a few weeks, on business, something to do with a foundation he was on the board of; he waved his hand. I told him about the divorce and he nodded, gravely, and said, "That nasty flea was never worth your pinky toe, my darling." Hot tears of gratitude rose in my eyes.

We had one drink in his hotel's bar, and he told me of his life, his new wife and their baby girl, how she was born with meningitis, but was fine now, a sweet girl, his joy. All this, looking at me, making an offer. I took a sip and considered his lovely face, smiling—offer accepted. We went up to his room in the hotel. It was gilded, full of things that glistened and chimed, a palace compared to my cramped closet. He took off his shoes, I took off my boots. I undid the yellow diamond from his tie and put it on the dresser. He undid his cufflinks and rolled them under his hand, then slowly took off his tie, watching me.

When I unbuttoned my dress from knee to neck, however, he stopped me. He drew the sides of my dress to both sides like a curtain, and looked for a long time at my body. I had lost some of my formerly vast embonpoint, but was still nicely endowed and used to men reaching and grabbing at this point in the unveiling. But Ancel de Chair wasn't looking at my chest. He sat at the edge of the bed and pulled me close, and looked up at my face briefly.

"Oh," he murmured. "I can see your poor ribs." And then, one by one he kissed them, gently, from bottom to top, and began again on the other side. I closed my eyes to feel his mouth, warm and delicate on my skin, and remembered those butterflies of Buenos Aires, how they opened and closed their brilliant wings.

But something heavy fell against the door to the corridor. We stopped and looked at it, startled. The knob jiggled; there were the shadows of feet in the crack beneath. An unearthly cracked voice, a woman's, said, "I know you're in there, Ancel, I know you're in there, you're in there, let me in." There was a sliding sound; the woman must have let herself fall against the door to the ground. I imagined her a beautiful young thing, drunk, her lipstick smeared. "Ancel?" she said. "Please? Oh, please?"

I stepped back, and Ancel de Chair gave me a rueful smile. I sat beside him on the bed and took his hand. For a while, we listened to the woman crying out in the hall, his fingers warm and dry in mine, until he sighed and gave my hand a kiss, and whispered, "There will always be next time, *ma bergère*." I whispered, "Of course, of course." I couldn't look at him as I buttoned up my dress, gathered my things. He put himself back together crisply, and I pinned the yellow diamond back in his tie. He kissed my eyelids, once, twice, then spoke softly through the door for a minute until the girl leaning against it moved. He went out, and she spoke. Their voices moved off down the long corridor.

I waited for a few minutes in a faux Louis XIV chair, under the stern glare of some dead white man in oil. As I left, before I stepped out again into the too-bright day, I saw the backs of Ancel de Chair and the woman at the bar, hers nearly boneless as she leaned against him, his sleek as a seal's. Beyond the ache of my body, my stomach also ached: I had counted on room service, some hamburger bloody with juices, some sundae topped with cream so rich it would make me want to weep.

Even had he not sent the extravagant chocolates to the medical office later that week, I would have been pleased to see him the next time I did, three or so years later, at a dinner party given by the sister of my second husband. It was a quiet bash in honor of our marriage a week earlier, my sister-in-law wanting to introduce us to the highfliers of her set: Ancel de Chair was on one of her boards. The first time I'd met my sweet and quiet second husband I had liked him very much, even though I had been fishing for a rich hubby and he was at that time only a low man on the public television totem pole. When he asked within two months of dating if I wanted to marry him, I said, somewhat to my surprise, "Oh. Well, of course, why not." At our party that evening, I saw my stock rising astronomically in my sister-in-law's eyes because of my friendship with Ancel de Chair, because of his affection. He led me alone to the corner of the room for an entire hour, and held my hand, as if in warm remembrance, though my poor sister-in-law would have had an aneurysm if she'd known what he was saying. A few months earlier I had begun to jog—it was the late sixties; I was long before my time—and he commented on how light and strong my body was, and told me the things he wanted to do to it. He made me laugh like a silly girl of eighteen again. I gave him our telephone number; he memorized it and said he would call me the very next day. We left with a great embrace and showy words about how we would meet again soon, and my face still felt hot in the car on the ride home.

My husband was struggling at the network in those years; he couldn't afford to alienate bigwigs like Ancel de Chair, who was instrumental in getting funding for many projects. I'm not sure if anyone knew what Ancel de Chair did at that time: it was said he was in international relations, which I interpreted to mean he was an arms dealer. In any case, he was heavily wooed by the types who wooed. My second husband had sat at his sister's all night, smiling painfully at us from across the room, not daring to interrupt our tête-à-tête. He was a gentle man, raised in the Midwest, and had a horror of confrontation; he said nothing about Ancel de Chair to me that night, or any night afterward. Still, if my old friend had called for me as he said he would—as I sometimes believed he actually had—I never received the messages. It was only much later, when my attorney was going through the boxes of documents during the divorce, that I understood the depth of my second husband's hatred for the man. There were old pictures of Ancel de Chair from the magazines, the seventies playboy aging a tad around the mouth and gut, but my husband had doodled on them goatees and devil's horns, slashed his face out of the society pages. He had mauled the sole photograph of Ancel de Chair and me together at an event, poked holes through his eyes while I beamed on, blonde and thin in my nice dress, my diamonds timid beside the giant yellow one in Ancel de Chair's tie.

Even today I wonder if the baron's sudden fall from grace had anything to do with my husband—there were some ugly rumblings of someone's pockets being filled with the wrong funds, an exposé on the network's news magazine that mentioned him unfavorably by name—but by the time I thought to ask my second husband about what he'd done to my poor old friend, I had three quarters of the man's money and didn't feel I had the right to inquire about such things. I'd learned, of course, from my poor first husband. It's perhaps crass, but a nice pile of money does go a long way to make up for the absence of a warm body in the bed, and I only regretted not doing it earlier, when I first suspected my mild-mannered second husband's interest in his assistant. *A true genius*, he'd called her, brimming with glee. I never thought to ask in what, exactly, her genius lay.

In any case, the collapse of my second marriage had left me sad, spent, my body racing toward the day when it would no longer be possible to have children. I yearned for one, but couldn't think of having a child on my own. There seemed nothing to do but laugh in the stern, wrinkly face of time. I lived the life of the gay divorcée for some time, until, one rainy night, my third husband came along and swept me up like the warm blast of wind that he was. He was a good man, a gallery owner who created his own wealth, so clever that he could craft any little creature out of whatever was at hand, so humble that it took years for me to realize that what he'd really wanted was to be an artist himself. My third marriage was the one to stick. Almost immediately we had a son who was a dream, a country house in Maine and the one off the coast of Florida, and vacations and parties and lobster bakes on the beaches. Once in a while at a party, there would swim into my view that sleek and smiling face that would bring back the old pangs, the thrilled heart, and I would feel my body respond as it hadn't since I was just a girl. Ancel de Chair would send a glance from across the room that seemed to laugh at the world and to include me in the joke. He'd smile at me so gently, kiss my hand, say, Ah, if it isn't my favorite shepherdess in the whole wide world. But never again would we find each other in a secluded corner, never again try our decades-belated rendezvous.

Still, he drove me wild, that man. As my girlfriends and I sat and chatted over drinks, I reinvented him as a different lover, my imaginary first, an Argentine with a suave smile who led me in a tango on a cobbled street long ago. I described him as he'd been, with the sleek black hair, the thin nose, the face with those ironic lights dancing under it, the sudden, ready tears in his eyes. I described his body as I imagined it, white and carved like ivory. I told those stories again and again until I almost believed them, and every time the aging face of Ancel de Chair showed up again at another event, I saw the man I'd invented superimposed atop the man he actually was. It was a mixture so heady that in the seconds between when we'd spotted each other and when, having sailed across the room, we kissed, I was overwhelmed by nostalgia, deep and heavy as a flood.

He was the only person I had ever met who was always so elegant, so right. When my husband died ten years ago, we received such a mass of flowers that my son spread them out on other graves in the cemetery. Among the heaps of lilies and roses, there came to the house a miniature bouquet of tea roses in an antique silver vase with no note, the echo of its mate so long ago in Buenos Aires. I put it by my bed. It was a great comfort to see when I opened my eyes in the morning.

In the past six years or so, though, I haven't once seen the man: at this age, it is not unusual to have dear friends one hardly ever sees. I had heard he'd retired to a place in the British Virgin Islands, was living a quieter life, blessed with sand and sea. Still, it was odd that only a very few days after I had shown my granddaughter the photograph in Buenos Aires, Ancel de Chair called me on the telephone. "My darling *bergère*," he said, "it has been far too long. I am in town this week and would simply love to meet you, if you have a free moment." Of course I said that I would be delighted. But I didn't want him to think that I wasn't as busy as he, and so I suggested a time one week later. Out of vanity, or pride, I don't know, I invited him to the apartment. I'm not sure what I expected, only that I am still fine-looking, that I have money now, the right apartment, wonderful pictures on the walls that my last husband collected so carefully. I am, at last, *comme il faut*, and maybe I only wanted him to know that. Maybe I wanted something more. I'm not sure.

In any case, the morning of the visit, just yesterday, I worked hard to gather the right cakes and tea, and Rosa flew about, trying to rub the surfaces spotless. I felt foolish, young again. I hadn't been so nervous about a man visiting since the day I sat in the women's dorm in Madison, shivering with excitement, my hair in curlers, waiting for the time when I would walk downstairs for my inaugural date with my first husband.

At last, the intercom murmured, the elevator whirred open, and my old friend stepped into the apartment. I had always remembered him tall, and had worn heels for the occasion, but he seemed shrunken, and when he kissed my cheek with his dry lips, he had to crane upward. His eyes were sunbursts of wrinkles, his hair, once so sleek and so black, had thinned and whitened and was combed over his bald spots. But when Rosa took his overcoat and scarf, his suit was as beautifully tailored as ever, and he wore the old, enormous yellow diamond tiepin. His canny eyes had seen my first distress, and he laughed.

"Old age humbles even the great, my dear," he said. He

stepped back, holding my arms, and said, "Well, not you, don't you look lovely. *You* look half your age."

"You old charmer," I said and felt myself warming, and led him into the sitting room, where he sat and admired the view, the wind in the bare winter branches, the flurries of snow kicked up from the treetops. He took a neat bite of his cake, and spoke of various things, the biography someone was writing of his life, an interview on public radio, how he'd invested rather stupidly in a business run by his son, only to see the company disintegrate as if composed of ashes. "Oh, well," he'd sighed, "isn't that life," and I agreed that it was, and talked of the boards I sat on, my granddaughter's wedding coming up, my third husband's death ten years earlier and how lonely it sometimes was in the great apartment all by myself.

Like this, we chatted amiably for an hour or so, until Rosa took the teapot away to refresh it. Then, when the kitchen door swung shut and we were alone, he leaned toward me with a curious smile. "As I am sure you have already suspected, this is not, unfortunately, only a social visit, my dear. I came to you," he said, "because we are very old friends, and I know you're a woman of tremendous delicacy."

"Oh," I said, putting my teacup down, very carefully. I studied the park, a crow bobbing on a branch, and looked back at him. "Please," I said. "Go on."

He sighed, ran his elegant hand down the length of his thigh. His voice purred on, telling me that, as I suspected, he was in straitened circumstances, a life lived rather too well, poor investments, et cetera. He had heard, from who knows where, that my granddaughter was getting married. He thought that perhaps I might want to offer the child a gift that would outshine any other gift. An only grandchild, the apple of my eye, deserves something invaluable. Something she could fall back on in a time of need, God forbid she'd ever have one. But, and he shrugged, one never knows, does one?

He lifted my hand from my knee, and placed very gently into it the large yellow tiepin that he'd detached during his speech. He said, "Maybe have it reset into a necklace. My great-great-grandmother, Henriette Ancel de Chair, wore it in a necklace," he said. "A lovely choker at her throat." He pressed my hand closed and nodded.

I stood and walked to the window, my back to him. I held the diamond before me, and it glowed, a living creature in the dim winter light, the brightest thing in the city. I had tears in my eyes like a foolish girl. Of the millions of things I had to offer now, it was a wound to find he'd ask for this. My throat hurt, and when I could speak, the words came out in a rasp. "How much?" I said.

He quoted a number. I looked at the diamond, blinking. A price like that was more than double what the diamond was worth: a price like that, it was plain, and he was asking me to give not one, but two gifts. He counted on my having learned enough subtlety in this life to know he was asking for charity and to understand that he had too much refinement to call it what it was. For a moment, I felt lost, a bumpkin again, stuck in a tight space with a dizzying ladies' man a hair away.

I considered owning this thing, his pride. I thought of reducing those many years to a transaction, one scribbled check. I thought of my kind last husband, of how hard he'd worked for his money, and with that thought, I grew a bit heated. Ancel de Chair was asking for repayment for what: graciousness to a country yokel back when he hadn't had to be gracious to me? Flirtation? Friendship? I never knew I'd have to pay for that.

My head was beginning to pound. I was not yet old, and I hoped my life was still long before me. I was not yet old and had given already to so many charities.

I turned around, holding the tiepin like a buttercup, and pinned it gently back into his tie. "I'm sorry," I said, softly. "I have already bought my granddaughter an entire set of china."

Ancel de Chair brushed crumbs off his trousers and stood, a small smile playing on his lips. "Of course, of course," he said. "I understand. One must think practically, and I shouldn't expect frivolity from you, my dear Iowa shepherdess."

"Wisconsin," I said. "Actually."

"Well," he said, "well. I'm flying to London tomorrow, and have a great deal to pack. Thank you ever so much for the tea. Very tasty, indeed."

He moved toward the door and took his overcoat from the closet. "Wait," I said, "just a moment. Wait," I said, but he was flushed now, and tucking his scarf around his throat.

"Oh, darling, don't worry about me, it is quite all right. I really must go." He leaned toward me to kiss me on both cheeks, but came close to my ear, and said a curious thing.

"By the by," he said, "your milk has gone sour. I thought you should know."

He entered the elevator and threw me a kiss as the doors closed. I stood, burning with shame, then hurried back to the tea things. I lifted the cream pot to my nose and sniffed it, took a small swallow from a spoon. It tasted fine to me. "Rosa," I called, and she came hurrying out with the teapot in her hand, confused that my guest had left so quickly. I made her take a taste as well, but Rosa also thought the cream was fine, and we shrugged at each other, and I retired to my room to let my headache hatch into the beast it would become.

It was only late last night when I awoke again to the night-glimmering apartment that I understood, at last, what my old friend had meant. That night in the elevator in Buenos Aires, the sniff of my neck, what he had smelled so many years ago. Milk. I lay awake all night, burning. My granddaughter came by this morning and took one look at my face and was gentle with me. Later, my son called and invited me to go with him and his wife to Tortola in a few weeks, and it's very possible that I will accept. I should like sun and beach and daiquiris, and a sky with some blue in it, some freedom from the inevitable winter.

Still, at moments since the odd last encounter with Ancel de Chair, I have found myself watching the bare trees move on my glistening walls, thinking of Buenos Aires. Many times in my life I longed to return to that city, and though I could have gone a dozen times, a hundred, for some reason I never did. I probably never will. I find myself wondering now, in the shining, expensive desert of my apartment during this endless winter, if that city I loved so dearly could have stayed the same, after all this time. If the tiny old woman still sits in the park on her bench, silently weeping into her hands. If that old man still presses his wizened cheek to the bosoms of plump brides, humming tangos in the gaslit streets. If the jungle-smelling wind carries great flights of butterflies into the streets. If, in the restaurants, the waiters are still elegant and the steaks still glisten thick as tongues; if there are those great rivers, those oceans of wine to dizzy us, to wash our bodies sweet again.

Fugue

THE WOMAN DOESN'T KNOW HOW LONG SHE'S been here, or where she was before. It doesn't matter: all that does is this hotel window with its sulfurous draft and the quiet street beyond. The trees scrape forklike against the sky, the mud is matte on the ground. This village rests in a hollow so deep the sun cannot reach into it. Up the street the abandoned hotels hunch in perpetual dim, awaiting the end of winter.

The only variation is the girl who makes the bed, cleans the bathroom, carries up meals. A strange one, all safety pins and pink hair, a new type, a punk. But gentle: the girl sometimes brings with her small gifts, evidence of the world's quickening. A crocus bulb with a tender flag unfurling. An abandoned nest with a speckled green egg. When the woman holds those tiny things, she feels something rising in her that she is careful to chase away before it can catch and seize her.

This morning, the girl cleans, then stands beside the woman until she grabs one of her hands in its constant flight. Ma'am? she says. You a musician or something? Because your hands. They always look like they're playing music.

In the girl's bitten fingers, the woman's hand is elegant, the type that probably played music well. I believe so, the woman says; she doesn't know for sure. The girl nods and leaves, her footsteps echoing in the empty hotel.

Alone now, the woman recalls her own body. The filthy skirt, the cashmere sweater, the mud-caked calves. Unpleasant: she has begun to stink. She goes into the bathroom, dropping her clothes on the way. Under the hot hiss of the shower she notices what has been burning all along: the long, swollen cut in her thigh, the blood black at its edges. The water turns pink. The wound is deep.

Only when it is stanched with great handfuls of toilet paper can the woman sit again at the window, look out into the town, listen to the roar of the wind corkscrewing down into the hollow. Only then can she recapture all that stillness, all that peace.

I BELIEVE, BETTINA SAYS as she cuts the gizzard from the turkey, that she's a ghost. A sad old ghost, yearning to go home.

Jason cracks pecans and winks at Jaime behind Bettina's back; he seems to believe that Jaime and he are in some confederacy against his wife. Jason is handsome in a military, washed-out way, with features that blur into one another and buzzed, rust-colored hair. His fingers are long and delicate and can craft woodwork that seems a marvel of sensitivity, but he tells the raunchiest jokes Jaime has ever heard. He keeps her off balance.

Bettina turns toward them, her violet eyes, overstuffed lips, a beauty mark in a sickle shape across her cheek. She reminds Jaime of an iced cake, all fondant and sugar pansies. She is plump and British, too refined for this dark place, the falling-apart hotel in its sulfur-stinking valley. Jaime, she says, what do you think about our guest?

Bettina has only begun asking Jaime her opinions, though Jaime has been with them for almost nine months. Jaime's family had come to Sharon Springs every year since her own grandparents were children, her Orthodox Jewish kin climbing the hill from the springs, their dark clothes damp. Bettina and Jason aren't Jewish, but are fixing up the village's grandest hotel, and Jaime's mother loves them for it. One morning last summer, over blueberry pie, Jaime's mother had confided to Bettina that her sweet girl had turned sullen, strange. Dressed in rags, wore makeup, refused her religion. Only the day before she came home in a police cruiser; she'd tried to buy cocaine from a boy at the Stewart's up the hill.

We don't know what we did, Jaime's mother had wept in Bettina's kitchen, her wig sliding slowly over one ear. How could a good girl become bad so fast? How could our little Jamina become so different? It is our fault, her father's and mine. We gave her too much, now she wants none of it. The eighties! Jaime's mother said savagely. Nowadays people think they can do whatever they want.

Bettina patted her lips and said, Why don't you leave her with us for the winter? What trouble will she get into in Sharon Springs? Give her a few months with us in this old barn in the wintertime, nothing to do. She'll run back to you.

That was that: at the end of the summer Jaime's parents drove off, and Jaime stood staring at their exhaust. All fall and winter Jaime has been at this closed-up hotel. School had been her choice—she was sixteen—and she'd said, No thanks, thinking of the cloddish boys and passive-aggressive farm girls she'd find there. Without school her days stretched long. She learned to cook, to love the town in winter, empty of people. She'd go for long hikes in the mountains, wander in the huge, abandoned hotels, finding the postcards in odd corners, the cellulose dolls left by forgotten children.

The night the woman showed up, Bettina and Jason and Jaime had been in the parlor watching the show they all liked with the wily Texas rich folk: the main character, a raven-haired beauty, had begun to act strangely, an evil new glint in her eye. Then came a knock on the hotel's dark window, and there was the woman, bedraggled in the rain, like a zombie from a horror film. She'd insisted on a room though the hotel was officially closed until May. She signed her name in an indecipherable scrawl, something like Danielle or Diane or Donna, then closed her door and has not emerged since.

Jaime wants to tell Bettina and Jason about this morning, when she'd plucked one of the woman's hands from its graceful scrabble in the air, and felt her flesh, and knew she was real. But she only says, blushing, I just think she's a really sad person. She told me she plays music.

Bettina massages butter and herbs under the turkey's skin, her imagination afire. She speaks of a cellist she once knew who had been in a coma, who had dreamed of her soul wandering, desperate to find its body again. Jaime has stopped listening. Jason is watching her, his face impassive. He puts down the nutcracker. Jaime flushes. Bettina natters, back turned. A quiet lunge, and Jason pins Jaime's hand on the cutting board, slides his own up her holey tee-shirt, cups her breast, squeezes it.

It is over: Jason is back to cracking nuts, and there is only the ghost-warmth of his hand on her chest. Bettina is still singing her little tale, tucking the turkey fat over the herbed flesh as if it were a coverlet. Jaime picks up a celery stalk and dices it.

This is a game, Jaime knows, but only Jason understands the rules. She believes the goal is to see how far he can go before Jaime squeals. For a month or so he has been catching her, squeezing her hips, letting his hand brush her ass in passing. A few nights ago, he caught her in the corridor on her way to the bathroom and pressed his body against hers hard and when his voice hissed in her ears for hours afterward, she didn't know if she felt pleasure or alarm. She dices, she does not look at Bettina or Jason. She waits to know what she wants.

LILY WATCHES HER grandmother from under the silken fringe of the table. The old woman is crumpled into a wheelchair against the window; behind her the winter sun sets over the city. She has a cigarette in one hand, a martini in the other; once in a while she puts down the martini to gasp into her oxygen mask. She never, Lily notices, puts down the cigarette.

She's like an old witch in your mom's stories, says Sammy in Lily's ear. Sammy is spiteful and bad, and Lily often has to discipline her because no one else can.

Shut up, Sammy, she says. The grandmother turns her head and sees Lily.

Come out of there, child, she snaps. Who's that you're talking to?

Lily worms out slowly, her hands floured with dust. Just Sammy, she says. Nobody. She can see herself now reflected in the glass beyond her grandmother's head: pale and plump, her hair stringy, her red-framed glasses enormous on her face. At least she's not like Sammy, who's fat and moist and googly-eyed, like a frog.

The grandmother sighs, rattling, and says, You with your everlasting imaginary friend. And seeing Lily's hand digging at her nostril, more sharply: Don't pick your nose.

Maria moves out in the hallway, humming. She went all the way to the West Side to pick Lily up at school that afternoon. The girl had been sitting in the principal's office for hours. Lily's chest had grown tighter and tighter until at last her bladder exploded and she wet herself. Lily often does. She has severe anxiety issues, Dr. Kramer says. Her mother calls her Our Lily of the Furrowed Brow, and at school, the kids are mean and call her Lily-Wet-Butt. But today Maria only smiled at Lily with her potato-plain face, and helped wash the girl off. Maria is like that. She puts out two plates when it's snacktime and always asks about Sammy's health. Even Sammy likes Maria and Sammy likes *nobody*.

She's real, says Lily to her grandmother now. Sammy's real. She considers for a minute and says, But she's ugly and dumb so you probably don't want to see her anyways.

Stop clutching yourself, says the grandmother sharply. Do you have to urinate?

No, lies Lily, and then, feeling the old tightness in her chest, she stretches the neck of her shirt above her nose and down three times. All her shirts are floppy at the neck because of it. Dr. Kramer says she should do whatever helps. Sammy unfurls her long tongue into the grandmother's martini, and Lily frowns: she's going to have to punish Sammy for that later.

A dense wave passes over her, and Lily is suddenly tired. All she wants is home. To finish her homework, to see her dad, who scoops her up when he comes home and reads or talks to her until she sleeps. Routine. She feels a sharp stab of sorrow in her gut. When am I going home? she asks.

The grandmother says, I don't know.

Lily blinks, makes a little squeak. Where are my parents? she says. She feels the pressure descending on her, fast. It's bad, and Sammy draws near to watch, breathing her moist breath in Lily's face.

We're still trying to figure that one out, the grandmother says.

But seeing the way Lily's face changes, seeing her slow collapse, she hurriedly croaks out, Maria, Maria, Maria as loudly as she can until, at last, Maria comes running.

KEY WEST, HYMN OF JOY: from the dark shadows of the room the girl emerges, a pale fish rising from the deep. Howie watches from the bed, heart throbbing in his throat, his own body struck to water. Hers is slim, smooth, a length of muslin, a sheet of music. Knees in-turned, gap in her teeth, the green moth tattoo on her buttock, turned away just now so he can only imagine it. Knowing it is there gives him such a pang, the last trace of her origins, the sad rundown farmhouse smelling of cat piss and mushrooms that he has imagined in full, though she has said nothing at all about where she is from. There is a part of him who longs for just this dirt in her. She is unlike anybody he's ever known.

Her white body moves, and moves him. She's just past adolescence, just a girl, young enough to be his daughter. Briefly there flashes in his mind his daughter's face, such a fierce, lost thing, tiny. He has to focus on the lovely girl before him to regain his desire.

Outside, the lime-flavored sunlight tries to peer at them through the plantation shutters: in the sky, the birds rill the world alive. Above, the sun beats down on the island and urges the sea to singing.

Now that sweet face nearing, now those bitten lips, now the eye clear and blue as mint, that tender hollow in her collar. The girl, so young, smiles down at him. Howie reaches for her. At last, he forgets himself.

THE WOMAN IS IN the shower when the punk girl arrives in the morning. As she comes back into the cold room, bringing a cloud of steam with her, she finds the girl furiously pulling up the bedspread, her eyes red-rimmed. The woman cannot help herself: she touches the girl's face and feels the soft childish skin, her warmth. There is something familiar about the loose mouth, the way it leaps and stretches wormlike with the girl's emotions. *Vulnerable* is the word: and she doesn't realize she's said it aloud until the girl turns and flees, the laundry bunched in her arms.

The tray has no gifts on it this morning, which disturbs the woman most of all.

By the window later, as the sun sizzles out in the wet treetops, she falls asleep. When she wakes, there is the last fog of a story in her head—she'd seen it somewhere, or heard it. Television, book, movie, she doesn't know where it came from. There was a woman, tall and beautiful: this she knows, though she couldn't see the woman clearly. A letter plucked from a heap of mail, without return address or signature, a photograph falling from it, a menace of flesh. And, somehow connected, a night, a pond rimmed by dark trees, headlights spinning the fog, a car sunk to its bumper in the water.

She considers this for a minute, but there is danger there, and she pushes it safely away.

Now, as she awaits the knock on the door, the hot early supper on the tray, a voice in her mind rises up, sly and dark, an old woman's voice. It says: Tabitha. It says: Sudden Pond.

The woman shivers: the radiator clucks out its warmth. Although she presses her hands against it, although she paces, counting her steps so she won't think, she can't get warm.

IT IS LATE. Bettina is in the kitchen popping popcorn over the stove; Jason is out, somewhere; Jaime's hair is still wet from her second shower of the day and she is waiting for *Roman Holiday* on television. There is something tragic about Hepburn even when she's happy. As if the princess knows that the one measly day in which she gets to eat gelato and smash a guitar over a secret policeman's head and swoon into Peck's arms will never be enough to compensate for her lonely life as a royal.

This makes Jaime think of the woman upstairs at her window. She pictures what she found when she was cleaning that morning and pushes her out of her mind again.

Bettina comes in with the popcorn as the credits roll. She

settles into the couch beside Jaime, puts her arm around the girl's shoulders. She smells of lemon balm and the camphor cow-udder medicine she rubs on her hands to keep them soft. Like this, leaning against Bettina's bulk, feeling a wash of love come over her, Jaime wants to confess everything. How, this morning, in the shower, she looked up to see Jason's head tucked behind the curtain and watching her, a grin on his handsome face. She'd clasped her arms over her breasts, her crotch. He didn't touch her. He went whistling away. Despite herself, she grew warm. She sat on the floor until the water turned cold, not knowing what she'd wanted from him, whether just to leave her alone, or to intensify this game, teach her the rules. Jason was not an unkind man (she'd seen him put out kibble for the feral cats; he'd been the one to hold her when her parents abandoned her in Sharon Springs and she'd wept with fury). She was sure he would obey whatever she asked of him. Ex-soldier, married to Bettina, he was used to obeying. Jaime studied a handful of her hair. After two weeks the dye had lost its hold, the magenta turning into strawberry blond. Considering her hair brought her back to herself, made her stand, turn off the water.

Tonight, on the couch beside Bettina, Jaime feels safe. She lets herself think of the boy from the park a lifetime ago, the flowers frilly as Victorian children. Jaime had cut through the park on her way home from school and the boy had followed her, throwing horse chestnuts, his clothes ripped, his head shaved save for the spiky band down its middle. Stop it, she cried, but he didn't until she ran away. At home, her mother, on the ottoman with her skirt hiked up over her knees, giving herself a pedicure: she saw Jaime's face and cried, Jamina, Jamina, what's wrong? her voice full of alarm as she followed Jaime through the house, her feet pigeon-toed as she walked to keep the polish from smearing on the rugs. Jaime wanted to push her away, to think angrily of the boy alone in private. Over supper, the endless questions, even though Jaime was still a good girl then. Top of her class, quiet, going to college. Horse-plain, the way good girls are. But even when she was amenable, her parents didn't trust her to make her own decisions. Oppressive, their worry, their expectation.

The next day the boy was in the park again. He offered her a box of chocolates, stolen, she found out later, from a drugstore. She ate three right there, not caring if they were kosher. An immense thrill.

A few days later, he took her home. He didn't live in the rat-infested hovel she'd expected, but a large apartment on the Upper East Side. Played her records imported from Britain: Punk, he'd called them, and leaped around the room to the noise. It sounded like some blistered creature's death howls, but he loved it. He showed her a photo, the tight leather pants he wanted. He pulled a joint from his sock drawer (socks in neat buds, arranged by color by the maid), and she felt the world slow and become delicious. She didn't even know his name when he pushed her down on the bed. He hiked up her skirt, and on his clean blue sheets shoved his way into her.

She knew him for one month; during it he dyed her hair, attacked her tee-shirts with scissors, played his music until she began to like it. In school, people gaped at her. She crept out at night and stayed in a club until morning. Pills, coke, acid. And then, just as she was beginning to not mind the moment when he climbed on top of her, her parents carted her off to Sharon Springs, and at the end of the summer they dumped her with Bettina.

No religion, no school, no good Jamina. It had been a relief, in its way. At first she thought she missed the boy. Now she can't remember his face.

She'd wanted for a long time to tell Bettina about the boy, but if she was right to suspect that Bettina read her journal, the woman already knows. The commercials come on and Bettina moves off to make another aluminum pan of popcorn. Jaime follows her into the kitchen, where it smells of the coffee cake for tomorrow's breakfast, cooling on the stove. She wants to confess, to come clean, but she can't tell on Jason, and though she'd like to, she can't make herself talk of the boy in the park. Instead she tells about the woman upstairs, what she'd found that morning when she was cleaning.

In her purse? Jaime says. When she was in the shower? I found a man's button-up shirt. And it was all bloody. Like *totally* bloody.

Bettina stops shaking the popcorn over the burner. Her face has paled. A bloody shirt? she says, glancing at the ceiling.

That's what I found, says Jaime. You think she murdered someone or something?

Bettina turns off the stove and sits at the table. I think, she says. Doesn't matter what I think. She leans forward and Jaime is swimming in those violet, black-fringed eyes. Jaime, promise me, she says, don't tell anyone else.

Jaime flushes, resentful. Duh, she says, then Hepburn's bell-like voice chimes from the other room, and Jaime returns to the movie, feeling as if she'd just escaped something.

In the morning, when Jason comes inside, smelling of whiskey, Jaime is arranging the cake on the guest's tray. Bettina is by the stove. Jason grins at them, settles heavily into a chair. His back is straight. He runs his hand tiredly through his grizzled hair.

Drinking, Jason? says Bettina calmly. Already or still?

Jason sighs. You don't know, he says, his tongue slightly thick. You don't know about what's happening around here.

Bettina goes still. What don't we know? she says in her softest voice.

Be quiet for a minute, I'll tell you, says Jason. So we're at the Springs last night playing pool, he says, the boys and me, when in comes Arnie.

Arnie snowplow or Arnie cop? says Bettina.

Arnie cop, says Jason. Anyways, Arnie says, Looks like we got us a missing person down in Roseboom, going to drag the pond, make sure nobody's in it. He said to wait till morning, but we got carried away, got into our trucks, went up there to see what we could do. And get this, there's this car halfway in the water, this Mercedes all filled with water. So Pete shines his light in, sees the seats, and they're all covered with dark splotches. And he rubs his hand on it, and then says, Fuck!—here, Jason looks at Jaime and says, Pardon the French, then continues—Pete drops the flashlight and jumps back. It's blood. A lot of blood. And so we wait out in the truck and luckily someone brought whiskey and just when it gets dawn we drag the lake. But not good enough, I guess, cause we didn't find a body or anything.

He looks at the women, pauses for drama. Pretty clear, he says, slowly, somebody was murdered there.

Murdered? says Jaime, and looks at Bettina with alarm, but Bettina is calmly placing a poached egg on the tray for the woman upstairs.

Huh, she says. Any idea whose car it is?

Muckamucks from the city. Some kind of doctor and his wife. They think there was a hitchhiker or something, killed them both. Is there any coffee?

Bettina pours the coffee into Jason's mug and looks at Jaime. Take the food up, Jamie, before it gets cold, she says.

Jaime weighs the woman upstairs and her bloody shirt against Jason, so bleary, his great paws around his mug, ears cold-reddened, making him seem almost childlike. At least she understands the danger that is Jason's, a little.

Bettina? she says, helpless. I can't.

Bettina's mouth knots into a silken bow. She says, All right. Go on and do the dishes, then. She heaves the tray upstairs.

IT HAS BEEN THREE DAYS: Lily hasn't been to school. She's sure this is illegal, but Sammy said that if Lily told, her grandmother was probably too rich to go to jail and Maria would have to go instead. At night, Lily dreamed of Maria in jail and woke up in a puddle. She'll never tell, not even if she was out for the rest of the year, not even if she was out for *ten* years and couldn't go to college and get a good education and would never be a veterinarian, and would end up poor like Maria.

She feels the wildness rise in her again, tries to push it back. When she was just three, she would have such terrible attacks that she scratched her own cheeks until they bled. She remembers her parents talking, her mother's slow drawl, her father's clipped voice—Is it our fault? he said. Did we do this to her? God, I'll never forgive myself if that's the case; and Lily's mother gave a small, tough laugh and said, For heaven's sake, listen to yourself. Of course we did. We're both neurotic as hell. In a softer voice her mother, who was never soft, said: Lil will grow out of it.

This is what Lily tells herself when she fears she will never be normal, when she feels the anxiety lurking in the corners of the room: I'll grow out of it. And when she says it, to herself, she says it in her mother's broken-glass voice.

Lily is on the couch between Maria and Sammy. Maria is watching her show and Sammy is itching for mischief. She's been naughty all morning, spilling the milk, knocking over the grandmother's oxygen tank, eating all the cookies from the jar. But Lily won't let Sammy be bad right now: she has to keep Sammy in check. It's exhausting.

On the screen a very beautiful woman with huge shoulders is walking across a wood-paneled office, a grin on her red lips. What's going on? says Lily.

Maria says, without turning her eyes from the television, Oh, it is incredible! This woman is not this woman, but her evil twin. Everyone thinks she is she, but, no, she has her sister tied up in a basement. She is trying to steal her sister's fortune and man. Maria pats Lily's face, her hand smelling of the fennel she'd turned into soup for lunch.

Lily's father knows stories about evil twins: he spends hours at night telling Lily stories, mostly fairy tales. Her grandmother has explained to Lily that her parents are lost. Now, as the show jitters on, she imagines her father out in the forest, barefoot in the snow, only frozen berries to feed him. Somewhere in a sleigh in the cold, her mother sits all dressed in white, her beautiful face icy, enchanted by bad magic into a snow queen.

With that, the great wave looms above Lily, threatening, keeping her from breathing.

Sammy has turned her froggy face toward Lily, is poking her in the side with a sticky finger. Together, the wave and the poke are enough to make Lily wail.

Into Lily's hair, Maria says, Oh, hush-hush. When Lily won't hush, Maria says, So you want to be a veterinarian? To doctor the animals?

Lily, crying hard, nods, and Maria stands and carries Lily through the French doors onto the veranda. It is freezing out there, the stripped trees in the park below bowing, the street noises billowing up to meet them. Maria puts her finger on her lips, and Lily tries hard to press her sobs into her chest. Maria carries her over to an enormous empty planter, where in the summer there sits a topiary in the shape of a swan.

They look down, and Lily gasps. There, blue with cold, peep three chicks, songbirds, opening their cocktail-straw throats to Lily, pleading for warmth and worm mash. They strain toward Lily, shivering with effort.

The world around Lily halts. In this moment, there is no Maria holding her, no grandmother smelling of sickness, no parents lost in the woods, no Sammy. Lily has stepped out of herself. It feels good. There is a rift inside her and on the far side of the rift, there are only the chicks, creatures so much weaker than even Lily that the girl feels herself filled with a kind of light, calm and blue; a light full of forgetting.

THE GIRL IS UP in the hotel room and Howie is swimming his laps in the pool, feeling the joy in his new muscles, how after these few days his skin has softened into tan. He dips below the water and comes up blowing in the bright Key West light. Salt on the air, terns screaming: he dips again to the blue water and its kind murmur. There, he imagines the girl inside the dim room, television washing her body with flickering greens. Her show is on, and she has never missed an episode. He'd tried to watch with her the day before, but got confused: it was about a woman who was seen in two places at once; impossible, and Donna's explanation only confused him. There's Texas in her voice, though she's never been. His own Eliza Doolittle has learned a great deal from those oil-slick wives, their great powder puffs of hair, their avidity, their boldness, even the slow caramel drawl of their words. From the show she knows words that just a few months ago were foreign to her: *yacht, Sauternes, carat.*

Howie swims and his heart swims, too, rhythmic, longing.

Before the girl, he was gray. New York City snowfall gray, exhaust-dogdirt-gray. Gray as his office with its pleather couches, black-and-white photos on the walls, even home's small comforts gray, all glass and steel. His wife is modern and loves all things modern, as well.

But one day he saw the girl on his couch in the waiting room, a peony in a sea of ash. When he walked into the exam room, he pretended to be taking notes, only looking up when the door closed to see that she'd forgotten the modesty gown. She sat there, slow-smiling, naked, cupping her breasts like nesting birds in her hands. Pretty girl, barely out of her teens, gaudy squares of zirconium in her ears.

I thought, she'd said, smiling at him, that I felt a lump.

No lump: also no further exam. He didn't want to see anything belonging to the girl in a clinical light. He drove home dazed and saw coronas of sunlight on the cold glass of skyscrapers. His classical music station bored him and he flipped until he heard Neil Diamond warbling "America": he listened, astounded. It was big and celebratory and bold, this song, like his heart put to music. This song was the zeitgeist, this new decade hungry and striving, where anyone could strike it rich and everyone was doing so.

There was a party at home when he arrived: he'd stood limply in the door, striving to place all those people in the house.

Then he shook himself, mingled, fetched drinks. Became again the good man his guests knew, the one without adultery thumping in his chest. Howie, tee-ball coach, kind father of a problem child, head of the Neighborhood Association, gentle gynecologist. His wife shimmered and dazzled, bon mots spinning from her mouth, and he laughed with the guests, Tabitha's perfect audience. He squeezed her hand in passing, subject as always to her acerbic charm. His persona felt odd on him, as if he were wearing a mask from a Greek play, features fixed, mouth a loudspeaker.

In the midst of it all, he went to the bedroom, rolled up his cuffs, dialed the number the girl had written on his wrist: *Donna,* she'd written, and he knew by the way she'd smiled when she said it, tasting the word with such pleasure, that it was a name she'd given herself. Even here, in Key West, he still doesn't know her true one.

Before she answered, he remembered those two small breasts in her hands and almost hung up. But she answered and what had to happen, happened.

Now, three months later, as March sludges on cold and gray in the city, he is dipping into sun, into water, into sun again. He comes to the end, clutches the concrete lip, and raises his face to the warmth. On the balcony, there is a butterfly flutter, magenta and gold, the girl in the fancy kimono he'd bought her. She's laughing down at a gardener who gapes upward, his hose flaccidly gushing. Then she looks out and sees Howie in the pool, his thin hair slicked back, watching her. His breath leaves him under her transformation: from a mere girl she turns into a whole-body beckon.

THE DAY BEGINS: the woman rises from the bed, climbs into her chair. But even in the sulfurous draft she can't concentrate a whit. The exact matte of the road mud holds no draw for her. She is restless, restless.

Her fingers fly off her lap and scrabble about. Her thigh-wound has made her skin taut and pulsing. It burns and leaks a clear fluid through her denim skirt. Worse, that voice has begun to speak in sentences and has not left her head. It is a stern old woman's voice that barks out names in staccato: Donna, she says, Tabitha, Miriam Dubonnet-Quince. Howard.

Now the old woman says, Sudden Pond, with a crow's

caw of a laugh. The woman feels ill. She tries to ignore the old woman (she knows somehow the old woman's fat, shrewd, a brusque old bat). She tries to think of other things. The water beneath the town, beneficial, beginning to melt: the veins in the ground, thick with ice, the sulfur, salt, magnesium water pressing up urgently against the ice. But there is something in this she doesn't like either. It reminds her of something very unpleasant.

The woman curls into her chair, presses her hands against her ears. She doesn't hear the door when it opens.

But rising to her, the scent of breakfast, lifesaving coffee, and she looks around for the girl. She finds tears of gratitude, of love, in her eyes. She loves the girl for something the girl reminds her of. She doesn't want to examine exactly what it is.

But instead of the girl, it's the large woman, the dark one with the British accent (the old woman in her spits out, *Surrey*, distastefully—how would she know?). The British woman is the wife of the gardener, he who chips ice from the walks—they own the hotel; she cooks the meals. The man is a Labrador retriever, earnest and stupid and simple. The woman is more difficult, secretive, and far too young to be the punk's mother.

She wills the British woman to finish her cleaning and leave, but the woman isn't cleaning at all. She's watching her, lovely porcelain face on a swollen body. Laura Ashley cabbage roses, poofy sleeves, ridiculous. Stillness of a cat.

Where's the punk? says the woman, nervous. I like her, she says.

Sorry, says the large woman. Jaime isn't well today. She leans forward and does a curious thing. She takes the woman's hands in her own and presses them.

For a long while, for the time it takes for the dawn to dip the highest chimneytop in gold, she holds her guest's hands. They stare at each other. Then the British woman says, The day you came. Do you remember it?

Despite herself, the woman does now. She sees a three-quarter moon, raw; headlights; her whole skin chafed and wet. She shudders and pushes it out of her head.

I walked down the hill to the village, she says. It was dark. My shoes were wet. Your windows were the only ones lit and I knocked.

And before? says the British woman.

Before, says the woman. The road at the top of the hollow and the truck driver. He stopped for gas. The truck smelled unpleasant, and she got out and began to walk. She doesn't say this. She shakes her head and says, No.

All right, says the British woman. She cocks her lovely head. Listen. I don't know what happened. The less I know the better. But this afternoon, my husband and I are going to Richfield Springs for groceries and we can take you. There's a coach, at three, to Boston.

Something in her voice when she says: Boston's a large, large town. Easy to begin anew.

The woman is not sure what the other is trying to tell her. Oh, she says. No, thank you. I like this very much, and she gestures at the town, her window, the stark little room.

The British woman looks at her, then sighs and stands. Very well, she says, and turns to make the bed. When she leaves, she leaves the television on to some show. A black-haired woman with a pistol stands over a woman who looks just like her, bleeding on the ground. The music dramatic and bright. Under it, the old lady in her head speaks up. Well, now, she says grimly. I sure don't believe that fat Brit is all she seems to be.

Hush, you, says the woman, agitated to standing. She turns off the television. The voice in her head goes silent.

The woman circles the room, feeling like a caged finch, picks up the musty books on the nightstand, puts them down again. Nothing is right anymore. There is no solace in the dead street, the dead town. She pauses before the television, but to invite such noise will make it hard to be quiet again.

After hours of pacing, she goes to the door. She has a vague idea that if she can find the girl she can talk to her. Jaime, the British woman had called her. The girl who reminds her of someone she doesn't want to remember, though she thinks it may be necessary that she remember now.

EARLY AFTERNOON AND the hotel is empty, save for Jaime and the woman upstairs. Though Jaime is in her little brown bed, her nest, listening to the foggy pop music on her clock radio, she feels as if she's tied to the woman with an invisible tether. She wonders what she had felt when she murdered her husband, the moment the knife entered his flesh. Jaime closes her eyes and thinks that she probably felt nothing. That she watched herself from the outside, and it was a wonderful relief.

In the past, when Bettina and Jason were both gone Jaime would wander the forbidden depths of the hotel. On the third floor, the begrimed windows and furniture hulked under blankets like beasts asleep. Pigeons entered through a broken pane, and when she came into the room the birds would rise and swirl about her in a confetti of down. There she'd found a box of old letters in the servants' quarters, misspelled, stained, banal, infinitely tender. Jaime would go into Bettina and Jason's suite, three rooms in ivory and pink, smelling of Bettina's flowers, Jason's things kenneled in their own closet. She loves to pick through Jason's nightstand, his careful cache of treasures: the hunting knife in the handmade sheath that stinks of summer camp, the misspelled list in his adolescent hand: *Things I Will Do Before I Die* (number three, *Be a Brigideer General;* number nine, *Be a Millionaire*), the photographs of a younger Jason and a stunning, thin Bettina laughing, at Niagara. She runs her hands over Bettina's floral dresses, searches through her lingerie.

In her journal she writes a loopy *Bettina*. It's not enough to write the name; it is all she has.

Since that February night during an ice storm, when Jaime and Bettina stood in the kitchen rolling out dough for mincemeat pies, and the lights went out, and Bettina laughed and lit great conflagrations of candles in the room and in the flickering light Bettina glowed, Jaime had felt bubble within her a certain new helplessness. At that moment, she understood why she'd been happy these past few months. She'd understood, finally, a small piece of herself.

Good girls wear wigs and long skirts and marry men their parents choose and become mothers. Good girls don't dream the way Jaime dreams about other women. With that bright pulse, she'd found a better way to escape her parents. She had felt powerful in the kitchen that night.

It was not impossible that Bettina knew. She read Jaime's journal, after all, kept Jaime on a leash she'd tug from time to time to make sure that Jaime was attentive. Still, if what Jaime wrote about Jason bothered Bettina, she had yet to show it.

That morning, after Bettina went upstairs with the tray, Jaime's face grew hot in the steam from the dishes and Jason sat at the table, watching her. Jaime, Jaime, Jaime, he said when she put the last dish in the rack. C'mere. I won't bite.

Nah, she said. I'm okay here.

Fine, he said, standing. Then I'll go over there. He was still a little wobbly from the whiskey, and Jaime stepped easily around the table to put it between them.

Jason laughed, leaned his fists on the table. Oh, Jaime, he said. You don't fool me for a minute.

A sea rush in her ears. I don't? she said, wondering what he meant. She strained to hear upstairs, and relaxed when she heard a door close, Bettina's heavy tread on the stairs.

Jason heard, too, and his smile fell off his face. Nope, he said. You and my wife are hiding that woman upstairs, aren't you? I'm not as stupid as I look. Soon as I heard about the people in the car, I thought of that woman. He sighed, sat down. He looked suddenly old.

Jaime, he said, Bettina's a complicated lady, you know. She's got her own reasons for what she does. I just don't want you getting mixed up in something you don't understand.

Jaime made a sound as if she'd been hit in the sternum, though it came out sounding like a laugh. And then there was Bettina in the door, frowning, with the empty tray.

Jason stretched, smiling. We should go into town now, he said. Ready, Bette?

In a jiff, she said. Jaime, you'll hold down the fort?

Sure, said Jaime, though she wasn't sure, at all. In a minute, they were in the car, gone.

They have been away for hours when she hears Jason's truck coming to a stop before the hotel. She weighs Jason against Bettina and finds him lacking. The doors slam, the kitchen door opens, the rustle of bags on the counter. Jaime waits until she hears Jason crunch over the gravel outside, heading to his workshop, and then she's in the kitchen, where Bettina has sliced open a melon and is eating a juicy crescent at the window.

Bettina laughs, guiltily. Couldn't help myself, she says. Then puts the sweet fruit before Jaime's lips for her to bite.

But Jaime looks at Bettina, and Bettina takes the fruit away. I have to tell you, says Jaime. I have to tell you about something. Up rises the kiss in the dark corridor, Jason's face behind the shower curtain; Jaime feels the prickles on the back of her neck, as if she's about to lob a grenade into a marriage. It's about Jason, she says.

But Bettina is already nodding. I know, she says. He's smarter than I gave him credit for. Called the police. While we were at the store, he took off and I know he did it then.

Jaime feels dizzy, and when Bettina smiles and leans forward, her pretty mouth close to Jaime's, Jaime doesn't at first know what is happening, and only thinks fuzzily of the woman upstairs.

LILY IS HIDING in her grandmother's closet. It is a palace in there, mahogany and crystal, whole walls of spike heels and furs in plastic shrouds. Lily is trying to listen into the bed-room, but Sammy is odious. She's pulled out the silk pockets from the grandmother's spring coats, spilling used tissues to the ground like shriveled mushrooms, and is now standing in a pair of red heels, shimmying on her bowed legs, her belly pulsing in and out.

Lily mouths, Stop it, Sammy!, but Sammy only chuckles and shimmies some more.

Her uncles are in the room with the grandmother, all stone-faced; her aunts are there, too, crying and patting at their cheeks with tissues. The lawyer is there, a family friend, a fat man with a big nose like a red lightbulb. Lily was standing on a chair on the cold veranda, peering at the birds, when

Sammy hissed and pointed through the glass door, and Lily saw the slow march of the relatives and the lawyer toward the grandmother's room. When she saw Maria pushing a cart full of drinks and snacks toward the door, Lily waved at the birds and their mother, who hopped in indignation on one foot. Bye, Winkyn, Blinkyn, and Nod, she said. Be good.

The lawyer is now saying something: a car found in a pond. Upstate. Howard. Blood. Missing. Tabitha.

Tabitha is Lily's mother. Howard is Lily's father.

And then the grandmother gives a curious sound, a half-shout, raspy and metallic. My Howard? she shouts. *My* Howard? Murdered?

Uncle Chan, the oldest uncle, begins to roar. Why?

A long pause. The lawyer honks into a handkerchief and folds it away. He says loud enough for Lily to hear, We're not sure. But the evidence points toward. Well, there was a manuscript on the desk, unfinished. From what we can piece together, there may have been some, er. Indiscretion. On the part of. We're running things by the credit card company, to make sure. And we're looking for Tabitha now. Or her body. We're just not sure.

Lily feels like she's swimming. She can't breathe. Sammy stands over her, staring down with a dirty finger in her mouth. Lily clutches a silk skirt and lifts it to her face, over her nose and down, three times.

Your mother, whispers Sammy, murdered your father. She grins a terrible grin.

Maria finds Lily hours later, folded into a ball beneath her grandmother's dresses, wet, mute. The girl won't speak through her bath, won't eat the soup. And so, when she puts Lily to bed, Maria curls up beside her and breathes with her until Lily sleeps in her own small nest of pillows. She is careful to stay on the corner of the bed so that when Lily wakes in the night, Maria will not have rolled over and crushed Lily's imaginary friend.

PARADISE, THE PARROT in the lobby on his brass hoop, Donna's pale to tan, blonde to white. Their breakfasts of fruit, melon and papaya and pineapple.

This, Howard says to the girl over the coffee, watching her in the breeze in her kimono; this is the best gynecological conference I've ever been to in my life.

She snorts. Real diamonds, his gift, glow in her ears. Aren't you glad I made us stay? she says, her voice still rough after all her painstaking finesse. What if we just didn't go back? she says.

Yes, he says, but with the word there swims up a small unease. His wife, banging pots in the kitchen, coming up with her sloppy dinners to go back more quickly to her imagined worlds. He was supposed to have returned three days ago: he left messages with the answering service when he knew his wife would be out of the house, making excuses: they asked him to stay to address a medical school class, then the plane broke down and he had to stay overnight.

What would happen if he just remained here, soaking his

flesh in the sun like lobster in butter, Donna beside him? Every day, this lascivious sun. He'd buy a yacht and sail it from island to island. Even in the midst of his fantasy, though, he knows he'd think of Lily, his pale, intense girl, and guilt would chase him. It would catch him, no matter where he was.

On the wind now there's a trace, a hint of sound: Shostakovich, moderato. Someone in the kitchens, listening to a grainy radio. The mournful piano, unsuited to this thoughtless place, brings him back to the gray grandeur of New York, and he closes his eyes. He must get back, he knows. It makes him terribly sad. There's his mother, sick in her bed, suffocating in broad air. His daughter, who breaks his heart. His wife. He listens to the movement of the music, the waves, the seabirds, until it is all smothered under the gardener's electric hedgetrimmer.

Donna is looking at him, rubbing her hand on his knee. She says, What? a little crossly. He looks at her, the music heavy in his stomach: he opens his mouth. Howie doesn't know what he's going to say, only that it may be unpleasant. Donna's lips purse, her pretty face suddenly waspish. And he hesitates just long enough for the phone to ring in the room behind him. He stands and answers it.

As he listens to that old, familiar voice on the line, he watches Donna on the balcony, drenched with light, her hair shifting in the wind like seaweed. The words at the end of the line put an urgency into his limbs. And a grief as clean as relief comes into his heart.

THE WOMAN CREEPS DOWN the curved stairwell in her bare feet, her heart bumping hard against her ribs. It is cold downstairs. Only her room has been heated nice and toasty; the rest of the hotel is frigid. There are voices, but in all this immensity, it is hard to tell where they are from.

Stink of the springs' sulfur, heavy from one open window. Transistor music, some country song cloyed with longing. She sees the gardener scraping the wrought-iron gate, the black chips falling into the mud, his pink ears bobbing to the beat. She slides through the rooms like an eel in the deep.

But the way the light hits the glass of the antique windows makes her stop: that slick ripple is much like water. That pond rises again in her mind. And she sees it now, more clearly than ever, the car up to its steering wheel in the mud, ice like broken glass, windshield a broken cobweb. Blood everywhere, from when she opened the door, caught her leg on a sharp branch. She wrapped her husband's shirt, ripped from the dry-cleaning hanger in the backseat, against her wound. The rain was hard as needles on her scalp.

Now she touches her leg and it burns warmly. Did she do something terrible by that pond? She feels that she did, though she doesn't know what.

Ha, crows the old woman in her head: but the woman goes swiftly through the house now, trying to find the kitchen, the voices, the girl.

Now she emerges into the kitchen. Grocery bags tumble-weed on the floor. Pile of fruit on the table, a melon split and dripping. And there, in front of the sink, standing before the window that looked into the dim stretch of the street, the fat woman holds the girl's face in her hands. The girl weeps. The fat woman gives her a long kiss on the mouth.

Not motherly, indeed, chuckles the old voice in the woman's head. When the girl backs away, her face looks slapped and childlike.

In her mind, another voice, a different voice, one that sounds like her own, says, Lily. It sounds like grieving. She doesn't know a Lily, she doesn't think. The pang in her chest says otherwise.

But she doesn't have time to examine it, for beyond the bodies of the woman and the girl, down the hill, come cars like birds gliding to water. Two are black and white, their lights discreetly off. The last a green Jaguar, sleek.

She watches these cars pass all the abandoned hotels. They park in the street before the window. The police emerge. From the last car there comes a bronzed, thin man, his hand-some face set in wrinkles of worry. She is certain she knows him. Her hands float toward her mouth, hover in the air there. They write wildly in the air as she watches him.

Oh, she says, and the two other women spring apart. They turn to her, then follow her look out the window, see the police cars, the third man. The gardener drops his tools and bounds toward them, grinning madly, already talking.

Oh, dear, says the woman, joining the other two at the

window. She feels a broad smile spreading across her face. As the four men move together toward the door of the hotel, she gives a happy laugh. And just before the men enter, the woman says, watching the bronzed man with his thin hair, Oh, I believe my doctor is here.

YEARS LATER, WHEN JAIME THINKS of this day, she will only remember the kiss. Not the subtle sighing recognition when the police reveal that the woman is famous, a writer whose books even Jaime has read, whose picture she had seen many times on dust jackets. Nor that Jason ratted the woman out and her husband came and took her away. She will remember Bettina, enormous and beautiful, pressing her lips on Jaime's own in the silvery light of the day. The kiss is what she will see every time she sees the writer's name, every time she sees one of her books on a girlfriend's shelf. She will remember the kiss when she finally finds the woman's novel in a quarter bargain bin. It had been an instant best seller: everyone loves a scandal. Only when she reads the book will she learn of the woman's amnesia, of the marriage certificate she ripped up and sent in flutters into the midnight water, the wedding band she sent skipping into the dark. She will learn of the troubled daughter, look up pictures of that lost girl, and feel a surge of sympathy, a strange recognition. But when she finishes the book and fingers the title, *Sudden Pond*, Jaime will forget all that she knew about Tabitha and only remember the kiss in the window, and a darkness will fill her and slow the world.

ON THAT DAY, as the three of them stand in the window, watching the woman carried off, Bettina squeezes Jaime's hand under the cover of drapery. The last icicle in the window melts a *ratatatat* on the screen. Jaime feels ill. Jason is laughing, counting the reward money in his head. When the cars are gone, he goes back outside to the wrought-iron fence and chips at it again, whistling intricate contrapuntal melodies to the music on his transistor.

Alone together, Bettina's warmth pushes Jaime's breath from her. The hotel without the woman feels empty and a little sad.

At last, Bettina says, Sit down, and she lowers herself on one of the overstuffed settees. Jaime traces the lilies in the fabric with her hand, feeling as raw and tender as a newborn. Bettina says, You know, Jaime, you remind me of myself.

Jaime is shaky and says nothing.

Bettina says, That's not a compliment, strictly. I mean that I look at you, Jaime, and see a girl chased by herself. Like me.

A silence: Jaime tries hard to understand. If you want, I can tell you my story now, says Bettina. How I got here, of all places I mean, she says, and Jaime nods.

Bettina's story is stark, has a strange ring to it. Childhood in the country, doting parents, bicycles and gardens and brothers and cousins and tennis and Pimm's; her aunt paying for public school; blazers and experiments in the dormitories under lights-out. A-levels, Oxbridge. Balls and visits in London; boys and cigarettes. She was beautiful. A wild girl.

One summer, home from school, she drank too much at a bonfire outside her grandparents' estate. She woke with the wild music playing somewhere, her face pressed into the dirt, a mouth full of cinders.

She could have just waited it out, until the boy heaved off her, and then walked home, taken a shower. But she found a broken bottle under her hand, and without thinking speared it up. And then his weight was a different weight, and there was a hot wetness spreading down her back, a darkness pooling on the ground. The boy was dead. The bottle in his eye.

Bettina panicked, ran back to her grandparents', stole cash from their safe, showered, and left. She bought a ticket to India, but in the terminal crept onto a plane to America. There she changed her body, name, hair color, age, became a nanny. She met Jason at Niagara and after one drunken night they awoke married.

She could have run away again, but she was too tired. He left the military, took her to Sharon Springs, his hometown, where they bought the hotel, in foreclosure, with his savings, a grand place almost rotted to its studs. Nobody looking for her could ever find her in this cold, dim town that smelled of sulfur.

I believed it, Bettina says, bitterness in her voice. I believed in the American dream.

Bettina's eyes are closed, lashes moving against her cheeks like wings. In the empty silence afterward, there is a strange metallic ring.

It sounds fake to Jaime. She cannot breathe. She has listened to it all, love flying from her like scales from a fish. Bettina is too composed, her story too composed. Something bad did happen to Bettina, clearly: she probably is from England, probably was chased away. But whatever happened was not what she just told Jaime. And the story feels like one so often told it has the warp of fairy tale to it. Worse, she suspects Bettina has come to believe it herself. Jaime can't look at Bettina, now, for pity.

So, Bettina says, to the scrape of Jason outside, the parlor cold and damp. There are goose bumps on Jaime's arms. We can do two things now. One, you stay in town, in our little arrangement. Or, two, you know what you know about me and can't forgive me for it. Go home and be a good girl and go back to school and become who you were before. You tell me what you want to do.

For a moment, Jaime becomes Bettina, sees her long days of work, her nights beside snoring Jason; she can feel Bettina's boredom heavy as a rock in her own torso. Jaime understands with this that all she'd ever been to Bettina was a plaything to stave off the tedium, the kiss only a promise, a way to keep Jaime around.

In this light, Jaime's freedom is vast and wondrous. She

is young, unfixed where she is. She can, she understands, do whatever she wants. She wants to laugh with surprise.

I think I'll go home, she says. A watery beam of light from the window slides like a cat across Jaime's legs and up the wall. The fast-falling night darkens the window. Jason comes into the kitchen, still whistling.

Bette? he calls, sounding lost. Bette? Somewhere in the hotel a draft plays a corner like a tin whistle.

Bettina sighs and says, We're in the parlor, darling.

Jason comes in, bringing with him the smell of his sweat and the crisp outdoors. Oh, he says, relieved. But he says, Oh, again, when he sees Jaime, hunched over, face twisted, and the word is saturated with guilt. He thinks Jaime has told on him. Poor Jason, who had joined the military to become something better, who married Bettina in an act of aspiration, but who in the end found himself only the man he was always meant to be: hick, redneck, country boy.

Bettina stands and walks to the door: the windows in their panes tremble with her steps. Wonderful news, darling, she says. Jaime feels she has grown enough here with us that she can face the world. We're letting our little chick fly. Isn't that spectacular, darling? Her face is creamily reflected in the dark window.

Spectacular, says Jason, his voice confused. He straightens himself up into a military stance: he does this when uncertain. Jaime finds him newly endearing.

Our little girl, says Bettina, leading her husband out the

door, and Jaime feels a heavy relief. Our little girl, says Bettina, is ready to grow up.

LILY IS SICK. She and Sammy are on the veranda in the cold March wind, watching the scattered clouds move, the shadows slide over the spots of sunlight in the park. Sammy has taken books from her dead grandfather's locked cabinet and is tossing them over the edge. She throws one now and it flutters in midair and whips its pages around. It comes to a stop on the neighbor's patio a few stories down, beside another book. The books riffle their pages at one another, communicating alarm.

Lily has no heart to stop Sammy. She is shaking, and even by breathing slowly she cannot control the wave that hovers above her, threatening to crash down. In the apartment, the grandmother had rasped at her father: *Howard, you are irresponsible, so stupid, what do you think you were doing in Key West with that trash, I wouldn't have blamed Tabitha if she had murdered you,* and is now breathing air from her machine, cigarette trembling in her hands.

Lily's parents aren't dead. Worse. They had abandoned her without a second thought.

They don't love her. She sees her mother as her mother had been the morning she disappeared, her sharp, elegant face drawn at the breakfast table, her coffee untouched, her cigarette spinning blue smoke into the air. Lily knew better than to approach her when she was like this. There were some times when her mother was brilliant, laughing, fiery with life; but she was unpredictable, and when she was working she was more likely to look at Lily as if she were a stranger. They were still looking for her mother, but it was her soft and kind father's abandonment that made the panic rise up again.

Lily sees the mother bird dart back over the sky, flutter down. She moves over to the planter, peers inside. The baby chicks are fatter today than even yesterday, and the mother ignores Lily by now. She spits brown-pink pap into her babies' gullets. Winkyn, Blinkyn, and Nod swallow and open their mouths again and again until the mother bird, emptied, flies off. The babies peep hungrily for more.

Sammy reaches down, but Lily says, No, in such a strange voice that Sammy backs away, sucking her finger and looking at Lily with her froggy eyes. And it is Lily who reaches down into the nest and cradles Winkyn in her palm. She knows this is bad, that the mama bird won't touch him because he smells of Lily. She brings him up close to her eye. The chick must think she's an enormous mother bird because he opens his beak extrawide. He chirps one sweet chirp.

Lily takes him to the railing and throws him.

Winkyn's little body hurtling through space, falling like a clump of dirt, landing with a thud next to one of the books. For a moment, it feels good to be bad. The wave hanging over her lifts away for a moment.

She turns around, her heart drilling in her chest. There,

behind the window, is Maria, watching her. Paper towel in one hand, spray bottle in the other, face stricken. Lily thinks, *It's not my fault,* but Maria slides open the door and at first says nothing. The wind rises and blows her dark hair from her forehead. Then she says in a deep voice: They have found your mother, child. She closes the door and moves off.

Below, the books flap like beasts in distress. She knows that if she looks, Sammy will not be there. Sammy died when Lily threw Winkyn. Lily sits now on the flagstone veranda, feeling tiny and alone in the wind.

BEFORE THE HOMECOMING, the dark stretch of their apartment, before they find Lily a wet shivering mass on the couch, he and she, husband and wife, ride home in silence.

In the car, he squints through the rain on the windshield into the darkening day. The trees seem naked, and at a rest stop near Poughkeepsie he sees buds spangling a tree. *Like nipples,* he thinks at first, then grows angry, says, Ornaments, loudly, to himself. His wife is silent, clutching the purse on her lap, one thigh twice as fat as the other (at the hospital the next morning they'd whistle in awe when they uncover it). In his haste to get her home, he had wrapped it in clean bandages and carried her over the mush of the street to the car.

He drives; he thinks. Is that dull, gray woman really his wife? Can she be Tabitha, who is sarcastic, skinny, too chic, too flippant? Is his wife really the one about whom the fat British lady in her tea cake of a dress had said, Oh, but she was such a dear, really no trouble at all, quiet as a mouse, so quiet we didn't suspect a thing. Those words rang so false he'd wanted to strike the phony British bitch in the face. In his fury, he'd paid them, thanked the officers, conferred with the psychiatrist from the local hospital, was reassured that it was probably temporary amnesia, and, at long last, left with his wife calm in his arms.

He carried her as gently as he could to the car, feeling the way they watched him in his shoulders. The punk, the hillbilly, the fat British lady: as if *he* were the horror show, not them. None of them had ever seen a chopstick in their lives, he was sure; none of them had ever found themselves with such yearning in their hearts like the yearning that lived in his. He longed to turn and shout at them. He did not.

In the car now he doesn't know what to say. His wife gazes out the window dreamily, watching the landscape roll by. When it finally grows dark and begins to rain, he feels something pushing behind his eyeballs. When he brings his wrist up to wipe his nose, he can smell the coconut of Donna's tanning oil. Lovely girl, whom he will never see emerge from a dark room into tropical light again, her kimono flapping like wings around her. One last time he lets his eyes flush and the golden headlights of oncoming traffic blur in the windshield.

Is it wrong? he thinks. Is it so wrong to want, just for a short while, to be someone else? Even when he asks this he knows the answer, has known it all along. When his eyes clear and everything is crisp again, his wife is smiling with her strange beatific smile.

She clears her throat. You're a very good man, she says; aren't you? She waits, smiling at him. She puts out her hand and pats him on the knee.

No, he wants to say. You know I'm not good. I'm not good at all. But when he looks at her next, the way she smiles, the way the light from the passing cars glints in her eyes, gives him pause, and makes him, for the moment, wonder if she is actually there, deep down. If, somewhere, she—the acerbic, the writer—does mean what she is saying. If this was all intricately plotted, as elaborate as one of her own Miriam Dubonnet-Quince books, that crusty old lady curmudgeon whom he'd never liked but all his wife's fans think brilliant. Did he, in the wash of light through the windshield, just see her inhabiting her face again, mothlike, alighting for a moment, flittering away?

He rubs his own eyes, briefly hating her. He frowns at the long, wet road in the window until it fades, a dark worm pulsing before him.

At last, slowing down for the bridge, he says, I try. She doesn't turn toward him, but he can sense that she's listening. The moon is a hopeful shadow behind dark clouds; the car swims through the rain, steady and true. I'm only human, he says, and I try.

Delicate Edible Birds

BECAUSE IT HAD RAINED AND THE RAIN HAD caught the black soot of the factories as they burned, Paris in the dark seemed covered by a dusky skin, almost as though it were living. The arches in the façades were the curve of a throat, the street corners elbows, and in the silence Bern could almost hear the warm thumpings of some heart deep beneath the residue of civilizations. Perhaps it had always been there, but was audible only now, in the dinless, abandoned city. As the last of the evacuees spun through the streets on their bicycles, they cast the puddles up into great wings of dark water behind them. Paris seemed docile as it awaited the Germans.

There was a fillip of sulfur and light as Parnell lit two cigarettes and placed one between Bern's lips. In the flare, Bern saw Viktor's eyes watching her in the rearview mirror and the pink rolls of the back of Frank's neck. Then the match went out again, and in the darkness she was no longer flesh, only the bright, hot smoke in her lungs.

It was all over. They had awoken in the middle of the night to unnatural silence, and rose to an abandoned hotel, the door of each empty room solemnly thrust open, the beds identically smooth. In the breakfast room, the geranium's soil was damp and their coffee was hot on the sideboard, but there was no one there but them. They were journalists; they had seen Czechoslovakia, Poland, Norway, Belgium; they knew what this meant. They hurried, and Viktor somehow procured the jeep, and Lucci bicycled off for the photo. Just an hour, murmured the little Italian and sailed off bravely toward the invasion while Frank spluttered and fussed and Viktor grew stony and Parnell rolled cigarette after cigarette, each as perfect as a machine's. They waited in the jeep and they waited.

Now the street gleamed with richer light, but still, no Lucci. Bern sensed the tarry massing at the edge of Paris where the Germans were undoubtedly pushing in, and felt a wildness rise up in her. But there was Parnell's hand on her thigh, squeezing, and she was grateful, though comfort like this was not what she was hungry for. She had to do something; she wanted to shout; and so she said, voice low and furious, Fucking Reynaud. Fucking Reynaud, handing the city over to the Germans. A real man would stand and fight.

In the rearview mirror she saw Viktor wince. Bern was the first woman he'd ever heard curse so, he once told her; to him, he said, it was as if a lily suddenly belched a terrible stench. From the looks of him, it seemed impossible that he'd never heard a woman curse. He was Russian and massive, had a head ugly as a buckshot pumpkin. One imagined that had the serfs never been liberated, he'd be a tough old field-hand today, swinging scythes and gulping vodka like water. But, in fact, he was the son of some deposed nobleman and spoke perfect tutor English and governess French, and was known as a reporter whose prose was as taut and charged as electric wire. He had shadowed Bern since the Spanish war. There were times she was sure that his silent presence had saved her from some vague danger. She knew she should resent it, but the way he looked at her, she couldn't.

Viktor, darling, she said, a serrated edge to her voice. Is there a problem?

But it was Frank, with his Kansas drawl, who said, If Reynaud fought, my dear, *poof*, up in smoke goes all your precious architecture. All the civilians, smithereens. He did the sensible thing, you know. Paris remains Paris. It's what I'd have done.

It's cowardly, spat Bern.

Frank rubbed his fat hand over his head. Oh, Bernie. Don't you grow tired of being the everlasting firebrand? And where the hell is that little Eyetie of ours, that's what I want to know. Let's give him ten more minutes, then scram.

Bern bristled. There weren't enough female firebrands in the world as far as she was concerned, she said; Lucci was the best damn photographer in this damn war; and why the hell *Life* magazine paired Frank with Lucci was beyond her when

Frank could barely write a story without bland-as-buttermilk prose. God knows she herself, by far the better journalist, even if she was a girl, had to bend over like a goddamn contortionist for *Collier's* even to get to tour the front lines.

But Frank wasn't listening. Viktor, we better get going, he said. Germans catch us, you know where you're all headed. Me, I'm the only one who'd go free.

Parnell rubbed his handsome forehead with a knuckle. What do you mean, Frank? he said softly.

I know it's hard, but make an effort, Parnell, said Frank. Viktor's a Commie, Orton's a Jew, you're a Brit, and they probably wouldn't let Lucci go, what with his wife causing all that trouble down in Italy. I'm inoffensive. He gave a snort-laugh and turned around, his face set for Bern's attack.

There was a pause, then Bern said, softly, Good God. Parnell gripped her thigh to hold her back, but the truth was that she was glad for this argument, for the dirty distractions of a fight, for just now two planes with swastikas on their wings roared overhead into the fields south of them, then separated, curved about, poured together like water into water and came back over the jeep. The journalists, despite themselves, cringed. In the silence of the planes' wake, Bern took a breath, ready to lash some sense into Frank. But she didn't have the chance because Parnell, his voice slipping from its cultivated heights back into its native Cockney, said, Bloody hell, if it isn't Lucci.

There he was, tiny Lucci with the camera like a millstone around his neck, throwing down the bicycle so it clattered on the cobblestones, leaping into the jeep, saying, Gogogogogo. And Viktor threw the jeep forward even before they heard the drone behind them, and they shot out from the city onto the tiny dirt road as the motorcycles came around the bend. Two hundred feet apart and even from that distance Bern could see the stark black of the German officers' armbands, the light-sucking matte of their boots, the glint in their hands from the pistols. Viktor cursed in Russian and spun the jeep over the dark and rutted road. Lucci was in Bern's lap, hot with sweat and flushed and trembling; she frowned and kept her head down and watched the lace of his eyelashes on his cheeks. And then, over the roar of the engine and wind and pebble clatter, as the motorcyclists rapidly lost their grasp on them, falling back, Lucci opened his eyes and said, Oh, Bernice, in his Italian way, Ber-eh-nee-che; Oh, Bernice, I have it. The best photo of the war. Nazis goose-stepping through the Arc de Triomphe. You shall see. Oh, it is the sublime photo. Oh, the one to make me live forever, he said, and Bern couldn't help it; she closed her eyes; she clutched Lucci's thin shoulders and threw her head back. Hurtling into the steel-gray dawn, she laughed and she laughed.

THE DAY WAS ALREADY full when they stopped in the hemlock copse. Bern was stretched over the hood, basking in the sun like a cat. They were waiting for Lucci to finish vomiting in the ditch; ten miles south of the city he had discovered that the Germans had shot through one of his rolled-up trouser cuffs, and he slowly unrolled the fabric and fingered the six neat holes. Turned green. Viktor had to stop the car. Now Parnell and Frank were smoking, looking back at the city behind them. For a moment, Viktor wondered if he could just take Bern and leave the rest behind; Lucci was all right, but Parnell and Frank he despised. Parnell for obvious reasons; Frank because he was a greasy toad. But he couldn't; they were not far enough out of Paris for abandonment to be anything but cruel. The last bicyclists they had passed were now passing them and an old woman with a chicken under her arm hobbled by, the chicken's head bobbing with each step. The Germans would be along soon. In the distance there were odd mechanical sounds.

Viktor flicked his eyes over Bern. Though she was the most beautiful woman he knew, she was not a true beauty. He should know; he himself was a warthog, but he had grown up around swans, long-necked sisters with velvety eyes and a mother whose grace was so legendary that, among her three dozen rejected suitors in old noble Moscow, there were still men who wept when they remembered her. Bern was too dark a blonde and too light a brunette, devoid of embonpoint, her face hawkish with its aquiline nose and her mouth like a pink knot tied under it. Too thin, also; war whittled her down, though she was always hungry, always eating. Still, even though she was almost plain when she slept, when she was vibrant it would take a strange man to find her unattractive. In the sunshine she radiated; her hair turned golden, her eyes green, and her skin seemed to pulse with health. In the sunshine, Viktor had to hold his hands in his pockets to keep from grabbing Bern's sole world-class attraction, her tidy rear, fleshed with a layer of smooth lard, firm and handy as a steering wheel.

The day Viktor met Bern, she was twenty-two, climbing up the stairs of a Spanish hotel just after witnessing her first battle. Her face was pink, her eyes sparked angrily. She was trembling, and shook his hand hard to introduce herself, then said, Damn! I mean, damn! and went into her room and tapped at her typewriter for an hour, until she came out to the veranda, where he was waiting for her and pretending not to. She thrust a piece of paper into his hands and demanded to know if it was good, because, you see, she was determined to be a war reporter, and she'd heard he was a good one. The man she came to Spain with, a lover, wasn't worth his weight in pig poo, she'd said, and she had to learn from *someone*. Viktor read the article, and said it was a job well done, B. Orton: but what does B. stand for? And she said in her French horn of a voice, Ah, well, it means Bernice but it also means that if I can fool *Collier's* into thinking I'm a man, I'm a war reporter for good, and don't you forget it. And Viktor said, To be sure. And she said he better goddamn not because they were going to be buddies, watch out.

But they didn't become buddies yet: he went off to a different section of the front and when they met up again, it was in a hotel right after Guernica and Viktor was having an awful time of it. He kept seeing flashes of things he tried to shunt away. Late at night he wept in the water closet, unable to stop himself; he tried to stuff his shirt in his mouth to muffle the sound, but couldn't. For fifteen minutes, there were two dark shadows in the crack under the door, Bern's feet, Bern's head on the door, listening. When she came in and took off her blouse and hitched down her trousers and smiled up at him, he couldn't think to say no.

Afterward, he kissed the delicate slice of her chin under her ear and asked her to marry him. And she laughed roughly, gave him a tweak of the ear, and said, Oh, well, Viktor, dear, now you've made a terrible mistake, and vanished down the dark hallway. And so, to Bern, it had been a mistake; it hadn't happened again. Instead, he'd watched time and again as she disappeared down other hallways with Parnell. And he had to swallow it because she was who she was, a woman so removed from the women of his youth as to be a whole new gender. In her every small movement she was the woman of the future, a type that would swagger and curse, fall headlong, flaming into the hell of war, be as brave and tough as men, take the overflowing diarrhea of nervous frontline troops without grimacing, speak loudly and devastatingly, kick brain matter off their shoes and go unhurriedly on. When he looked at Bern, Viktor saw the future, and it was lovely and clean and as equal as things between men and women, between prole and patrician, could be. And he also saw that any impulse to pin her down would only make her flitter away. Some days he hated her.

He must've sighed, because Bern shielded her eyes with one graceful hand.

Viktor, you're wearing ye olde death-head again, she said. What's the matter?

But instead of saying, for the hundredth time, Oh, Bern, why Parnell and not me? or Oh, Bern, why won't you marry me?, he gave a grimace and ground out his cigarette and said, We should be off, then, if we don't want the Krauts to catch us.

Now the others climbed up the embankment and Bern let herself slide off the hood, graceful, winking. Come on, chaps, she called out in her high honk. *Vite vite.* We've got to make it to Tours before the Nazis bomb the bejeezus out of it.

IN HALF AN HOUR, the dampness had burned from the ground, and dust rose in a haze and saturated everything. The oaks that drooped over the avenue and the pocked road were so lovely in the dust-cloud they seemed to drip with honey. Strange, Parnell thought dreamily, that on a day like this there should be beauty left in the world. For a while they had been going increasingly slowly, passing thicker and thicker clumps of evacuees, whole families like packhorses, even the smallest pulling little red wagons full of bedding or small dogs or even tinier children than they. Terrible shame, he thought, terribly sad.

But later he saw a number of parties in the fields huddled over blankets spread with food, picnicking as if the occasion were a merry one, and he murmured, How lovely, wishing himself out there, with his own little ones—how the girls would enjoy it!—and Sally presiding over it all with her neat sandwiches and birdly chatter about gardens and whatnot. He longed for home, longed for the house in London and his shoes shined in the morning and a proper cuppa. Looking out in the fields, he murmured again, Oh, how lovely, and hadn't thought he'd said it aloud until Bern turned her head to him and snorted, They're idiots, Parnell. Germans flew by they'd be blown to bits.

He stared at this brusque American, appalled as ever. Then she softened and cuddled against him, a good kitten, and he reminded himself that she never meant it, not really. She talked a terrible hard streak but was a dear thing inside. Reminded him of Sally, in some vague way, not that Bern would ever do if he had a mind to introduce her to his wife. Sally was so peculiar in that way, refusing to take tea with so-and-so for somesuch reason or other, and he knew that Bern in his wife's parlor would be a frightful thing; the snubbing going on over the tea and poor Bern never seeing it for a moment, honking on the way she does and getting on Sally's nerves. It was odd, wasn't it, how people changed; he was only a housepainter back in the day when he met Sally, and she didn't hold it against him then, although she did make him take elocution lessons and become something. He was about to follow this thought into another daydream of Sally, young and naked and smelling of his house paints, when Bern interrupted, saying, So, did anyone think to bring food?

There was a long silence, until Parnell, wanting to be helpful, said, Well, rather, I brought that half a can of petrol, you know.

And I the jeep, said Viktor.

And I the stupendous photo, said Lucci.

And I the water, said Bern.

The back of Frank's neck turned red, but he said nothing. Bad-tempered fellow, Parnell thought, but doesn't seem to mean any real harm.

Frank? Bern prompted sweetly, but he just turned and said, Darling, you being the only female of the bunch, I thought provisions were your field.

Not now, said Lucci throwing his hands into the air, but Bern seemed too tired to curse Frank to hell more than a few times. Then she bent down and rummaged in her valise and pulled out a bottle of Scotch, brandishing it like a tennis victor with a trophy.

Looks like a liquid lunch again, fellas. She grinned and cracked the seal with her fingernail. I liberated this from the hotel bar this morning.

Now Parnell wanted to take her in his arms again. This was why he invited her into his bed every night, propping the picture of his family up on the windowsill first, a plea for them to forgive him the sin he was about to commit; *this* feminine thought for the comfort of others. He felt a bubble of elation rise in him as he took a swig of the Scotch; this is why the men were out here in the fields, fighting: for their women, for knitting and stews and flower arrangements, the wondrous small things that keep a fellow's life pleasant. If he weren't so blasted old, Parnell would fight for it, too. And Bern had a great womanly capacity for comfort, though she kept it hidden because she thought it made her seem like less of a chap than she wanted to be. Silly duck. She shouldn't hide it; it was what he liked about her. He resolved to tell her so, maybe sometime when they were alone and not so pressed for time.

Bathed in a warm dust and a warming buzz, Parnell drifted into a pleasant waking doze as they passed the growing numbers of refugees on foot, on bicycle, on carts pulled by peasant women like pendulous-breasted oxen. They went down that insignificant road from Paris until it emptied out, at last, into one of the major southbound arteries, to the northeast of Orléans and about sixty miles south of the city.

It was then that, pulling out onto the autoroute, Viktor cursed and stopped the jeep, jolting Parnell out of his lovely trance. Before them roiled a scene of such chaos that they, all veterans of chaos, had to take a moment to sit, absorbing, before they reacted. For, instead of the neat, small clumps of refugees who had decided to take the small road they had just left, the autoroute was teeming, impossible: cars that had run out of gas were abandoned by the roadside, women in summer dresses had fainted in the heat and were fanned by wailing children, a teeming mass of man and mule and bicycle and machine was pulsing down the road as far as their eyes could see, and everywhere were wounded people. An old woman, haute bourgeoise by her chignon and her gray silk dress, had a dried magnolia of blood blooming on her chest. Two men carrying a makeshift stretcher bore a tiny boy, waxen and still, with a tourniquet on his thigh and nothing where his knee should have been. Filling the air were the claxons of the few cars still running, hushed talk, a faraway keening.

And, out in the fields beyond, as if this migration were not a hundred feet from them, the backs of an old farmer and his wife as they bent to pull weeds from their crop.

Shit, said Bern, and she flew out of the jeep, into the maw of humanity, asking questions, scribbling answers. Parnell felt a tad sheepish: this was not his beat; the British people were under attack enough—they didn't need more bad news. His orders were to write about resistance and bravery, not innocent civilians fired upon when they fled their homes. From where he sat in the jeep he heard *bombed, machine-gunned, massacred,* the airplanes strafing the émigrés about twenty miles south of Paris. Numerous dead. A two-week-old baby shot in the throat. An old man had a heart attack, seeing it. Parnell watched as under Bern's pen the story formed, neat and relentless, threads ordered from chaos.

Frank trailed slowly behind her, gleaning, having little success at asking questions himself: his French was poor, and people did not warm to him as they always did to Bern. Viktor glowered in the jeep, keeping it a meter behind Bern as she walked beside her subjects, protecting her; dear Lucci darted hither and thither taking photographs until he returned to the car to hide his face in his jacket, unable to see any more. For a while, Bern held a baby so its mother could shift her bundle, and she held it awkwardly. But Parnell wanted to tell her she would make a marvelous mother; as she looked down into its soft fist of a face, he knew she would. His admiration only grew when, after a while, Bern held the hand of the boy on the stretcher when he awoke and sobbed soundlessly in pain.

When she at last returned to the car, when the first bats began swooping over the fields, she wiped and wiped at her cuff where a small coin of the boy's blood had darkened it. She moved close to Parnell and looked up into his face and he saw the kind of searing look she gave him when she wanted to take him into a corner and have her furious way with him. As always, he was taken aback, though he would have complied, had there been any real chance, but he looked around at the boiling mass of humanity, at the others in the car—poor Viktor, he tried not to be so obvious around him—and shook his head, just slightly.

Disappointed, Bern turned away and said, I have four stories just dying to be published. And no fucking wire to send them.

That is why we are going to Tours, darling, said Viktor.

That's our problem, said Bern. People out there told me. The wires are cut in Tours, too, the government's fleeing to Bordeaux. Nowhere to sleep, even the barns forty kilometers out full of people. No food. No water. General panic. What have you.

A long silence, broken at last by Lucci, saying, So what is it we're to do?

And Frank unfolded the map, whistling "La Marseillaise," as he was wont to do when he wanted to calm himself. There's a road, he said, three miles to the east, that's smaller than this one. Takes us to Bordeaux, looks like, if in a bit of a roundabout manner.

Bordeaux, said Parnell, thinking of good wines and soft beds. He hadn't eaten in a day and his hunger had been replaced by a dull ache. How he longed for the buttery melt of pheasant in cream sauce on his tongue. How fine it would be to take a warm bath, to sleep and sleep without awakening to the sound of artillery. So Parnell said, Oh, yes, let's go on to Bordeaux, and he wondered if he spoke more strongly than usual, for Bern looked at him, a smile flickering across her face, and Lucci made a little noise of approval.

It's decided, said Viktor. On we push. He turned into a cart path through the nearest field. When that path dead-ended in a long, lush field of barley sprouts, he drove through the young crops. The jeep left a path of broken plants in its wake. Parnell felt sorry for those small broken plants, he did. But when he was about to mention this to Bern, he felt foolish for it, and said nothing, after all.

THEY MADE THE ROAD by the time the sky had immolated itself in sunset. Bern would never admit it to the chaps, but she was beginning to shake with hunger; always a bad sign. When she began to shake, she needed to eat soon or suffer fits of nasty temper. The jeep pressed on valiantly until the moon had risen, but presently it began to make a coughing sound and slowed to a crawl. There was an electric light glimmering through the trees. Though they urged the engine along, the jeep died before they reached the light. Parnell got out, uncomplaining, and Frank got out, complaining, and together they pushed until they reached the settlement.

There she saw a group of three stone buildings that, in the thin wash of moonlight, seemed to have sprung up organically from the ground, as if a natural geologic formation or a mushroom ring. In the hard-packed dirt courtyard, two skinny dogs skulked and rattled their chains. One weak bulb hung over a door, which was thrust open when Viktor honked, and an immense, bullet-shaped body filled the light pouring from within.

Oh, he is very large, said Lucci. He will be sure to have food.

Our savior who art in hovel, said Frank, his sharp good humor returned.

When they saw, however, that the man had the unmistakable silhouette of a rifle in his hand, and that he spoke to two other creatures who came outside behind him, also with what appeared to be rifles, the reporters did not climb out of the jeep, as they had been about to do. They waited, still and quiet, in the car, until the man came up and pointed a flashlight at their faces, one by one. When he reached Bern, he paused, and she winced in sudden blindness so that she didn't notice that he was fondling a lock of her hair until he tugged on it. When she batted at his hand he had already pulled it away and she was left clawing air.

Excuse me, sir, said Viktor in his impeccable French, but we are hungry and tired, and would gladly pay for some food and a place to rest. And some gas, if you've got any.

The man, still invisible in the darkness, grunted, and the soft voices of the two others murmured behind him. Yes, he said in an earthy provincial French, yes, we've got all that. Come inside and bring what you've got.

Now they all slowly slid from the jeep and walked behind him, the two other strangers dark shadows at their backs. And when they were inside the cottage all Bern saw at first was a tiny old woman paring potatoes in a dark corner, a fairy-tale grandmother who smiled, though her eyes watered, rheumy. Bern's eyes adjusted in a moment, and only then did she see the small photograph of Hitler over the mantel, one plucked daisy and a guttering candle before it, as if the Führer were some syphilitic-looking saint.

Bern spun toward their host and found him grinning down at her with his dark eyes and his oily but handsome face. His arm was jutted out, his hand upraised, and on his great biceps there was an armband embroidered with a crude swastika. Heil Hitler, he boomed. Today is a great day, is it not, my friends? Please, sit. Are you hungry? Call me Nicolas.

She didn't know how she bore it, but in the next moment

she was eating, and to her surprise it was good. A smooth white wine, hot bread, potage of carrot, even a small tin of potted meat. She scowled. It would do no one any good if she were to starve to death, but she didn't have to enjoy it. Viktor sent her warning glances from his side of the table, and Parnell kept his hand on her knee, for good measure; not as if she were really so stupid as to open her mouth and let fly; they were just making sure. By the fireplace at the far end of the room sat the two creatures who had come outside with their host to greet them, and now Bern had a hard time seeing any threat in them: they were two teenaged boys with guns in their arms, but so skinny, and cringing, they may as well have been girls cradling their dolls.

My sons, Nicolas had said, gesturing at them. My wife died many years ago. The boys kept their eyes averted, and on one of them Bern noticed the blue-green stamp of a fading black eye. The watery old woman kept peeling her potatoes, nodding and smiling vaguely.

For his part, their host was leaning back in his chair, watching the reporters eat and smiling his approval. When they had finished and Frank had speared the last hunk of bread with his knife, Nicolas spoke again, softly. I am so glad my meal was to your liking, my friends. Now that you are satiated, I hope, we can come to an agreement, can we not? You mentioned that you could pay for my hospitality, did you not?

We did, said Viktor. We can. We have money. Francs, pounds, dollars. For supper tonight, of course, plus a roof over our heads, plus provisions for tomorrow. And enough fuel to get us to Bordeaux. Perhaps fifty francs would be a good deal. That is, if you please.

I do please, said Nicolas, smiling his charming smile. I do, indeed. I will give you all that you want, the food, the gas. But I do not, most unfortunately, accept currency from those places. Those countries will presently be crushed, and all that will be worthless. Just paper, a few tin coins. Now, if you had reichsmarks, that would be something, he said, and sighed a voluptuous sigh. How I am glad that I share this day with you, he said. I must admit that I have been dreaming for this day, my friends, for years.

Since the last war, said his mother from her potatoes. He has not let up about it. Germany this, Germany that. Takes a correspondence course. German. All sorts of books. Always a very smart boy.

I was a prisoner of war during the last one, Nicolas said, but, really, I was kept better there than here: they valued me more there, where I could not at first speak the language, than they do in my own country. We had schnitzel for luncheon every day. Schnitzel! A marvel of precision, the German mind. These boots here, he said, rapping his vast foot on the ground, are German-made, given to the prisoners, and they're still as good as the day I got them. I lived among those people and knew they were superior. The Germans rise, he said, dreamily. And with them a better race of man.

Oh, Christ, spat Bern, feeling herself flush with rage.

Indeed, said their host. Bern saw his eyes drop to her lap,

where Parnell's hand was clutching her thigh too tightly, too high on her leg. Nicolas raised an eyebrow and gave her a private smile. Bern was not prepared for the pretty dimple in his cheek.

Viktor rushed in. Well, we have other goods. I've got a gold watch, he said, and put his father's watch on the table, looking sternly at the others. I'm sure we can rustle some more up.

Parnell gamely took the photographs of his family out of the silver frame, tucked them back into his pocket, and put the frame beside the watch. Then he added to the pile two diamond cuff links (*What*, Bern thought, amused, even now, *does he imagine he's doing with cuff links in a war?*), his engraved cigarette case, and a still-wrapped bar of Pears soap.

It's unused, he said with a significant glance at Nicolas.

I don't understand what's going on, said Frank in English, but he can have my flask if he wants it, and threw into the mix a horn-and-silver flask that he had kept hidden from all the others until now. Parnell gave him an odd look; Frank only shrugged.

Bern threw in her gold bangle and it made a furious jingle on the pile.

Lucci fumbled, and found a pair of clean woolen socks in his pocket. All I have, he said cheerily in French. The watery old mother by the woodstove creaked out of her chair and hobbled up and took them, muttering how nice the wool was, how soft, what lovely socks they were, worth a lot, she was sure, and she patted Lucci on the head like a good child. The boys by the fireplace watched the pile hungrily, their eyes large in their faces.

Ah, sighed Nicolas. A pile of riches. Surely more than this family has ever seen in one place before. He played his hand around in the pile for a moment, moving this bit, then that, but shook his head, and pushed them back toward the reporters, save for the socks, which the old woman stroked in her lap like a kitten. Alas, said Nicolas, this is not what I want, either.

Well, what in bloody Christ's name does he want then? said Parnell in English. But Viktor shushed him, and it was only when Bern saw the face of her good, strong Viktor pale, as if washed with bluing, that she began to feel cold. Frank gave a small whistle, like a kettle releasing the pressure of its steam. In the wake of this sound, Nicolas looked at Bern.

Her, he said.

Into the vast, frigid silence came a snicker; Nicolas's boys, eyes like darts.

Never, Bern said. Never, never, never.

Not forever, no, Nicolas said, seeming not to understand her. I'm not a sadist, young lady. For a night. No more. Then you will be on your way tomorrow. Plenty of gas to get you to Bordeaux. Plenty of food, my mother's delicious chicken. I have been far too long without female companionship, and I am a man with strong desires. You remind me of my wife, you know. Same hair. Same, excuse me, behind. Lovely behind. Now tell me, my cabbage; I know you're American, but is there a chance your people were German?

A sharp blow to her ankle: Lucci kicking her, and she knew he meant to remind her that this man was both bats and had a gun. So she said, grimly, Oh, in a way.

I knew it, he said, sitting back with his charming smile. You are the purest Aryan I have seen for some time. I knew it when I saw you.

Oh, did you, said Bern, and couldn't help herself, saw herself telling this story to a whole dinner table of guests, saw herself shrieking one day with laughter, saying, My God, he was telling a Jewess she was the most Aryan creature he'd ever seen; even now, she gave a high little bleat of delight. Viktor, she noticed, had grown huge, was sitting up in his chair as if ready to spring; Frank was gaping, red, having apparently understood; even Parnell's handsome brow was knotted and black. Lucci's eyes were bowed to his lap, as if in shame.

Your answer is no, Bern said. I would rather gnaw off my own foot.

Very well, said Nicolas, making his mouth twist painfully. You may soon be doing so. I am sorry, but I'll have to keep all of you fine foreigners here until the Germans come, won't I. Prisoners. And who knows what they'll do when they find you.

You can't do that, said Viktor. We're reporters.

Oh, can't I, said Nicolas and it was not a question. Now, boys, he said to his sons. Lock them in the barn.

He stood and nodded at them all, thoughtfully, and said, Good night, and after he climbed the stairs they heard his footsteps on the boards above them, so heavy they feared that great rocks of plaster would fall down on their heads. Then they moved, one by one, into the night, Lucci kissing the hand of the old woman in thanks for the meal.

The barn was one of the buildings of stone, dark and chill, more a cellar than a barn. Inside was a great mass of hay and a mound of potatoes and one ugly old donkey that bit at Lucci when he tried to make friends. The boys shoved the reporters inside and made a great to-do about running the chain through the handles outside and locking them in sturdily, and when the reporters were alone, with just a chink in the roof for a weak light, they settled into the hay in silence. But Parnell stood up presently and began to pace between the donkey and the door, and at last spat out, How disgusting, really. That delivered, he sat down again.

There was another long silence, then Bern burst out, Filthy. Filthy, filthy. I would commit hari-kari. Spectacular fucking brute. Never in my life would I sleep with a Fascist.

From his corner, Frank cleared his throat. No, Bern, he said. No question. I would shoot you myself if you did it. For the principle of the thing. If there's anything we Americans know, it's principles. His voice in the darkness held a tremble, and Bern, who was never quite clear where she stood with him, felt a small easing inside her.

No, said Parnell. Nothing of the sort can happen, of course. Barbaric, really. So what, old chaps, do we do?

Bern said, Well, we sure as hell can't wait for the Germans, and they will be here sometime soon. And even if this old barn weren't a fortress we couldn't escape, not without gasoline.

I say, said Viktor, so quietly they could barely hear him, we murder the son of a bitch in his bed. And his two whelps. And leave the mother trussed outside for the vultures.

Wonderful, wonderful, murmured Parnell, standing, then sitting again. Your fury, Viktor, it's wonderful. In his agitation, he fumbled for a cigarette and failed to light it three times before it glowed a sudden orange in the dark.

Yes, but, said Lucci. But how is it we escape this place?

And you forget, said Frank, that there are three of them, and they all have guns.

After this, a black silence enveloped them. They sank deeply into their thoughts. Without conferring with anyone, Lucci eventually rose and made a thick bed of hay, and they lay down together for the warmth. Bern was in the middle, between Viktor and Lucci, Frank and Parnell on the outside; and when Frank began to snore and Lucci's nose let out a sleeping squeak, Viktor turned to Bern, and put his arms around her. There, safe against his smell of body and sweat and his own clovelike undertones, she realized how unsurprised she was.

Even as she was now—unbathed, unkempt, exhausted—Bern knew she had it, that same old something. She'd had her first great love affair at sixteen, was still notorious because of it. The man in question had been three times her age, the mayor of Philadelphia, but even so they blamed her, a child. The father of a schoolmate, he had given her a ride home from school one day in his chauffeured car, and that was that. Over the year she was involved with him, his wife grew skinny and sour, his daughter turned the entire school against Bern, and her lover took her to Montreal for a week while her parents were visiting family in Newport News. She was enraptured; she felt free. She took it as her due when her lover fed her vast meals and put her in bespoke lingerie and took her to burlesque shows and, the last night, to a dinner party given by the kinds of friends who would be amused by a sixteen-year-old mistress. In that gilt-and-velvet world of closed curtains and secrets circling like electricity, there was another girl there not much older than Bern, but uncertain and clumsy with her hands, her face in painted roses like a porcelain doll.

Bern had still been vibrating with her strange new joy when the butlers set the silver domes in front of them. The lights had dimmed, and the lids were whisked away. There, on the plates, Bern saw the tiniest bird carcasses imaginable, browned and glistening with butter. There was a collective gasp: L'ortolan, a woman murmured, her voice thick with longing.

A bunting, whispered her lover, bathing her ear in his wine-warmed breath. Caught, blinded, and fattened with millet, then drowned in Armagnac and roasted whole. A delicacy, he said, and smiled, and she had never noticed until then that his eyeteeth were yellowed and extraordinarily long.

With the gravity of a religious ceremony, her tablemates

flicked out fresh white napkins and veiled their faces with them. *To hide,* someone said, *from the eyes of God.* The porcelain girl held hers like a mantilla for a moment before she dropped it over her face. Bern did not: she watched, holding her breath, as each person reached for his own small bird, and made it disappear behind the veil. For a long time, at least fifteen minutes, there were the wet sounds of chewing, small bones cracking, a lady's voluptuous moan.

A stillness came into Bern as she observed this, a chill, as if she were watching from a very distant place. Later, she would read of what the others tasted just then: the savory fat, representing God, followed by the bitter entrails, which is the suffering of Jesus, followed by the bones, which lacerated their mouths so they tasted their own blood. All three tastes commingled became the Trinity. Bern, to whom Christianity was a gorgeous myth, like literature, saw then the barbarism at the heart of all the beauty.

The bird on her own plate cooled and congealed, and she didn't even look at it when she wrapped it in her napkin and placed it gently in her evening bag. She watched as the others, radiant with badness or shamefaced and shaky, came from behind their napkins, wiped their lips. A tiny bone—a wishbone, a foot—stuck to the carmine lipstick of some opera singer. Bern saw thin wet streaks in the porcelain girl's cheek powder, saw she was still holding something in her mouth, and Bern gazed hard at her until the other turned away, flushing for real under her paint.

That night Bern let the tiny carcass drop from the hotel

balcony, setting it free, she thought, though it dropped like a lead weight to the ground for some prowling beast to eat. Like that, she who had been perhaps too amenable, too obedient—why else could she be seduced so easily?—felt herself harden. When she returned to Philadelphia, Bern never spoke to the man again, and the story formed the foundation of the first piece of fiction she ever wrote, in a hiatus between wars. After the magazine ran it, people in Paris and New York began to call her behind her back L'ortolan. Bern Orton; Bern Ortolan. It made a certain awful sense, Bern herself could admit.

Now, so close to Viktor's peculiar scent, Bern felt something stirring in her again, and with her silent cool hands undid his belt. This is what she needed, a man coming alive in her arms, such comfort; and though she preferred Parnell—there was no complication in him, and he was gentle and sweet to Viktor's large roughness—when Viktor put his hand on her waist and slid it under the band to hold her rear, she let him, eager. She loved this, and not because she ever had much pleasure from it; it was a gift, the men wanted it. Their gratitude made it good; the way that Bern was the white-hot center of another person's world for those minutes or hours; the way for a moment it made them both forget everything but this other skin, forget the shattered souls drifting over the world, how it was cracking in half.

But Viktor put his two hands on hers and stopped them. She could see a glint in his dark eyes as he looked at her. He lifted her hands to his mouth, and kissed them both, on the palms and on the backs. Then he turned her about so that her back was facing him, and he held her gently around the chaste arc of her rib cage, his arm for her pillow, the deep beat of his heart a current, eventually drifting her off to sleep.

Frank was up earlier than everyone else because his blasted hands wouldn't stop shaking. Hungry, too. The others useless logs in the hay, Bern cuddled with that mad Russky Viktor. In the back the donkey stinking in his own muck. The dark barn, the stench, the longing to leave made his skin crawl. When he went to the doors and peered out into the half-dark, he saw the refugees along the road. Pale as death, a huddle, waiting.

Frank remembered an assignment he took to Haiti long ago, when he was young, not the fat sad sack he was now. He remembered the stories, the fear in the people's faces when they talked of the warlords who would steal souls and turn the emptied bodies into slaves. Those people out there moving in the dust and dawn seemed to have their very souls leached from them: war zombies. When they sensed someone awake in the cottage, they knocked, loudly; when nobody answered, two of them moved on. The last, a young man, waited for an hour until the sun rose fully, and then halfheartedly stole a chicken from the yard. The son with the bruised eye stepped from the roadside and cocked his rifle under the man's chin. The man released the chicken and limped away.

Crazy, Frank muttered, what war makes people. Animals.

There was a rustle and he peered behind him, saw Bern sitting up with her lovely sleepy eyes, hay in her hair. Frank? she said uncertainly.

What I wouldn't give, he said, for a fucking drink. His voice was shaking, he noticed. Bern stood, and Frank's heart lifted as she moved toward him, but then the group in the hay began to stir and his mood darkened again. Always there were others around. Frank was no match for handsome Parnell, or Viktor, who sweated virility, or even Lucci, with his easy charm. He'd seen it, there was something going on there between Bern and the photographer. He might as well forget about it. Not that a cold bitch like Bern would be good for him, drive a cold dagger through his heart, more likely than not. There was something so phony about her.

They rose and stretched and tried to forage for food and watched the sunbeams slowly rake across the floor of the barn. Still no Nicolas, none of the sons, not even the weepy old hag, no food but the scent of some kind of ham wafting from the cottage. He couldn't ignore Bern: just by existing she commanded attention. She needled him. There was that one time in Oslo, anyhow, when they were drunk on aquavit and everyone else had gone to bed. Frank normally resorted to whores, peroxide and bosom, but that night when the electricity shorted out, under the smoke of the cheap tallow candle there was something so dark and appealing about Bern that he put his hand on her and raised his eyebrow. She went still, and carefully raised hers back. Bern had tasted of alcohol and copper, and in the night, rumpled and sweating, he wept and confessed that for years he'd dreamed of killing himself. Usually a noose, he'd said. Sometimes a gun. Sometimes I step deliberately on a land mine.

It was this that got him. That he'd said this to her, of all people. That she'd taken it in and stored it away and might use it someday. He couldn't shake the idea that maybe she'd only done it out of pity, slept with him because she'd felt sorry for him. He couldn't take pity. Frank turned away and counted his breaths through the morning to stay steady.

The day passed. Lucci sat staring through a crack at the clouds skimming across the delicate sky. Viktor did fifty pull-ups on a beam. Parnell smoked the last of his cigarettes and flipped the photographs of his family over and over again like playing cards. Outside, there were the sounds of a few more passersby. A French owl, someone working nearby, the clang of metal, the blunted clock of wood.

In the midmorning, Frank couldn't take his hunger, and bit into one of the raw potatoes from the sacks, but spat it out again when he saw its black heart.

Before noon there was a rumble in the sky, and the way that Viktor scowled, Frank understood that the Russian had recognized the sounds as Nazi planes. If the Nazis could fly this far south without firing, their troops would be only a few days away. Then, the camps, which he had heard of. Bullets in the head, inmates thin as bones. Frank was not so sure now that he would get away easily.

At midday, the mother came out into the yard and scolded

her chickens; Nicolas and the boys clomped back to the house for their meal. Afterward, Nicolas unlocked the chain on the barn and thrust open the door. In the overbright sun that poured into the dim barn, Nicolas did not seem quite so frightening. Just a peasant farmer, and a not bad-looking one at that. Younger than Frank, at least. He gabbled something inquisitive in French at Bern, and she spat back her answer, saying *cochon,* which Frank knew meant pig. So: the answer was still no. He felt his insides twist at this and a fury rise up in him when Nicolas laughed, then slammed the door shut again, locking them in the dark.

Germans are advancing on Orléans, Viktor said for Frank's benefit.

I got it, Frank said. He hadn't, though he couldn't let Viktor know that.

Damn Bern. In the light of day, he didn't see what all the fuss was about. She'd slept with everyone and his brother, so why one more peasant meant anything, he didn't know. The first time he knew he was going to report on this war (how young he seemed then, my God, not that long ago, either), the fellows back at *Life* raised their eyebrows. Say hello to Bern Orton for us, Frankie-boy, they'd said. We hear she's a hot number, and when he said, What do you mean?, admiring a woman whose moxie let her do what only men had done until then, they laughed. Showed him a photograph of a young lady. Said, She looks all prim, distant cousin to Eleanor Roosevelt, Main Line, all that, but don't be fooled. They told stories: the mayor she'd seduced at sixteen, the marriages she'd broken up, the painter who'd shot himself in the heart over her. Pussy of gold, they said. And gives it away for free.

Lucky bastard, they all said, and clapped him hard on the back. Queer, he thought now, how those men were equally right and wrong about Bern.

By evening Frank's shudders made the wall behind him rattle. He had nothing in America, no family, no wife, no children, nothing but his job and baseball and a small house near a decent brewery, but he just wanted to go home again. When night fell and the moon rose in the chink in the roof and it became painfully evident that there would be no dinner, Frank began to curse. The curses rattled out of his mouth like gravel, like spittle, he couldn't stop them. He cursed Nicolas, the boys, the dogs, the chickens, the old hag; he cursed God, France, the world, the United States of America, the *Kansas City Star*, *Life* magazine, his mother who urged him to be a reporter, his father who had gotten him his first job, President Roosevelt and his ugly old wife, and, because Bern jumped in roaring to defend Eleanor, he spun about to curse Bern.

Dammit, girl, he said. Just do it and get it over with and we can go. I'm dying here. I feel like a fucking beehive was set loose in me. Just do it. Then we'll never talk about it again and we can reach civilization and I can have a fucking drink.

Viktor grabbed Frank by the collar and shoved him up against the wall. Frank struggled to breathe, his vision blackening from the edges. And then, saying nothing, Viktor let him go and Frank slid to the ground and wheezed there sullenly for a long time, watching the straw before his eyes dance with his breath, watching Bern at the far end of the room as she combed and combed her hair like a cat licking itself calm.

HE WAS IN THE GARDEN in Fiesole eating figs and Cinzia was there, her hair short like a boy's and blown by the warm wind. She opened her mouth, about to say something—Lucci's very limbs tingled, waiting for her voice—when Parnell sat up beside him, shouting incomprehensible words. Lucci sprang up in the darkness of the donkey-smelling barn, his heart splitting in his chest.

Oh, he cried. Viktor lit a match.

In the spit and flare they saw Parnell's face, seized by fear. Then he was weeping. No, he said, No, no, no, and Bern was beside him, holding his face, saying softly, Parnell, wake up, wake up, it's okay, sweetheart, it's a dream, and Frank scrambled to the wall, and Lucci sat down again, wearily, and the donkey kicked, and Viktor lit another match when the first burned out in his fingers.

Parnell rested his head on Bern's shoulder until he stopped weeping, until his breath came naturally again. He told them what he had dreamed: ranks of soldiers, black as beetles, marching in lockstep down the Strand, a child swung by its heels against a wall so its brains splattered out. London burning. Bombs falling like hailstones on the Houses of Parliament.

I want to go home, Parnell said. Please, Bern. Just let us go home.

See, said Frank from the wall, where he sat, shuddering. See, Bern. You're hurting all of us, you know. Your *morals*, he said, are hurting all of us.

Viktor moved toward Frank, but Lucci stepped between them. Frank's ill, he said quietly, and he knows not what he talks. Viktor glowered down and for a moment Lucci steeled himself for a blow, wondered if it would kill him, but Viktor turned and sat, abruptly.

When they settled again, Lucci could no longer sleep. In his mouth he could still taste figs. He could almost smell Cinzia's hair. He thought of her as she would be now, if she were alive, in the camp at Bolzano. Probably gaunt, no longer pregnant. Still as fierce as she was as a partisan, going into the night, doing what she needed to do. All that time Lucci had tried not to worry, stood under his red bulb, pulling images from the baths, but growing more frantic as their child began to show. And one bright afternoon he watched as, down a street too long for him to run to her, she was hustled into a dark car.

Now the Germans were coming, perhaps only a few miles down the road. A great ugly inkstain on France, spreading. And when they overtook this barn, who's to say where the journalists would go. Perhaps Lucci would walk into the camp and see Cinzia look up from whatever work it is they make women do; sewing, or weeding, and she'd blanch, be furious with him for being caught. Wishful thinking, Lucci knew: more likely he'd be killed on the spot. Journalism was no impediment to evil. And only the willful say they do not know what's happening in Europe anymore.

Yet, he thought, there are still people like Bern, and this is good. White-hot people. Lucci had met Bern long before the war, when she was a debutante visiting Europe on the arm of some man. They'd met at a nightclub and she charmed him. That night, Cinzia, in the presence of a woman so beautiful, was dazzling herself and danced the way that only Cinzia could dance. Bern turned to Lucci in the dim flickering light and brilliant bleat of horns, and said, Giancarlo Bertolucci, your wife is spectacular. And he said, This I know, Bernice, and she laughed her smoke-filled laugh. Later, in his despair with Cinzia gone, when he took the job to photograph the looming war, they met up again in Czechoslovakia. When one night he knocked on her door, she opened it a crack and said, Oh, Lucci. Oh, darling, no. I make it a point of honor not to see the husbands of women I adore. He said, I understand, but it is probable I am a widow. And she said, Widower. And don't think that. Never Cinzia, she's a strong one—you can't let yourself think that. She opened her door a little wider and gave him a long, soft kiss on his mouth. There, she said, now I know she's alive, and she closed her door.

They were going to die there, in the barn. Starve. Already, they were at the end of the water in the donkey's bucket and he had seen Parnell try to eat the oats. A terrible shame to die now; it made him want to weep for the glorious world out there, weep that he would not be able to see it grow healthy again. To find Cinzia, or to avenge her. Now, in the bleak night, he hoped his heart would break and kill him before the Germans did.

Lucci heard a scraping at the door and sat up. Probably rats; still, he crawled over to see. It was morning but still dark, and he pressed his eye to a crack and saw the teary old woman creep back across the yard and close the cottage door with exquisite care. Lucci was heartened; perhaps there was still good in the world. Then he smelled a smell that made him heady—crêpes—and he could isolate each of the ingredients as he never could before: butter, sugar, flour, milk, even a little rum. He felt the ground until he found the plate, and pressed his fingers into a soft stack two inches high. If he were Frank, he would eat them himself. But he wasn't Frank, so he said, loudly, Excuse, and the others grumbled in the hay. Chaps, he said, and they sat up. Breakfast is served, said Lucci. Courtesy of Madame Lachrymose.

It was enough to keep them alive, not enough to satisfy, and by dawn they were starving again. Nicolas came early to take the donkey to the fields and recoiled at their smell. My cabbage, he called to Bern, Have you come to any new conclusions? But Bern sent a scathing stream of curses in French at him and Nicolas chuckled and led the donkey into the light and locked them in again.

Frank and Parnell sat together by the wall and conferred quietly. Lucci did not like this. He stroked Bern's hair, telling her little tales that his mother had told him as a child so that she would not have to see the others in their low discussions. Viktor paced. Lucci wasn't looking at him when Viktor suddenly, around noon, turned pale, sank to his knees, and fainted.

Though Frank looked close to death, he was quick enough as Bern knelt over Viktor. He stood over her and shook her shoulder roughly. Listen, he said. You don't have to prove anything to us, you know. You're the most courageous woman we all know.

The most courageous *person*, rather, called Parnell from the wall.

I've seen you with my own eyes, said Frank. I've seen you kick a wounded man from a door so a cottage full of women could escape. I've seen you walk through brains and guts and viscera without gagging. If you could do those things, you could sleep with Nicolas to set us free. It'd only take an hour. One hour of courage and then we can go.

It's not about courage, said Bern. Shut your trap.

Viktor stirred on the ground and blinked confusedly, drawn and pale. She leaned over him again, cradling his pitted face. Lucci felt ill to see Viktor as low as this.

Nicolas is not even that bad-looking, said Parnell, in a rush. A bit greasy, but overall quite all right. It'd be a kindness to him, actually. He hasn't had a woman in years and years, he said. Think of yourself as doing a kindness, Bernie.

And, listen, said Frank. You can write about it when you're done. Imagine, a short story. Like that one you did, "L'ortolan," that won all the prizes. It's material. Be a good chap, Bern. Be a good sport.

Lucci leaped up, shouted, Enough, she will not do it. That is enough. He pushed Frank back, and though Frank was far larger than Lucci, he stumbled a little. As he waited for Frank to raise his fists, Lucci thought he could hear everything there was to hear in the world: distant planes, the shuffle of a weary family on the road, the wind rustling under the skirts of the trees, voices hushed and murmuring, moving in, moving out, one great tide. He could hear, somewhere, singing. No: it was Frank, whistling "La Marseillaise" softly under his breath. Lucci looked toward Viktor, who was struggling to sit up. When he looked back at Frank, a curious glint had come into the fat man's face.

Frank said, slowly, Why the hell not, Bern? Everybody knows you're a slut.

Shut up, said Viktor, voice deadly, quiet, but Frank gave his sour little smile. Oh, Viktor, I'm surprised you didn't know, he said. She sleeps with just about everyone she meets. I could name hundreds.

I do know, Viktor said, rubbing his head wearily. She's had a few lovers. It is her right, as it is yours. As it is Parnell's, and Lucci's, and mine. At least unlike Parnell, she's not married. Bern, at least, is not a hypocrite.

Ha! A few lovers, well, said Parnell, his voice turning

Cockney, ugly. Don't you wonder, Viktor, why she won't sleep with you? I do, very much. She fucks me, you know.

I know, said Viktor. I know.

She sleeps with everyone, said Parnell. She slept with Frank, if you can believe it.

What's that supposed to mean? said Frank, but nobody heard him because now there was a hole ripped into the air in the barn, and Bern was alone in the middle of it. She reached out to take Viktor's face in her hands, speaking low and seriously, but Viktor shook her off.

Frank, he said, very slowly. Frank? I knew about Parnell. He's handsome, it's uncomplicated. But Frank, Bern? Him?

Bern sighed and tried to find the sauciness in her voice again, but it came out strained. I don't understand it myself. I guess I felt sorry for him, she said.

Viktor stared at her, and though it was dim in the barn, Lucci thought he saw his eyes fill. Well, Viktor said. I suppose you felt sorry for me, too.

No, said Bern, but he had already turned away, already walked to the muck and stink of the donkey's area. Viktor, she said, but he raised his hand to quiet her.

Do what must be done, Bern, he said. It shouldn't make a difference to you, should it.

They were all looking at Bern, all of the men. She took a step back and leaned against the door to catch her breath. Lucci saw that Viktor had changed something, had turned something with his words, and Lucci himself couldn't resist the change. He saw the light again in Fiesole, Cinzia, the million small colors of that world, and longed to be in them. He longed.

In a minute, Bern stepped closer to Lucci, searched his face. She tried to take his hand. But Lucci couldn't breathe, and he stepped away, turned his back.

Bern blinked and her voice came out ragged. Et tu, Lucci? she said with a grim little smile. Then she took a deep breath and turned her back and waited at the door. When one of Nicolas's sons passed by, she called to him in a muted voice and told him to fetch his father. The minutes that she stood there, with her back to the men in the room, seemed to Lucci like weeks, like months. Her hair was lit golden in a sunbeam that fell in a long strip down her delicate back. He wanted, terribly, to say, Stop, to say Bern's name, to stroke her soft cheek where it was bitten by the light. But, in the end, he didn't do anything at all.

A SOOTY DUSK. It had begun to drizzle, and the men waited in the jeep. Under the seats were boxes of food: terrine, bread, cheese, pickles, bottles of wine. A full canister of gas. They had washed themselves with water the teary old woman had heated, they had eaten their fill beside a fire, warming their bones. The old woman would not look at them, though she wore Lucci's woolen socks in her clogs. She held out food with a closed face, turned those perpetually watering eyes away. The two sons had stalked in and out of the house with their excitement, loading the jeep with provisions. At one point, they had both disappeared upstairs, and reappeared an hour later to sit whittling by the fireplace, dogs licking their paws, satisfied.

In the car, Viktor held his face in his hands. Frank held a bottle and his normal pink flush had already regrown across his cheeks. Parnell held an unlit cigarette and stared at his hands. Lucci held his camera, but did not take a photo.

At long last, the door of the cottage opened, and Bern emerged. She had lost a great deal of weight in the last few days, and her clothing hung on her; she moved as if sore, and her lip seemed torn and bleeding, as if she had bitten through it. She climbed up beside Parnell, who glanced sideways at her, his eyes liquid and fearful. Viktor turned on the engine, and looked at Bern in the mirror, willing her to look back; Lucci, tentatively, put his hand on her cheek. Her skin was icy and white as wax. The world seemed to slow for a moment—there was the moon like a half-closed eye—the wind had died and so everything seemed to hold its breath. But Bern would not look at Viktor and grabbed Lucci's hand and threw it back at him.

Don't, she said, very softly. Don't touch me. Don't look at me. Go.

But they didn't, at first. A hawk over the trees darted down. There was the wail of a distant plane. When it passed, they were able to hear the silence of the woods, as if it had gathered itself in and was waiting for the conflict to end. At last, Bern said, Go, again, and Viktor started up the jeep. Frank cleared his throat and turned his face toward the sky; Parnell sighed. The engine throbbed and the jeep pulled away from the cottage, into the trees. And for hours they drove like this, in silence, southwest, toward a certain kind of safety.

ACKNOWLEDGMENTS

→>-<←

I OWE MY GRATITUDE TO MANY PEOPLE AND ORGANI-
zations, chief among them:

Everyone at Hyperion and Voice, especially my editor,
Barbara Jones, who dove in like a champion and made this
collection (wildly) better, Ellen Archer, Sarah Landis, and
Allison McGeehon, all of whom believed; and Pam Dorman,
at Viking now, but not forgotten.

The faculty and my fellow students of the MFA program
at the University of Wisconsin, where half of these stories
were written, especially Lorrie Moore, Jesse Lee Kercheval,
Judith Claire Mitchell, and Ron Kuka.

The editors who selected some of these stories for their
journals and anthologies: C. Michael Curtis, Heidi Pitlor,
Stephen King, Natalie Danford, Richard Bausch, Susan
Burmeister-Brown, Linda Swanson-Davies, Don Lee, and
Bill Henderson.

The Corporation of Yaddo; the Vermont Studio Center; and Anne Axton and the University of Louisville's Creative Writing Department for the Axton Fellowship.

My agent, Bill Clegg, an honest and true friend of my work.

My brilliant posse of readers: Steph Bedford, Kevin A. González, and Sarah Groff.

My family and beloved (though neglected) friends.

The brave and beautiful women whose stories inspired this collection.

And, mostly, to Clay, my first reader, who was there at the birth of each of these stories and whose constant love made them come alive.